The

of

Alexander Castle

by

Sasha Newborn

MUDBORN PRESS SANTA BARBARA

The Martian Testament copyright © 2013 Mudborn Press, for Bandanna Books   ISBN 978-0-930012-63-2

Sport, Adventure, Fantasy, YA

The First Detective: 3 Stories. Edgar Allan Poe   **Hadji Murad,** Tolstoy
Frankenstein, Mary Shelley   **Surfing,** Jack London   **Ski,** Doyle
Benigna Machiavelli (YA)   The Martian Testament

History

Mitos y Leyendas/Myths and Legends of Mexico. Bilingual
The Beechers Through the 19th Century   The Basement (60s)
Uncle Tom's Cabin, H.B. Stowe   Berlin: Divided City

Schooling

Don't Panic: Procrastinator's Guide to Writing an Effective Term Paper.

First Person Intense   **Ghazals of Ghalib**
The Gospel According to Tolstoy   Gandhi on the *Bhagavad Gita*
The Everlasting Gospel, William Blake   Italian for Opera Lovers

Love

Dante & His Circle. Love sonnets   **Vita Nuova,** Dante on Beatrice
Aurora Leigh, E. B. Browning   **Sappho**   **Eight2Two**

Shakespeare Director's Playbook Series

Hamlet   Merchant of Venice   Twelfth Night   Taming of the Shrew
Midsummer Night's Dream   Romeo and Juliet   As You Like It   Richard III
Henry V   Much Ado About Nothing   Macbeth   Othello

plus

7 Plays w/ Transgender Characters   Falstaff: 4 Plays   Venus and Adonis

Teacher Texts

(*Q & A, glossaries, critical comments*)
Areopagitica, John Milton   **Apology of Socrates, & The Crito**
Leaves of Grass, Walt Whitman   **Sappho, The Poems**
Uncle Tom's Cabin, Harriet Beecher Stowe

INTRODUCTION

The Martian Testament peels back the myth of creating a new Earth on Mars. The view from the red planet is startlingly different, and deeper, than anyone imagined. Going to Mars? Throw away the rulebook.

Four main characters descend on the red planet for their own reasons: one marooned, another on assignment (so he thought), a third as a lark, and a fourth as an extraordinary power play. As to which is the hero, the reader will have to decide.

To keep the interwoven narration straight, notice the treadmarks in each title. Left pointers indicates Earth and Earth-ward (later in time) episodes. Right pointers show the journey to Mars and the Mars experience. And the inward pointers denote Jim Weston's Journal, the twenty-year diary of the First Martian. The pieces will fall into place, as needed.

Let me acknowledge Ida Stein for correcting my school-days French.

As of this date, an audio version of *The Martian Testament* is online at www.bandannabooks.com/radio.

Sasha Newborn

March 2014 (Earth calendar)

CONTENTS

The possibility of life is a probability

‹‹‹1. GOING HOME‹‹‹

Lord, I been on this ship too long.
Can you hear me sing this song?
Captain says, "Find that man,
And shoot him, shoot him if you can."

Got the night watch every night,
When everyone's out of sight.
I thought I heard the ghost
Of a buddy, an old pal I lost.

No telling what is what,
Is it is or is it not.
Well, I'll go on singing this song
Until I know that I was wrong.

Good old Billy. At last I have paper to write on, so I won't be forced to deface Weston's notebook, yes, the one he kept in those first years (see Appendix). But, Bob, if you think that's something, there's a hell of a lot more. When you get a handle on this story, it'll be worth every penny you paid for it. But a travelog it ain't. Never mind the craziness; without it, there'd be no story.

I'm aboard the *Fledermaus* now, cramped into a locker under the space suit of a man I left back on Mars; it was a cheap ticket, considering that I might have paid with my life. Not that I'm out of danger, you see, but the worst of it is over. Now there's Billy.

Billy... God, it's good to know he's aboard. He's not in very good standing... a captured ship-jumper... what did he expect? But not all of it is his fault... the kitchen duty let him in for hell, when missing food was noticed... food I had sneaked out only two or three times since takeoff. But he figured it right: after the cook, who might lose his job over it, Billy himself was the most likely suspect... only he knew that he hadn't been snitching whole meals. Ergo, someone else had, someone who wasn't getting fed at mess. Namely, me.

That song at the beginning, that was Billy's way, just a song, boss, that's all. But that was enough. On the strength of his words, I crept out hours after everything was quiet... above the insistent hum of the power drivers. I found him in Control, blowing the saddest blues on a worn harp, feet propped against a patch panel. He never finished the phrase... we were too busy hugging each other.

He kicked the door shut, and I started talking in a rush... it'd been more than a week since I'd dared to open my mouth, the news kept gushing out.

I told him my locker number, the locker of the missing Shelton, and we set up communications this way: I'd hear the news of the day from his songs, and he'd tap out a signal as soon as it was safe for me to get out of that box.

And paper. After food, paper was most important to me. This paper I'm writing on now, stolen from the radioman's wastebasket. Billy can do better, later. He's a scrounger, just what I need right now. Maybe he can find me a roomier apartment... an unused airlock or something. The stakes are higher than he knows; we'll have to play this one through to the end.

2. INTRODUCTION FOR RUPERT CARSON

I came a fool, and left, knowing that I am one. But I am coming back. Angry. And alive.

Hear that, Carson? You'll hear plenty when this book hits the stands, and there's nothing you can do about it now. I'll see you fall, if I have to get up on that pedestal you've built, and push.

Your friends are outside the locker now. Friends, ha! You have no friends. If you don't buy people, you ruin them.

Carson, I learned one thing on Mars, one thing that makes me not a fool any longer: you are the greatest fool of all... fooling yourself. Fooling yourself into power you can't handle, didn't earn, can only keep by a stranglehold grasp on the lives of everyone around you. By strangling a planet.

Men will stand up against you, Imperator Carson, men and women like the Lawrences, and Pyotr Smek, and I too will be proud to stand with them. Think you own Mars? You thought you could own me, but that wasn't true. And it isn't anything more than a fiction... because your power ...[I'm so pissed, have to finish this one later. Probably never get published anyhow]

3. NOTE FOR ROBERT BARTLOW, PUBLISHER

At last. God, Bob, you asked for a book, sent me a quarter of a billion miles to research it. And this is the first time I've had the chance to sit down and write it, cramped in a space two feet square, minimal light through the metal louvers... I can't even tell what color they painted the inside with.

But you'll see a book before I get home... that'll be most of a year from now, if I'm still alive by then. All I hope for is that, somehow, this gets to you, and you can do the rest.

You might have heard that I'm a wanted man. It's true. Why, just a couple of weeks ago, I wounded a man, and almost killed another. I should have finished that one... but then you never would have gotten this book out of me... I might never have left Mars. Yes, laugh over that, it was you who talked me into coming here... there... in the first place, with a line of phony baloney I didn't have the sense to recognize. From my first step on the surface, I knew right away that every promo ever written about "the red planet" had been pulled straight from science fiction... but you must have believed it, or you wouldn't have sent me here. Would you?

As I was saying, I escaped with my life... through the aid of a beautiful lady, Sadie Lawrence... God help her now. I was decorated and humiliated at the same time, barred from the few friends I had found, by an act of unwitting heroism that never happened... it'll take some time to explain it all, so be patient. I'll have to be patient, too, in this position. Patient, very patient. If I make a sound louder than pen scratching on paper, it's all over.

This isn't the book I was going to write. Nothing ever comes out quite like you'd expect it. Don't be surprised if I'm the hero...they're my experiences after all, that I write about. But there are plenty of heroes in here, when I think about it, people whose lives touched mine, changed mine, briefly, but with that humanness that makes me hopeful for the future of a planet headed pell-mell for civil war... when I know that people like these exist now, with the real possibility of coming together on a new world, a fresh start at the sticky business of humanity governing itself.

I write now in the hope that what I say may have some effect before it's too late. Too late? It's already too late for some. Pyotr, Wolfgang, Lawrence... they may not even have known they were fighting on the same side, but they each had a clear understanding of the problem. And the same helplessness.

4. INTRODUCTION FOR MARS

I promise to come back,
I will come back.
Friends I have lost,
Be my friends,
And listen.
I have been a fool,
A damned fool,
And I listened and did not understand, but I
            pretended that I did.
I have lied.
I have wished better of myself than of you,
And I suffer now, please forgive me.
My unwitting tricks were in words,
And words deepen my trouble.
Words, damned words, never speak from the heart.
Weasel words, false words,
I know them better than you,
I have traded lies for money.
And the lying makes my heart small.
I killed, needlessly,
wasted, squandered, split brother from sister, father
            from son.
I know the pain of it,
All of it.
I dedicate this book to you.
Please read,

And if you find lies,
Then you say to me already, before speaking,
"Go. You are no friend."
I dedicate this work to Pyotr,
And to Marta,
To Homer,
To Harry and Sadie,
Especially to Jim Weston, for all that he has done,
With all my heart, I dedicate this gift
That you may live free again.
In my best way,
Through words that I have learned to understand,
I am doing what I can for you.
And I will do more,
I promise.
May you feast on me,
And enjoy.
This book is my blood and my muscle and my mind.
From here, all I may do is speak to you,
For you.
May it bring you together with every man and
                    woman
Whose shoes walk Mars.

[a matching intro —really a different
audience who also need to hear this story]

5. INTRODUCTION FOR EARTH

And you, Earthlings who read this book, you have no loyalties to a distant world, except a common humanity with it. I come to plead before you a long and complicated case, an indictment. But it is also a story, the story of all of us, facing a crisis in human development. The question is, can we really make the journey outward without destroying ourselves?

Mars is a test case, the first and most developed of worlds other than Earth capable of supporting human life on any level. The Argonaut expeditions into deep space, that is, beyond the eight planets, have reported ambiguous evidence at best for the possibility of human settlement. Only Mars offers even odds for self-sufficient human colonization. And Mars is now in the fight for its life.

Earth Assembly has voted no confidence, and minimal funds, for space. I know the attitudes well; I helped shape some of them. From Earth, it looks like one big sinkhole out here, a place to waste extravagant amounts of money. True, all true. From the point of view of Earth.

Now step out with me, into the universe. Glance back now at this mother planet, still young, beautiful, unforgettable. A mother who demands all attention for herself, for nothing else. A mother rich in life-giving oxygen, precious carbon compounds, useful iron... but poor in scandium, isotopic elements, the rare earths. Bountiful, even profligate, Earth is a mother bound and blinded by a magnetosphere which prevents her from seeing much of what is outside. Blinded by her cozy warmth from the sun, as if no other suns existed... as if nothing else existed. That was the Ptolemaic system: there was Earth, center of the universe, with crystal spheres in orderly geometric rotation, a cosmic clock, the sole function of which was to register twenty-four hours in a day. One man spoke up about it, though he spoke timidly, almost from the grave. His name was Koppernigk, or Copernicus.

And after Copernicus, Einstein. And after Einstein, Van Dutton. Now, say that Earth is the end-all and be-all of everything. Say it, let it choke in your throats. Earthlings I call you, and I apologize. Yes, we are all bound to a world, while we live... bound to obey its rules, observe its customs. But do not let that world blind you, Humankind is greater than one world can contain... you know it if you read any newspaper. When horses were unknown, many different tribal worlds evolved on just one planet, and relative peace could last as long as the living space held enough room, as long as one culture didn't rub too hard against the next. Times are hard now, you say; things will get better. When? How?

The Argonaut vessels were honest scientific attempts to find life and/or living space. But politics and bureaucracies inflicted budget cuts to wound that great growing kitten, took away its sustenance until now it's starving. Satellites! I hear from the Assembly... that's all we need, and they're cheap: Remember what I said about Ptolemy? Satellite... think what that means, for a moment. A follower, a subordinate. Yes, Earth will keep her little court of space junk, fancy technological mirrors so that she can see what she looks like. But dammit, that's not enough,

What's the matter with living on Earth?—you say. And with good reason. Certainly anyone would choose Earth over Mars, wouldn't they? I agree. Most people would, if given the choice. The point is to keep alive the possibility of choice itself. Except for the rich or the brainy few, who really has that choice, now? And if something isn't done, and done quickly, the choice of Mars will be gone.

But that is only the perspective of me talking, somewhere outside Earth, outside Mars. Let's for-instance a man, say, Harry Lawrence of Mars. He's a Martian, been there fifteen Earth years... can you imagine it? It might not seem that long on Earth, but we're not on Earth any more, we're right alongside old Harry, a former Port-of-New-York boy from Brooklyn, who'd hardly even seen the USA when he signed up for a lark on a Mars-bound freighter.

Stay with me a moment, while we visit Harry, and his wife Sadie, on their homestead—yes, they're not in a government compound—on Mars. They aren't very far from the "country store," just about half a kilometer. He built his own home there, dug the rocks with his own two hands, and he trades with the townsfolk for some food. Doesn't hurt anybody, minds his own business. Except, by the time I left, there was this crazy coot there who claims he owns Mars and all the Harrys and Sadies in it, and he's going to revamp things a bit, tilt the board his way so all the chips fall into his pockets. He's played the game before, and he knows when... and how... people break. My friend Harry, he was sort of ornery. He didn't cotton to nobody telling him what to do about his own life, nor what was going to happen to his pregnant wife.

I wish I could write a happy ending to Harry's story. I hope to God it hasn't ended already. But I don't want to make anything up. There is a Harry, and there are a lot like him, and a lot more who sure wish they could be like him. But, there is also a Rupert Carson. Without him, this would be a very different book.

My part in all this is that I care about human beings and what happens to them... for past and future (there is no present; things are happening so fast I can't tell whether we're leaping or falling. The present is only the rate of change of us with respect to time), and in particular for the men-women of an embattled world.

But does this mean that I care also about Rupert Carson? He's an opportunist, and I despise the man. Yet his abilities are truly unique. Given other circumstances, he might have been a hero instead of a villain. However altruistic or positive his actions may appear from Earth, I am here to tell you different. Cruelty spurred by personal ambition, lives ruined, deception... that's what I saw.

And, reviewing the course of Earth politics, I know where his support comes from: the ignorant, negligent attitude that found political expression in the Federal space monarchists' pre-lunar conception of Earth supremacy. What can that mean, though, on the Moon? On Mars? On an Argonaut mission? It means one thing: a dream of empire, limitless power, ruling the universe from one place.

I learned better as soon as I stepped off the Mars ship.

An invisible sign hung over my head at every step: Earth Standards Do Not Apply. At a distance, power becomes transformed into tyranny, just as Cortes and Pizarro used their loyalty to the Old World as an excuse for extravagant adventures of robbing, plundering and annihilating whomever they didn't like. Carson is no better.

As for Mars-Earth, what can we look forward to? Across an ocean, Spain and Portugal found it hard to keep their colonies, once the idea of human dignity and freedom was loosed upon the world, first in the United States and Haiti, then in France. Boundaries were redrawn, but more importantly, the conception of a national boundary shifted. It shifted once again in our own century, when the Earth was declared.

Mars has not yet written its independence proclamation, but not for lack of agitation. Mother Earth is too near and too far... the lines between worlds are annually threatened by budget review or irrelevant intramural wars. Fate may depend, as never before, on a negligent comma or an ambiguous phrase.

The most isolated Stone Age tribe now knows, and fears, that Somebody rules the world, in this case, Earth Assembly. From the first cities of the Indus Valley and Mesopotamia, men have bowed to power, scraped the ground before a man standing as representative of... themselves. This paradox of power psychology enabled laws to work, straight-lined roads to be laid down, pyramids to be built, armies to be trained.

I could talk politics endlessly. I really mean to say just one thing: Mars is its own can of worms. It may have troubles of its own... those can be solved. But the enormous crime now being committed... aside from Carson's personal ambitions... is that Earth decides for Mars who are the bad guys, who are the good guys... in other words, dividing and deepening divisions between people who must depend on each other for basic survival.

The story I have to tell is a complicated one; you will have to draw your own conclusions, and act accordingly. I am forced to limit this narrative to what I saw. Very early on, I became involved, that is to say, I made enemies, powerful ones. Nevertheless, I will describe, to the best of my ability, what happened, who is who, and, occasionally, why I think it happened.

Which brings me to this book: "The Mars Book," or whatever Bob Bartlow and his marketing team end up calling it. I'm sure he expected a book like my previous journalistic ventures... an examination of the corruption etc. in the Martian government, and specifically tracking down the insistent rumors of revolution, including the legendary journal of Weston. That's what I expected, too.

Revolution... such an aura about that word. It means, strictly, a turning over of power. In that narrow sense, Mars will have no revolution. Too many groups hold too many pieces of the puzzle, and nothing holds them together except survival, and sometimes not even that.

Until Carson. The man is unwittingly manufacturing his own destruction. If unhampered, I give him two years Martian... that's five years on Earth. But by that time, the planet may well be ruined for decades... physically, psychologically, economically. We can't afford it, this time ...not Earth, and certainly not Mars.

[Hmm, overlong—need to trim it down.
Less rant, more specifics]

>>>6. BEFORE>>>

2028. The whole thing happens before you notice a difference. And when it's over you can't remember a thing. Worse, it's as if you never had that piece of your life, as if you made it up.

It all starts when you begin to have a suspicion that not everything is hotsy-totsy. You can even name the ways it has all changed to shiny surfaces: the automated highways, the plastic food, the plug-ins, the media panes of glass between you and any real human contact.

Individualism... that's what we fought for, fought so hard that the rest of the world let us alone. Isolation, death of the arts, an insulation of self... silence broken only through the circuitry that carries voices and faces... and even those, devoid of human value.

I was what you might call a success. The books sold well, but then there was the head-to-head show, my own private two-way holochannel. Big ratings, syndication, plenty of exposure and they never got tired of it. I'd take them into the bathroom with me, let them watch me take a dump, just for kicks. Very human! the papers wrote. They loved it, all the heads and eyes floating in media space... sometimes even a whole body, and those would be the rich ones, the ones I might like to get to know for business reasons. Why did I waste my time?

My latest hologram ploy was to leave the equipment going even when I was not there. The only moving object in the apartment might be the sweeper bot, which was programmed, among other household duties, to entertain my dog; the gentle chunkchunk would pad around after Brutus, catch him at his food dish, or napping. Some viewers loved it. But I was never in the picture, never in the ghost room. And it held them for a while... "Oh, did you see what Castle's doing now? New approach to theater." Bullshit.

No, something had happened, maybe not in me, maybe just in the air, a time of change, when, in a few short years or a few hours, we all decide on a new thing. Only maybe nobody else had caught the media sickness. Then what?

It didn't matter, I decided. This was my life, my media trip, and if it was time to quit, then I'd quit, no more questions, case settled. It took three weeks to clear it, and I was free.

Then George-my-agent called.

"It's bigger than big, Alex, this time it's for real. No more living room pantomimes. No more squirrel cages for you. I've been working on this for you for months. You can't pass this up..."

"The fuck I can't," and hung up.

Half an hour later, he was at the door. I almost didn't let him in, but it wasn't George I was angry about, not then.

"Sit down, George. Don't say anything." Impossible command. He fidgeted for fully half a minute before speaking. The ice cubes in his glass clinked nervously. He was his own show, but he lacked the confidence to go public... that's why he was an agent. At the moment, I was more concerned with forgetting the whole business. What I would live on, well, that would be decided as things went along.

When he hit me with the proposal again, just as Mood Mellow was breaking into the first mind-throbbing chorus, I kicked him out. "Yes, yes, tomorrow. Your office, sure. Now, get out!"

>>>7. OMEN>>>

The next morning, on my way out, I saw a man end-playing his way through the avenue traffic toward me. In the same moment that he reached the curb, a shot echoed between the buildings.

He fell almost at my feet. I leaned down to help him.

The side of his head had caved in from the impact of a detonating shell. But his eyes were open, staring at me.

Fingers clawed at my leg, his jaw twitched out a pain-filled incomprehensibility.

"Lay quiet," I told him. Passersby had formed a silent ring around us.

He tried again. "Alex..." between gasps, struggling to keep back the blindness. Stark fear, a growing weakness. I tried to puzzle out who he was; obviously, he knew me, though because of media overexposure, that was common enough. And he was expending his last remaining efforts to say my name. No, even without the blood, I'd never seen him before, I was positive. On the street, perhaps?

He pulled me down to him for a last try. I put my ear next to his mouth. Heavy, awful breathing. And then I could make it out, repeated over and over, two words: "Don't go."

"I'll stay right here by you. Don't strain. Help is coming."

By the time an ambulance arrived, he was gurgling, in what I took to be his death rattle.

Strangely, I could not remember why I was on the street

at all, what errand I was on, or even which direction I had been heading toward. It's not my habit to "take the air," especially without my dog. I do remember, finally, looking up to see where the shot must have come from. Nothing visible. Still, I went back upstairs to wash and change.

>>>8. MANHATTAN>>>

"You're the greatest writer in the world, Sandy, It's a chance in a million. Wing it, boy, you can do it."

I was looking fifteen stories down, watching a pretty secretary water her plants, puttering about the great glass shield that kept her from falling 200 meters to the mall below. Off to the right, a steeluminum bridge arced gracefully from building to building, joining a mass of square pimples-cum-glass to an unimaginative Mondrian façade in black and silver. Above, the tinted plastic triangles of PONY, a memorial to Old Bucky by one of his protégés. And in the jungles of Indochina Roquentin's hand, and in Manhattan mine, appeared grotesque, utterly out of place in this world-as-it-is. Vertigo, an inability to connect the pieces into a meaningful Gestalt, I closed my eyes.

My agent continued, "Sandy, you've got to do it. Do you know how many people depend on you, trust you, fawn on your every move? Besides, after that book on the power monopoly, you need a vacation. Let things cool down a bit here."

"Bullshit, George. You stink."

"That's beside the point. McDellum made this bid unsolicited, nobody'll know where you are; you can work in peace." Yah, George knows my weak points, now he'll hit 'em one by one, Privacy, check. Vanity, check. Reliability, check. He was a damn good agent, dammit, that's what I paid him for.

"I don't know anything about Mars, George, you've got the wrong boy."

"Who knows anything about Mars? The Martians? No, this is your kind of job, Sandy. You can make scandals where you find them, and this Mars business is ready to bust." His eyes gleamed with an emotion known only to agents.

The secretary was gone; someone two down and five over adjusted their blinds. It was just possible. "Let me think about it,"

"I knew you'd see it my way, boy, Sure, sure. Sleep on it. An all-expense paid tour to Mars. A travelog, anything." You do it, I'll peddle it, right?" He slapped me on the back, pumped my hand, and shoved me out of his office in one practiced, oily motion,

§

One thought occupied my mind, one person I had to see. The third phone was intact, and her image flashed on the tiny screen.

"I gotta see you, Maggie."

"Alex, what's wrong?"

"I gotta see you. Meet me at your apartment, two o'clock."

"But I've got too much to... meetings... are you all right?"

"I gotta see you," The whine worked every time.

"All right," she sighed, "Two? Alex..."

"Two. Love ya." And clicked off.

She was a real person, my first wife, If I hadn't been crazy about her, I'd never have married her, but it was a crazy time, and we were both at the height of youth. I must have been tripping, but it didn't matter. We sent telegrams to the folks: HI IM SANDY I MARRIED YOUR DAUGHTER; HI IM MAGGIE I MARRIED YOUR SON. And had a party, a glorious bash in Art Kildeen's Soho gallery. The ceremony was a work of multimedia art madness, everything and everyone invited. After all, she was an heiress, and I had three plays off-Broadway and my own 3-minute spot on the news. Hell, I *was* news. Nothing could stop us then.

We lived precariously on the publicity ladder for more than a year. And then angry words, a falling out over the Guru's sex kick. She maintained it was the supreme height of supraconsciousness, I went along for the ride, until she started bragging about the Guru's prowess. He would have fucked me, too... Maggie could have arranged it...but that was just too much, too fucking much.

By mutual consent, it was over. I, free and miserable; Maggie already involved with three other guys. How she ended up on Sixth Avenue, I don't know, but her women's lib rap broke down a few doors and brought on the Secretaries' Strike. Then I didn't hear from her. I was busy picking up the pieces in the Lower East Side, gathering my talents into one bundle, one big book on the entertainment scene... naming names, every line trembling on the verge of libel. Friends and enemies alike went into that book, and they all came out smelling like hamburger. The public ate it up. That's when I started being known as an honest man. Bull crap. That's when I descended into the pit.

The cab let me off at the corner... no cars permitted on Harriman Square... and I walked leisurely into the little park. My favorite sycamore had a new scar... a spray-painted grafitto. At least it wasn't the civic orange band that marks trees for destruction.

The gently modulated strain of a string quartet hovered,

about navel-height, from projector speakers in the benches.

The music clotted in my ears, a solid texture of city-garden tea party morality strung through technology of incredible subtlety to recreate the Eighteenth Century in the virgin years of the Twentieth-First. The violin quavers almost seemed to match the leaves' tumble and restless shuffle across the path. She was coming up the steps.

"Maggie!"

"Alex,what is it? Are you in trouble?"

"Ever since I met you. Sit down, you're not here yet."

"It's damp here, can't we ..." She pulled out a Kleenex, blew her nose.

"Of course. How thoughtless of me. After you," In the bulky forties-ish man's suit, she looked less like the woman I had given up bachelorhood for, more like a child lost in her blankets. The heavy overcoat flopped about her ankles. I patted her behind as we entered the elevator,

"Please, Alex, I'm a married woman."

"I don't believe in marriage. It's all a hoax."

She reached for a cigarette. "That's not funny, Alex. You know it's not."

"Troubles of your own?"

"I thought I came here to talk about you."

I nodded, opened the door. "A good fuck wouldn't hurt."

"You're not a child any more." The mother attitude; she was good at that, getting better as she got older. She'd had a child once, lost it. Maybe it was mine; she never told me. Maybe she didn't know.

But she wasn't unwilling. The old joke was really true... I could talk to her better with our clothes off, lying next to her, being with her intimately, motion by motion, kiss by kiss, the years that had worn us down into accepted roles dissolved under the sexual assaults of need and existential hunger. She was as hungry as I, and as dissatisfied.

"Male and female created he them."

"What's that supposed to mean?"

"You and me, we're two of a kind. Two, not one, we were never really married. That old fiction, 'the twain shall be one,' how did they ever get us to believe that one for so long?"

"Did I come all the way up here to discuss philosophy? Really, Alex, you're the end."

"Let me stoke up the pipe. You got time?"

"Oh, all afternoon! It doesn't matter that I'm not on top of things while the conglomerate is crumbling. It doesn't matter in the least!"

"Stop shouting, I'll give you your clothes back later. Madge, I'm in trouble."

"So? All right, I'm listening."

"It's been six months since I sat in front of a keyboard. It stares at me from the corner of the room, those rows of teeth grinning at me." I puffed, long and hard. The little ball of red glowed brighter, "I don't know, Maggie, I just don't know."

"You've got some good hits out of that creative high you've been in. Don't you think it's time for a downer?"

"Who needs it?" I demanded. "Sorry, I didn't mean to explode like that."

"Sure, get it out of your system. Is that what you called me for, a good lay?"

"Only in the very back of my mind, love. No, you understand me, at least. Molly never did, and Endira, well, I hardly ever saw her."

"Get to the point, Alex."

"Hold me. Just shut up and hold me." I couldn't have told her what was in me any more; she was too involved in other things... money, family, everything to make you happy. God, it must have been hard to give up... what?

She hadn't given up anything but me, and I still had a string around her heart, like she had around mine. If only she'd yank at it once in a while, If only...

§

"I'm going, Alex," She was fully dressed, her hand on the knob.

"Wait!" Too late. I ran after her into the hallway.

"Alex! You're naked,"

"That's not important. Come with me, Madge." Mad, I didn't know what I was saying.

"Where are you going?" Nervous, she was.

"To Mars."

Her mouth formed an O; the elevator door slithered shut between us.

I watched the ancient dial until it pointed at G.

>>>9. CAPE>>>

Maggie didn't show for the blast-off, but George, my agent, did. Checking up to make sure I'd go through with it, I guess. And he was right to do so; I almost didn't show.

They have fantastic procedures for these things. As soon as I arrived at the Cape, they shuttled me to a little building just inside the gate. Took forty-five minutes to shuffle the papers and find out that I actually was going, that my passage was paid for, or otherwise arranged. That was George's business; he knew what he was doing.

After that, they rode me to a little runway, looked like one of the originals from World War II, and after some more shuffling of papers, they put me aboard a helicopter to fly out to the site. A space lieutenant rode with me, and riffled through the pages of a little blue looseleaf book entitled "Rules and Regulations, Space Corps, USA." The lieutenant, his name was Anderson I think, was very friendly, but overly helpful in turning the pages. I couldn't really hear him through the prop wash and the motor noise, but he went ahead with his crash course in space safety, apparently because that, too, is in the regulations.

So I smiled and nodded in the appropriate places, pointing once in a while to a long paragraph to indicate that I was interested. And he would go into an animated sequence, his hands shaping the space in front of him, his mouth opening and closing, though I couldn't hear a word, until he was sure that I understood and was satisfied with his explanation.

One thing he did though, was to keep me so occupied that I didn't know where we were when we set down. On one side, the ocean, and all around, vast concrete flatness. In the distance, three or four steel derrick towers, and right in front of us, another of the same. A rocket was lashed to the tower, and on its side it had grown a short stubby airplane.

"That is going to take me to Mars?" pointing at the space toy.

"No," young Anderson said. "That will just get you into space."

"You mean I walk the rest of the way?"

Not a smile. "Hardly. You'll fire off from Skyhook. Don't worry about a thing. You'll get there all right."

A squad of braided men came over, dressed in the handsome black and silver of the Space Corps. One of them had the stylish Comet insignia of the space-borne. I nodded at his patch and said, "Do I get one of those?"

"When you get back," he laughed. "I'll attend to it personally."

"If I get back, don't you mean?" The group burst into nervous laughter and titters, but no one replied. Apparently, it's bad luck to bring up the subject. In my state of mind, it really didn't matter. There wasn't anything left for me on Earth. And Mars, they said, was a cold, bitter place.

The group, including the lieutenant, accompanied me to an office half-underground, in a low profile concrete block building with thick slit windows facing the launch pad. The first room was filled with a milling crowd of men, one woman-in-white checking them off on a list.

But we went straight on through the crowd to a second, then a third room, where I was introduced to the commander of the base.

"Morning," he said crisply. "You're Castle?"

I nodded.

He looked at his watch sternly and said, "We've been waiting for you for two hours."

Big deal. "Well, here I am."

"So I see. We'll have to skip the preliminaries. Hold up your right hand. Do you swear allegiance, etc., etc. So help you God?"

"I do." These were the essentials?

"You've read and understood the Space Code? Sign this." He turned a page. "And here." Another page. "And here. Now then, this is your health card, this your customs blank, your executive verification, security clearance, luggage allowance chit, this is a radiation detector, and oxygen deficiency indicator, identification card, you can sign that later. Now hold up your right hand again.

Do you swear, etc., etc., without question?"

I nodded.

"I hereby confer on you the honorary title of Spaceman Fourth Class, United States Space Corps. Congratulations," he said, a bleak smile creeping across his iron face. He grabbed my hand, pumped it once, and turned to the others. "Suit him up, let's get moving."

We went back to the second room; I was thrust into a chair, while two young technicians removed my shoes, and stuck my feet into what looked like a pair of canvas waders. They stood me up, still zipping, while another two came behind, and forced my arms into the armholes of the coverall. Then an iron ring was passed over my head, fastened and sealed around my neck, and a big plastic bubble fastened on it with a smooth click. Suddenly, I couldn't hear a thing. One of the young men impatiently motioned me to move my chin to the left and down. I brushed against a soft round knob, which activated two tiny speakers by my ears. Another moved my right hand down to my belt, which was loaded with pockets and straps, to a little valve on a thin tube.

I turned it, a steady hissing came all around me. And little currents of cool air circulated around my face. In two minutes, I felt my arms moving upward, and when I turned to find a glass or mirror, found that my legs were encased in two huge tubes. I almost fell and almost felt hands catching me. Yes, there I was, blown up like Mickey Mouse in the Macy Thanksgiving Day Parade. I pushed my arms in front of me, trying to make my two hands meet. And after much effort, succeeding. The boy in front of me grinned, and did a pantomime waddle across the floor, his arms stuck out straight, and his head stiff. I tried it, and this method of locomotion seemed to be most satisfactory in the suit.

The commander entered then, and I tried a salute, but he scarcely glanced at me. I was put on a low cart with a railing, told to hang on, and we moved swiftly out into the first room, where the crowd gathered were now suited, except for their helmets. Only I was puffed up, feeling like an idiot, a child at a Halloween ball.

The confusion settled out as the commander stepped onto a small platform, with a chalkboard behind him. An easel with charts and diagrams stood at attention beside him. I wasn't wearing my glasses and there was no possibility of putting them on, so I glanced around at the intent faces.

Very white, this group. No, there were two black men there, almost a darker shade of the prevailing color scheme. One wore an Afro, the other was beginning to bald on top. The woman stood at the side of the platform, looking like a prison matron.

"Captain Wentworth is your ship's captain," the commander

said. And a slight young dapper man stood and nodded to the crowd. A thin mustache emphasized the permanent sneer in his features, his thin nose flashing like a knife.

At that moment several heads turned toward the left at a noise, and I tilted myself around to see a second bloated figure coming out of the room I had just emerged from. He stationed himself by the back wall unaided.

I envied him this status, and made a move to step off my cart, but I could hardly bend forward, and the height of six inches seemed an impossible jump. Besides which, with every move I made, the wheels slid the cart precariously under me.

"Will you stop that nonsense, Castle? We're trying to run a meeting here." Heads turned toward me.

I stopped shuffling about on the cart, but as soon as the commander began again, I nudged my chin down to the left to shut off the sound. Now all I could hear were tiny tiny voices. The sooner it would be over the better, as far as I was concerned. The whole ten-month trip would be an enormous drag. It might give me time to think. There wouldn't be anything else to do.

Finally, the crowd broke up, the commander left, and the other figure waddled over to my cart, and with the help of a technician, stepped aboard. The two of us were then wheeled out, following the rest to the derrick, or launch tower.

I switched on as soon as we got on the elevator, and found that my companion had been talking to me ... nonstop apparently ... since the meeting hall.

"... last year, but Ardie and I always figure on long vacations, too bad she isn't coming on this one, don't you think?" And before I had a chance to reply, he plunged on. "No sir, no two rockets go up the same. You know what I mean? They scheduled me for one of these things, just a routine run to check out the Skyhook facilities, but the Berlin committee was meeting at the time, and I had to cancel out. Good thing, too. Damned rocket exploded before it left the ground. And where'd I be now, eh? But on the whole, they, run a pretty good track record here, I'd say about 80%. Successes, that is. Of course not all the failures explode. What do you think, eh? Think this one's a dud? Can't tell from the outside, but that captain looks like a sweetheart. I bet he sleeps in cellophane. You aren't superstitious, are you? Well, the flight number for the Space Shuttle is 1,013. I just thought you might like to know, and this buggy's getting kind of old, don't you think? Of course, it would cost a fortune..."

I clicked off with my chin again. My own thoughts seemed more important than the chatter of a man I didn't like even before I met him. Once on board, I'd find a nice quiet place at the opposite end of the ship. And that would be that.

We emerged at the top, and I was motioned off the platform onto a little runway, with rails on both sides, that stepped out into space.

The distance down seemed infinitely greater than it had looked from the ground. One by one the men in the line in front of me were helped into the capsule by a pair of well-muscled lads in white coveralls. The doorway looked more like a rabbit hole, and I didn't see how I could bend my arms that close to my body. My companion went in just ahead of me, and he made it look so easy that I was determined to do just as well. It took both of the doorkeepers, though, to fold both my arms over each other and stuff me in. I think I closed my eyes and let them carry me to the launch seat, or liftoff seat. These seats were arranged in a circle of double layer. And except for the gravity, it was impossible to tell from the shell-like interior of the shuttle which end was up. I rocked back and forth and the seat slid around on a liquid cushion with me. One of the crewmen strapped me in.

I looked around at the instrument panels, above, and on each side. Everyone was seated now, helmets on. I tried to make out who were the functional crewmen on this run. The captain was seated on the next level up, on the other side, in no way distinguished from the others, except by a brilliant red patch on his shoulder, surrounded by two gold bands. His rump, pointed toward me, was decidedly thin even in the space suit.

I nodded peacefully back in the seat, but suddenly, felt a shaking at my right shoulder. It was my talkative friend, shouting something at me. I twisted back to nudge the knob with my chin.

"—THE COUNTDOWN," he said. Eleven—"SHUT OFF YOUR—ten—SOUND—nine ..." And he motioned with his face to the left.

"KAWHOOOOO OOOOSHOOOO IIIII," and I clicked off again, my ears ringing. How could I be so dumb? But even without the speakers on, the noise was overwhelming, and I felt it in every bone in my body as the shuttle blasted off, and I was thrust back mightily at the same time the seat above me threatened to fall in my lap and crush me. The terrific acceleration continued, though at a lesser force, for an interminable five minutes, and I remembered that I had a terrific headache. It wasn't the only time I asked myself What am I doing here? No argument seemed to satisfy the question. Except for the one that said, Well, you're here. The real question is—What are you going to do about it?

When the shudders of the engine stopped, I switched on again. An object dangled in front of my face. It was attached to an arm, and a whole human being—a glove, unbuckling my straps. I couldn't see the face in the helmet until the big white grin opened up.

"Hi, I'm Billy Brown. You're Carson?"

"Castle."

"Oh, yas, very sorry, Mr. Castle. I though you wuz the other gentleman here."

Carson. Carson. Where had I heard that name before?

"Glad to meet you, Billy Brown. Call me Sandy"

"Sure thing, Mr. Sandy. We got about an hour and a half now, and you can move yourself around a little, look at the knobs and dials and such. But don't touch, you hear? Doooon' touch!"

"Bad luck, eh?"

"Bad somethin' or other. You gonna get all our asses in a jam if you do."

"But I'm an honorary Spaceman Fourth Class."

"Why that don't mean shit. That's just to make you feel good. Come on along, you want to see what ol' Mama Earth look like up yere?"

"Sure, lead on."

"This here ain't exactly no guided tour. I mean, you can see practically everything from where you set."

"You mean this is it? And everything else is outside?"

"Well now, we're sitting on a powerful lot of motor. You might of hear the putt-putt getting us on up here."

"What'd you say? There's a rocket in my ear."

He grinned. "W're gonna get along all right, you and me. Just stick by old Billy Brown. We're going all the way."

He maneuvered me out of the seat with a firm grip on my arm. "We go this way, Sandy, and watch out when you kick you don't kick too hard. Just aim yourself and push off lightly. You'll be all right."

Already I was looking back down at my seat, and not falling into it. The hangover from the night before still formed a fuzz around my brain. Billy pushed off across the great room, threading his way between poles to reach the other side and a small platform that had looked like a grille before. He beckoned.

I gripped a railing on the wall, pointed myself for the sidestroke, and shoved off. But I miscalculated the first strut that stood between me and Billy Brown. My right wrist hit it and I started whirling around like a gingerbread man. I must have grazed another person or object, and I started spinning in two directions at once. I bunched up my knees toward my chest, my arms in as close as I could get them, but the spin only increased. I hit a solid object, a person or the wall, and caromed off in a new direction, unable to straighten out. Hands grasped me, and I was propelled again, no spin this time, just a slow somersault, toward Billy Brown, who was laughing his fool head off. He grabbed me, and I looked up weakly.

"Helmet! Can you take this damned helmet off! I've got to retch."

He reached into one of the many pockets in his suit, brought out a familiar paper bag, the kind I'd never had to use on airplanes. I held this while he unscrewed the headgear, and just in time.

"Hold it over your mouth real tight now. Don't let any get out. That would be a mess."

Awkwardly I snorted in air through my nose, and let out the half-digested food, the bacon and pancakes that had been my last Earth meal. When I was finished, he took the bag and offered me a napkin-wipe, coated with a chemical.

I wiped, he tossed it in the bag with the rest.

"Y'OK now, Sandy? You better put your helmet on so you won't lose it. OK. Now come over here, to the window."

And there it was. It was like we were flying the highest jet in the world, so high you cold see the edge all around, but so close it looked like the blanket I used to have on my bed when I was a child. Soft, like that. Slightly fuzzy. The brilliant blue of the ocean, darker around the edges, almost melting into the land. I could see by the familiar shapes that we were coming over Australia just now. And down far to the other side, a white bank, more solid than the fleecy cloud wisps, that would be Antarctica, the only continent I hadn't seen before. And the land was moving under us at about the rate of the minute hand on a dial watch.

I was above it all, suddenly exhilarated by the feeling of power. It was all there before me, the enormity of it, all at once, the vision of the Earth Rising, but this was no symbol, this was the thing itself. I had thought I would see a little ball out there in space, but we were only a few hundred miles up, barely out of the atmosphere, and it was huge. And we were passing over the zone of darkness, to where a few spots were lit by tiny sparks in clusters. Those must be cities.

"What do you think, Sandy?" Billy Brown said.

"I love it, show me more."

"That's it, Sandy. Ain't nothing in between till we get to Mars. Except for Skyhook, of course. We'll be coming on into that pretty soon now."

"Hello there, Castle. It's me, Carson. You probably couldn't tell with this silly monkey suit on me. What happens next?"

"I was just showing Sandy here the Earth," Billy said. "Care to take a look?"

"No, no thanks. I've seen it before. Close up. But you know, Castle, it's like I was saying before, they just don't have any imagination about space. Now take a man with some talent, give him some resources to work with, and you'll see, the space program won't die on its feet. There's millions out there, man. Billions. Just waiting for someone like you. Or me."

A quiet but insistent buzzer started sounding.

"That's Skyhook coming up," said Billy Brown. "Going to do some maneuvering. That means it's back in the seats, gentlemen. All right?"

"Sure, Billy."

Carson scowled and pushed off with one foot.

"Billy, can you help me?"

"Sure," he grinned. "We'll walk it around."

The docking was time-consuming, but not otherwise painful. And we were soon shunted through a tube into a large round chamber like a tube built on two levels, except that the tube bent upward on both ends. I sorted Billy out of the crowd, and pushed off toward him as soon as I emerged from the passageway, but a force impelled me toward the floor. I tumbled lightly down on the grating, and it did seen to be "down," though at what point this weightlessness shifted to weightedness, I hadn't noticed.

Billy came over, helmet off, unzipping his suit, and invited me to do the same. I sat up, and with his aid removed the headbowl, and asked him what was happening.

"This ain't no banana," he said. "You're in Skyhook. It's a big wheel."

"So how come it's got gravity?"

"Well, it ain't gravity, but it amounts to the same thing.

41

Don't worry your head about it. Just put your feet on the ground, and come with me."

>>>10. SKYHOOK>>>

Just as we were coming back from our tour...Billy exclaiming "Look at that there, will you" at every new thing he hadn't noticed before, and me much more interested in the genuine enthusiasm he displayed than any of the gray banks of black knobs and red lights... we stumbled onto the Captain and Carson behind a series of tubes and valves in what looked and smelled like a boiler room. Carson, as usual, was dominating the tête-à-tête.

"...opportunities would be quite tempting...Why, hello, Castle. Didn't expect to see you here."

"I took the same subway you did. You met Billy..."

"Cadet Brown," the Captain broke in, "This is not an open area of the Station. Skyhook is not a museum."

"Sorry, Sir, I..."

The Captain aimed his nose 60° to the left, directly at my Adam's apple. "Hope you're enjoying the trip, Castle. We aren't a passenger line, you know. No comforts of home, or video in every compartment."

"Just as long as I'm not in your way, Captain."

"Brown, will you escort Mr. Castle back to quarters. Then come to my cabin. I want to speak to you."

"Yass, sir."

"See you later, Castle," Carson said. "We've got a lot to talk about, too."

Oh, no. Singled out by the bore. It wasn't bad enough to be

forced to share a room with him. As soon as we were out of earshot, I said, "Sorry, Billy. I seem to be nothing but trouble for you."

"Oh, that's A-OK, Sandy. I been busted before. 'Nothing trouble my mind Like the gal that left me behind.'"

"Nice girl, eh?"

"Shoot, thas just a song. Long as I can sing about it, ain't nothing bother me too long. That Cap'n, though, he's a mean sonamabitch. When I drew his ship, I almost up and quit."

"Quit? How can you do that?"

"Well, if they ain't a legal way, I know a few others. You been around, man. Can't tell me you ain't. I can read it in your eyes."

"You're right. But you shipped out. You going all the way?"

"To Mars? That's what my papers say. And they ain't no stopping place on the way."

"How about Skyhook? Is this place big enough to get lost in?"

"Hell, no. You seen it, the whole thing, in half an hour. Man, I'm tied."

"Suppose you refuse to go."

"And float back down? No sir, not ol' Billy Brown. I mighta been stoned to sign...but that nice cool jail cell back on Earth just ain't big enough for Billy. You know, I been to the Moon, I rode the Venus flyby, I been places, man, and I aim to see some more."

"Mars, for instance?"

"And I been there. Let me tell you, Jack, that planet's a

kook. Crazy cats go there. Why you going, Sandy?" -

"To write a book."

"See, I knowed you was crazy. Why don't you just rent an ocean to sit by? Plenty of time to goof off, write a little, nobody bother you. Mars? Man, you done took the wrong road."

"But this is a book about Mars, Billy. I'm a political writer."

"Hooey, you in trouble for sure. The Cap'n know? You talk to anybody? 'Cause if you open up in front of the wrong people, you've had it. And Mars is just full of the wrong people."

We stopped in front of my cabin. "Come on in, Billy."

"In a minute. You hear what the Cap'n say, I mean, under his breath? He say 'Billy Brown, I'm going to get your ass, ten months out and ten months back, I'm going to run you over with a Cadillac.' That's what he say."

"No shit. Well, my door's open, anytime, Billy. Thanks for the tour."

"Thanks, man. We're going to need each other. I'll keep my ears open for the poop. Two days, and we're zingo, downhill all the way to base four. Don't let it slip, Rosehip." And he was gone.

I had barely had time to bump my head on the second bunk when Carson walked in.

"There you are, Castle, we were just talking about you."

"I don't want to hear it." The direct approach.

"The Captain says you're a big name writer."

"Shove it, Carson, I'm going to sleep."

"He said…"

"Shove it!" I rolled over, not in the least sleepy, but determined to avoid this blabbermouth, at whatever the cost. Tense, rigid, I fantasized the Pirates of Penzance, as many lines as I could remember.

Billy stuck his head in, fifteen minutes later.

"You've got the wrong cabin, spaceman," Carson said.

I remained where I was; the door clicked softly shut.

§

At dinnertime, I waited until Carson left, then rolled out, brushed my hair, changed my shirt. If the military would be in uniform, the least I could do was provide a little color. I found exactly the right item…a Hawaiian drape-over jungle bumply-fabric short-sleeved open-neck shirt dominated by orange and puce patches, with Chinese tigers running from buttons to back. Shoes…why not the acrylic striped pneumatics? A whiff of Desert Passion, and I was all set. I would miss the nuzzly little turn-off knob inside the space helmet, though.

In the corridor, I passed the Captain's aide, Major Hanley.

"Afternoon, Castle. You'd best dress for dinner. It's time, you know."

"I am dressed."

"Oh? Oh, ho, ho, you civilians. Sometimes I envy you." He looked me up and down. "Well, cheerio."

On that promising note; I marched into the dining hall. Most of the fifty or so officers already sat around two long tables draped with white linen tablecloths. I found an empty place and slid into it. A middle-aged Army man sat on my immediate left, a black-suited Yeomaster on my right. I tried the Army man first.

"Been up here long?"

"Excuse me, sir. Were you addressing me?"

"Yes. Yes, I was." It seemed innocent enough to admit it.

"I don't believe we've been introduced."

"I'm Alexander Castle, from PONY. And you are...?"

He took my hand after looking at it for a second. "PONY, eh? Lived there once myself, before the secession. Awful place. I'm Lamar, Major Edward T. Lamar."

"Pleased to meet you, Ed. Say, you should try it now. Without the rest of New York, things are a lot different. Definitely twenty-first century."

"So I see. Excuse me." He turned away to adjust his cuff, then to stare at the empty head of the table.

I turned to face my other dinner companion, but he was involved in a three-way exchange across the table on a technical publication I'd never heard of. Billy Brown was nowhere in sight, though I should have known better than to expect to find him at the Captain's table.

One more try. After all, I was on assignment. I might learn something. Specifically, "What do you know about Jim Weston?" at the olive-garbed gentleman busy ignoring me "Weston? Never heard of him. I don't know anything."

"He was the..."

"The Commander. Rise, please," he whispered anxiously at me. We stood, in trooped a tall well-built man in Space Corps black, with rows of 'battle' patches, who took the central chair, followed by the Major, the Captain...and Carson, grinning affably. Something was going on between them. Even the Ivy League Wentworth was smiling through his lips.

Dinner proved to be already in front of us... the 'place mats' peeled back to reveal vari-colored blocks and chunks. A tiny spoon tweezer was the only implement provided. A limp package unfolded as an antiseptic napkin.

"I have the honor," the tall man announced, "of presenting to you tonight the Captain and crew of the *ESS Fledermaus*. Captain Wentworth would like to address you." The slight vapor of steam from my food was vanishing.

"Ladies and Gentlemen," he nodded toward the left side of the table...I noticed for the first time that the downy-cheeked lad with a shag at the next table had a decided bulge in the jacket. So, we would have a woman on board!

"Fifteen years and some months ago the first ship to Mars landed and returned, opening the way for settlement, exploration, and development of that planet within our system. Much has been done, and much remains to be done. One of the significant names now associated with this extension of Earthmen into the universe, a man who..."

And then it clicked. Carson, Rupert F. Carson, from Columbia. He'd been born poor but ambitious just across the border from Alaska; a little town of no importance called Lower Post, on the Al-Can Highway. He'd made his start stumping through the boondocks, spreading a message of self-determination of the "forgotten people," mingled with irresponsible, outrageous statements on popular topics. His Roman candle sputterings lit up the bleak wilderness with promises that couldn't be fulfilled...yet his failures nearly always resulted in his own aggrandizement. He caused a sensation in the Canadian Parliament by tricking through a bill that joined British Columbia to the depopulated, but mineral- and oil-rich Yukon Territory as one legal entity, called simply Columbia. But Rupert F. Carson was not to be stopped by success. The next year, in a close election, he was defeated for Premier of Canada...a ballot recount disclosed widespread ballot box stuffing and sabotage of voting machines in the cities where his provincial party was weakest. Even before the new Premier was inaugurated, a swift series of legal maneuvers by outraged legislators ousted Carson from office and forbade him to practise politics within the boundaries of the Dominion.

He countered by the direct method...if he couldn't win, he was going to take his province and go—amid further charges of bribery and irregularities, he connived with a doddering political anachronism, the Queen's representative, Lieutenant-Governor MacDougal, for a constitutional convention in Columbia, masked as a referendum on Indian rights. Poor MacDougal probably never did understand.

Under Carson's tutelage, the new founding fathers, dominated by upcountry first-timers ready for action, declared themselves a loyal but independent colony of Great Britain. The Queen and Prime Minister, predictably, refused the offer...and Carson was home free. He then declared Columbia to be a free and independent state.

Japan and China were the first to recognize the new government...the reason given was that their economic interests on the Canadian West Coast had grown too important, which was a subterfuge: since the matter was termed an economic question among nations, Earth Assembly had no jurisdiction; besides, the Great Powers were not interested in setting a precedent of that sort.

Too much was at stake.

Canada practically declared war on Carson; the orders fell just short of that wording. That action only made Carson himself into a popular hero in the backlands. And this emotional support, together with the winter season in the

Rockies, frustrated the government's attempt to retake Columbia by police action.

Meanwhile, sympathetic power groups of Carson's ilk within the U.S. saw a way to profit from this turn of events. At the lowest ebb of Carson's Columbian enterprise, a surprise bill came up in the U.S. Congress… a resolution to admit the Port of New York (PONY) as the fifty-first state, and Columbia as the fifty-second. Though absurd on the face of it, both East and West were satisfied that the balance of political forces would be maintained, So, it was done. The Canadians fumed, but by now they were legally and militarily restrained.

As for the U.S., this acquisition of the entire western slope of the Rockies…a seven-hundred kilometer swath… provided a solid overland link to the increasingly important Alaskan region. A short but intricate two hundred kilometer stretch of the Al-Can was rebuilt to place its entire length within the borders of the New! Improved! USA. But even this measure proved unnecessary, for by the time the road had been completed, Canada was already falling into pieces.

The renegade French-speaking province of Quebec seceded, splitting the country in two. Chaos, disruption bankruptcy…for two years, indecision in Ottawa. Then, martial law. The military, humiliated by their disgrace, set up a "temporary advisory junta." Elections still have not been called. Rebellions still spring up in the Maritimes or Saskatchewan, based mostly on the simple folk who don't understand why their lives changed so drastically, or what to do about it.

Now, what was Carson doing here? As a bonafide U.S. Senator, he might reasonably inspect Skyhook as a step on the way to what?…the Presidency? But Mars…no, he couldn't annex that…it was just too far-fetched.

"...Senator Carson." Applause broke out, and Carson had to raise his hands to stop it. Why was he so popular?

Whatever brand of charisma you called it, it stank in my nostrils.

"Thank you, Captain Wentworth, Commander Hevern," he began, swinging his body into each word. "I stand before you, not as a political candidate..." laughter, cries of yeah! "...but as a member of the Committee on Outer Space...and as an honorary Spaceman Fourth Class. Do I outrank any-body here?" Laughter, sounding tinny in the great tube. He knew how to reach them, all right.

Real down-home showmanship.

"I spent a lot of my time Earth-side rearranging real estate. And I'm proud to say...now that I'm allowed to say it...that I'm an American." Applause. "For a while, it looked like Japan was making a better offer. But we turned them down." Appreciative roar. He clowned an Oriental face.

"You might wonder that I came all this way to speak to you tonight. On the way up, I gazed out of the porthole and saw a little blue ball dancing among the stars. You don't know what that did to me. What am I doing up here?"

Laughs. "What are you doing up here?" More laughs.

"But then the blue ball drifted out of sight, and there were the stars." Lento, pianissimo. "And among them, a red point, moving slowly by, and I thought to myself, Rupert, there's work to be done, new land to develop. Why aren't you there already?" Andante. "And I began to look around at all the machinery...it's all steps on a ladder that we're climbing this very minute, a ladder marked 'Man's Destiny.' And I looked at the men...and women...around me who had built this ladder, and who were climbing, step by step, so that I may now stand before you here, at the top of the world..." Glorioso.

"...and talk to you about what we are doing, and why we are here." A master politician at work. Yes, he'd win some votes from these folks. Only, he hadn't said a thing. Why was he here?

"There are some that say we're taking an evolutionary step into space. Hell, I didn't notice any extra toes this morning when I put on my socks." A good laugh, breaking tension. "But then, we're only on the bottom rungs. We won't know until we get there, will we? In the meantime, I'd like to hear from you, all of you, just a bit later. After we finish this gracious standardized meal."

I didn't wait for the end of the applause and the standing ovation to dig in. My caked peas were distinctly cold, and the meat...or meat substitute...had lost all but the chemical flavor. I had finished the edible portions, and was about to belch and leave when the Captain dinged on his plastic glass. "May I have your attention, please. We should not overlook" (obviously he had) "that we have another guest tonight, the celebrated novelist Alexander Castle. Would you like to say a few words, Mr. Castle?" Novelist? That was quaint. He'd probably never looked at any of my books.

I stood, looked at the blank faces, the bobbing heads who had cheered on the demagogue. That, combined with the food, made me sick to my stomach. "No," I uttered. "I wouldn't." And left the room.

>>>11. BILLY >>>

Billy Brown's Blues, he called them. With an ingenious guitar made of scrap metal and a set of contact mikes, he could manufacture a tune out of the slightest bit of ship gossip. No two songs were ever alike, but those old chords must have come right out of the Mississippi Delta mud.

He was only Communications Second Class, and afraid of going outside the ship. Why he came spaceward was a mystery, but that was Billy Brown, he'd say, as if that explained everything.

After supper on the ship, the crew would relax wherever they were, but most came amidships to watch him invent endlessly with his fingers and his mouth. It was Billy Brown's hour; not even the Captain could have safely interrupted the ritual.

First, there's be a request, and if he didn't know the tune, which was likely, he'd make up snatches from this and that. Then he'd settle in to run over some old favorites, mix up a batch of lazy easy rhythms, and hook up words to them. I wasn't the only one tapping background, but his "sidekick," the only other black man on board, could wail into a half-open metal cabinet like a speedfreak at a conga contest. His name was Lathaniel Williams, from Jamaica, and he was a howler, too, but not like Billy. Their duets tended to tie up melody lines in knots, but they always came out more or less together.

You won't see me, when I get to Mars
No, you won't see me when I get to Mars,
'Cause when I step down on Mars, gonna hit all
       the bars,
Smoking them big seegars.

If you want, you can come along, too
If you want, yas, you come, your brother, too,
You come along, too, help drink up the brew,
The govament's paying for you.

Captain, Captain, get us there on time,
Captain, won't you get us there on time,
Captain, get us there on time, if it takes a double
       line,
Captain, you're doin' just fine.

>>>12. SPACE>>>

By the time the Fledermaus was two weeks out Billy gave me the picture, Carson hadn't been just idly sticking his nose into everybody's business; he was talking about a Plan. The reports of incipient rebellion on Mars had reached him, right in the Congressional responsibility. Rumor had it, Billy told me, that he was being urged to run in the next Presidential election, three years from now; Mars was to be his shining star, his crusade.

Captain Wentworth, apparently, was no random choice; he had a spotless political stand...as far right as Carson himself...and a reputation for succeeding where honest men failed.

"But what's he hope to accomplish, Billy?"

"Oh, he's been reading the Sunday supplement...right next to the funny papers. You know, 'Mars the Edge of Space,' 'Go Up, Young Man,' that sort of thing. He's crazy, though, if he thinks he going to get any prizes up there. Anybody goes, a damn fool. You and me included." He leaned back on my bunk, stuck his feet against the opposite wall, crossed his legs executive-fashion.

"You damn cynic. Aren't you ever serious?"

"Man, I am serious. I ain't been seriouser since my wife up and left me. Check this out: One, that planet's going to freeze your balls off. Right?"

"So I hear."

"OK, now. Two, it's unpredictable. One minute, you're

watching the sunset. Next thing you know, your feet is buried up to the ankles in talcum powder, and that wind is tearing the clothes right off your back. Savvy?"

"OK."

"And three, and foremost, nobody's got no business there in the first place. What for? We got Antarctica right there on Earth, plenty of room in between the penguins and the igloos."

"What do you mean, no business? Endicott Industries has..."

"Hasn't get shit. They grind enough rocks to pave half the planet, for what? To get littler pieces of nothing. They got plenty of that already; Lunar Enterprises is a bust. You just wait, oh man, just wait until you're crying dry to get that stuff out of your eyes. And there ain't no water."

"Wait a minute," I dodged for my fact book. "It says right here there's a milligram on every single square centimeter."

"That's what I said, no water. You'd have to lick an acre dry to get a drink."

"Maybe they live on alcohol," I suggested.

"Hunh?" He rolled his eyes around. "They couldn't...but, hmm, yeah, maybe they could. Requisition Form Triple A960 hereby request one freighter full to the gills with booze. Hey, not bad! Speaking of which, Sandy, old man, I been meaning to ask... I know civilians don't get inspected, but if you just might have some... I'd sure appreciate..."

With a twinge of regret, I reached under the bunk and drew out my second bag.

"Hooey, Sandy, you done saved my life. Can I just..."

"Hold on a minute. Get your hands off there." He put back the Scotch reluctantly, "I want you to promise me one thing, no, two things."

"Anything, man."

"That you don't drink on duty, or when you're likely to be discovered... I already got you in trouble once."

"Sure, Sandy." He lunged forward.

"Wait. The other thing is, there's only five bottles here..."

"Only five, he says."

"...for ten months..."

"Nine months, twenty-two days."

"...and I want to have half a bottle left when we get there. No drinking more than I do. Get it?"

"I got it. Uh, ain't you thirsty, Sandy?"

"All right. Two swallows." He tilted the bottle straight over his head. "Easy now. Let's make it last."

After we relaxed, Billy get sentimental and whipped out a Marine Band as worn as any I'd seen. The notes wailed right through my head and bounced off the walls... more than anything else, it now reminded me of a jail cell.

That old cold Space is getting in between my bones
They's empty space between my bones
Space is in my bones,
I can't find the way back home,
That Space is going to get my tired bones.

Oh, Sandy, Sandy, you look so white and pale
Sandy, why do you look so pale?
Why you so pale, we just ain't gonna fail,
O Sandy, don't you look so pale.

Oh, five bottles of hooch is in the bag
Almost half a dozen in the bag
Oh, you better not lag, for fear I'm gonna grab
The five hooch bottles in the bag.

He'd just finished the last bent note when Carson came in.

"Get off my bed, nigger," he bellowed.

It was the last straw. "Carson, you son of a bitch, you apologize to Cadet Brown right now, or I'll make your life miserable!"

He glared at me, but then he dropped his guard and looked down. "I'm sorry," he said in a tired voice. "I don't know what's got into me."

"To him!" I commanded.

He threw a sideways glance at me...pure hatred...but something else was on his mind. He didn't want to hassle.

"Go ahead, shake hands."

It may have been an act, but he straightened up, like the politician he was, and stuck out his hand resolutely.

"I apologize, Cadet Brown," he offered, then looked at me again. "All right?"

Billy grinned, wiped his hand on his pants, and clasped Carson's. "Call me Billy," he said.

"No thanks, Brown. But I won't call you..."

"Don't say it!" I said. Billy tightened... that old familiar resentment... but with me, he always put on Mister Bojangles-cum-Satchmo.

"What's the matter?" Carson said, with an evil smile. "You radical?"

"You know me better than that, Carson. I play my cards the way I see them. Right now I see a redneck."

"You better shut your mouth, mop-head."

"Unh," said Billy, "I be going now, Sandy. When things're a bit cooler, eh?"

"So long, Billy."

The door closed, and I heard a distinctly muttered "Nigger" from Carson.

"Why do you hate Billy?" I said.

"Oh, hell, knock it off, the spook's gone. I don't hate him. I've got more important things on my mind."

"Such as?"

"None of your goddamned business!" He turned away to

examine his chin in the mirror. "Well, I don't know why I'm snapping at you, Castle. I've just had a bad day, that's all. About as bad as your dinner-party poop-out on Skyhook. Hey, what happened, anyway?"

"Nothing. Absolutely zilch. Zero. No connection possible."

"Hm," he said. "That's never been my problem."

"So, what's bugging you?"

Carson shifted his bulk...gram for gram, he must have cost twice as much as I did, though in space, he could maneuver with the best...onto the top bunk before he replied. "Let me tell you something, Castle...this is strictly off the record... I know why you're here."

"You've got better sources than I do, then. All right, you tell me then, why am I here?"

"You're here to cause trouble, and you will, whether you want to or not. You already have. What do you think I've been doing all this time... covering up for you."

"Covering what? My shit?"

"Yes, in your quaint country way, you could put it that way. Ever since you stepped on board, there's been trouble."

"Look, Carson, I'm on assignment to do a book. They don't care what kind of book, as long as it has my signature. Because that's the way people will buy it. Do you know how much they'll pay for that phony autograph?"

"Yes, and I know where the money came from. Do you?"

That one stopped me. It hadn't even entered my mind that someone other than a money-grubbing publisher had the slightest use for me. I didn't like the idea of selling out to an unknown buyer. Not that I could do much about it, now that the train had left the station.

"I presume that you don't. Just as well."

"Now wait a minute, Carson. You threatening me? Because I don't buy that from anybody."

"Not even for ten million, and a free ride into the future?"

Well, he knew the price, and maybe, just maybe, he wasn't bluffing. I had to remember who I was dealing with. "No, not even that," Strange, though, the way it had happened; and George had gone to the trouble of making sure that I was gone.

"But you did. You're here, right? Castle, I don't like you, but that's not going to stand in the way of us understanding each other. I'll tell you why you're worth it. It's not because of Mars. Nobody on Earth gives a hang about Mars. That's only an excuse to get you out of the way. You know, your last book, on the United Power Utilities hit hard. But not hard enough. And nobody's blaming you...there's a well-kept secret in that industry. You got close enough to make things hot...but it didn't explode, did it?"

"They control a certain percentage of everybody, including, as I understand, some members of Congress." This for Carson's benefit. He didn't bite.

"Oh, now don't mistake me, Castle. You did a great job. But they're afraid of you...that's what this Mars thing is all about. They figure to put you out of commission for a couple of years to give them time to...breathe a little."

"And by that time, it's campaign season, right? You want your hands clean so you can come home and smite the dragon all by yourself, eh, Carson? Why didn't you do something before? Why did you let me go on this trip? What's your part in all this?"

"We're discussing you at the moment. There's another thing you ought to know, but it won't do any good to broadcast it. If you do, your life is a bad investment. But I can help, I think, better than anybody,"

"Carson, if you were the last man on Mars..."

"Watch it, Castle. I'm not your friend, but I'm not your enemy. Yet. You'll come to me, crawling. Because the ticket they gave you is strictly one-way."

>>>13. BEGINNING>>>

The ship arrived like en elephant coming to roost. On the screen the orange disk of Mars grew visibly now, until it overfilled the screen, and we were told to find gravity seats, fasten in, check suits in case of problems, lock on helmets. By this time I had gotten used to the routine; I'd even talked my way into my own private space walk. Once was enough.

Now we were coming in. Carson's words had stuck, they just wouldn't stay down. Every face—could it be he, that he would—no, they'd do nothing. Mars was expected to finish me off. Better not look worried, they might notice.

So, space had its spy games, too. Not the clean image agency, not at all. I'd seen, heard too much these three hundred days, been too near the touch, had my own compromises, engulfed in the gossip that cast me in the role, Carson-devised, of clown.

And in hours, minutes, we'd have open space, no more smelling armpits, cabin fever, stingy water allowances—but Mars had a problem there. No, I'd stink. The plasticized uniforms made sense in space—my dry-clean-only duds had had it.

As for Mars, I didn't know what to expect. Billy had hinted at this and that, but his considered opinion rarely extended to examples. Fifteen minutes after first fire, we were down.

The landing site appeared to be a flat sandy plain. The dust kicked up by the rocket settled down in thin layers about the ship, like smog.

The first time that the alarm bell rang, I didn't know what was happening. The ship had set down perfectly; I remember that we were under real gravity again, and the little butterfly could at last settle to the bottom of my stomach.

"Alex!" A voice from the bloody pavement of PONY stuttered through my head. "Don't go!" Memory played tricks, now, bunching together the words that had taken the remnants of a lifetime to utter. "Don't...go...don't..." and the face, the face had come back so often I neither knew whether that face had a real past, belonged to a man I might indeed have met—near a power station in Utah, perhaps?—nor whether the components of racial memory had reconstructed a vast metaphoric omen whose warning I'd disregarded.

And I almost didn't leave for irrelevant, selfish reasons. My kidneys felt the pull, my head knew it wouldn't, hadn't worked. In the end it was my pocket that talked loudest of all: ten million bucks, it said. Loud, very loud. It was hard to hear anything else; I feared more than anything those times of no money and little recognition. My time had come, so I'd sailed off on the romance ship, a steely bullet pointed at the heart of the greatest story I ever lived.

What I'd left behind was the critical mind that got me to the top. I thought I could take off my claws—not a chance.

Success had gone to my head, made me into a softie, and I hadn't even noticed. But the time for rehabilitation had not yet come.

And now? Shouts could be heard right through the sides of the bullet-express—angry cries, fighting, death in the air. This was to be my home for the next two years.

One screen pointed at the sun, low in the sky, apparently sinking toward sunset. Its rays through the dust made a short rainbow effect, the predominating orange gliding into red, and probably infrared.

Billy had briefed me on the landsuit arrangement, a jump suit of flexible material, and diver's gear—headmask, tanks, tubes. I hadn't realized it consciously, but he said we had already been experiencing a gradual decompression of air pressure on board, though the partial pressure of Earth standard oxygen had been maintained. Now even that would be reduced. He'd warned me not to scratch... my body would be going through extreme changes to adjust to the one-fiftieth Earth pressure, nearly nothing, it felt like. You don't know what naked is until the air is stripped away from you. Presumably the red corpuscle count was up... each of us had been checked by the medic.

There were three crewmen, nobody I knew, who were put into a special chamber of a higher pressure. Apparently their bodies were having a harder time of it, and they might be quarantined thus for weeks. I was glad not to be one of them, especially now. For now, it was confusion inside, crew hopping in all directions, Billy among them. I grabbed his shoulder.

"What's going on?"

"It's beginning, son. It's just beginning. Gotta get to the arsenal. You got a gun?"

"No."

"Hmm. Well, don't sweat it, I'll see about that. Now just get out of the way."

I obliged, took a vantage point on the side near the door.

The Captain's orders were booming out over the tin speakers when I heard a noise from outside, a rhythmic heaving, and a tremor shook the whole ship from one end to the other.

"Battle stations battle stations contingency red contingency red, rifles at the ready. Sheffield! man the airlock, get those men out of there as fast as you can."

Hickory dickory dock. The levity was gone, the smirks of the knowing replaced by lines of worry.

Again a shock. This time the room visibly tilted. They must be trying to take the ship apart with us still in it.

The raucous speaker blasted in my ear "Get the lead out, Sheffield. Decompression time one-half. One-quarter."

The hiss of air escaping back into the ship rose to a shriek.

I pitied the men inside the airlock cell. But if they didn't get out there quickly, no telling how long before the ship cracked open like an Easter egg. With a firm click, the outside airlock opened. Shots were fired. The creaking hadn't stopped, though, and about once or twice a minute, we leaned further over.

Billy rushed back through, slipped me a hand gun, disappeared again. I didn't take time to look at it...a gun is a gun, no matter what came out the end. I only prayed that it would work in the thin Martian air... and that I'd never have to find out. If we even got a chance to step down onto the planet.

Then I noticed Carson in the second group, dressed in uniform like the rest. He seemed to be avoiding my eye, so I went over.

"What're you doing here, Carson? Aren't you a bit anxious to get killed?" One of the crewmen flinched.

"Nobody's going to get killed if I can help it, Castle. Just shut up. We've got a job to do."

Bravura all the way through. He believed his own bullshit.

"Have it your way." After ten minutes with the guy, I had learned to recognize when he was really serious, and when he was being a politician. Right now it was hard to tell. A lot about him was hard to decipher. For all his bluster, he still held quite a few surprises.

Billy had talked, in the last few days, pretty strangely.

Getting to Mars was like a sailor coming into a strange port... he sort of knew what to expect, but he knew what was waiting for him on the ship. Captain Wentworth had really gone out of his way to make life difficult for Billy.

The half-bottle of Scotch, well, that was gone. We drank it in the last two days, each for our own reasons maintaining an artificial happiness. We hop-heads stick together. And now we were here, but just getting off the ship was proving to be the hardest part of the whole journey.

Then it was time for the second group to decompress and debark. The metal door swung open, and as they filed through it pellmell, a single man tumbled past them, at my feet, his hands over his ears, his face distorted with pain.

"I can't hear!" he yelled. "I can't hear!" His leg had a red stain dribbling down into his boot.

"Medic! Doctor!" Several men came running up to us, carried the wounded man to the sick room, now a story up from where we were. I helped them heave him up the steps, then sought out the Captain. Others might have battle orders; I had none.

In the control room, microphone shaking in his hand, he was pacing, pacing in formation. He hardly saw the walls around him, so rapt in thought, so West Point commanderly.

"Captain..."

"You!" His eyes blazed up instantly when he spotted me. "Get out!"

I bumped into a crewman on my way out. He muttered

something that sounded like "Don't tread on me," though I couldn't be sure; he was gone almost immediately into the whirlwind.

Sounds of shots bludgeoned through the shell of the ship, incredibly distant, unreal. Then the second crew must have gotten through. A last volley peppered out, one ricochet.

The silence that followed could have meant anything. But Carson now, I was glad in a way that he had chosen to go out. One thing about the man, he knew how to get a job done.

My blood pressure began to decline when I debarked with the tail end of the crew. He stood in a string of rifles circling the stanchions of the ship—one of which had been severely damaged, presumably by the ground-folk.

My companions rushed to the line without awaiting Sheffield's orders, and I stood alone inside the ring of rifles.

Through the spacemen-turned-soldiers, I saw a crowd—a motley group, mostly men, some of them not too young. Among the beards and homemade hats, three or four strong men, taller than the rest, stood at intervals a bit ahead of the others, partway toward the ship.

Captain Wentworth wavered back and forth on a little lashed platform, facing the largest collection of the Martians.

"...They warned me about you," he was saying, "and it's true, isn't it? Disrespect for law and order. No value for human life...and here, of all places.

"Never mind that. We have orders, sworn to carry out by Earth Council." The expected gasp did not emerge. "I will live by them to the death! And so will every manjack of us. Do you understand?" He was verging on the irrational now, the veins of his temples bulging from the effort to be heard in the thin air.

A low murmur from the crowd. Wentworth calmed down, patronizingly.

"I hereby inform you of these relevant passages from Earth Council's instructions to me regarding our mission here: 'The responsibility of the Space Captain shall be: (a) to maintain strict discipline and morale among officers and men under his command at all times; (b) to take whatsoever action he deems fitting to conduct his ship according to Earth Code, and to maintain the integrity of his ship under all circumstances...all circumstances consistent with the Declaration on Exology;

(c) under no circumstances to interfere in the ongoing cultural life of any peoples whatsoever, or lend his office to the knowing destruction of such a culture...'"

A guffaw from the crowd. The Captain tried to ignore the interruption, but before he continued, a burly man stepped forward.

"The goods. Where are the goods?"

"I will discharge supplies only to an official delegate of the government of Mars. Is anyone present empowered to receive them? I see no one."

Pandemonium broke out. Most of the shouting was aimed at the Captain. His mustache quivered from side to side. A rock was thrown, missing him by a meter. He stiffened. "Sheffield!"

Then, at a gesture from the Captain, he barked out commands. The reserve of about fifteen men fanned into a double line just beyond the circle, nearest the Captain. The crowd moved back slightly, then stood, hostile, expectant.

"Hold!" The man who had spoken first raised both hands

high and turned to face the mob. A hush. He spoke again. "In loss," words forced into English, the common language, probably from German, "of Krag Jensen, I speak for all. Yes?"

A huzzah of Yesses followed hard on his, but amid them, a strong Noooo that held in the air when the other sounds had died away.

"Who dare to No? Who?"

"I," admitted another of the tall men, this one with bristling orange beard and a large red nose. "I, Tamrak."

The mob between the two men scattered to get out of the way; a semicircle of bodies formed an arena containing them, and a spry oldster jumped in between them, looked both ways, then said, "Two hands, two feet. One-Eyed Jacks. Yes?"

"I break him clean," the first man said. "Hands, yes, enough."

And he dropped a broad-bladed knife and several other metal objects to the ground.

Tamrak grumbled, but he too set his weapons aside.

"Wait," shouted the Captain. "What are you doing?"

Several voices from the crowd booed him. "No interference.

This is election, Martian-style!" the loudest said, and laughed. The referee leaped out, and the battle was on.

Number One snarled and charged for the head of Number Two, the challenger. And in a mêlée of fists and feet, heads butting, knees gouging, the worst of all the S & V vids I had seen now in real life, tearing flesh with fingers, first one, then the other dropped to the dust. The fantastic leaps made Siamese footboxing possible for the heavy men, but neither of them had the agility to dodge the other's blows.

The kick had been out of favor for more than a century, when John L. Sullivan, was it? lost to a barefoot foreigner, but now the force of it had been rediscovered, the enormous muscles of legs scissoring up to chin-height delivering deadly power.

"Stop this!" the Captain sputtered. "Sheffield, do something, stop it."

"But sir..." the stout major protested.

"That's an order!"

Sheffield reluctantly but efficiently led his trusty fifteen right into the center of the brawl. Three of them caught one unsuspecting contestant around the arms from behind. The other used this unexpected advantage to make a last charge at his helpless antagonist. Held back, but not far enough, he managed to pluck out the prize, an eye from his opponent's head. Tamrak was the loser of this round, though he was still on his feet and bellowing worse from the indignity than from the pain. The Martian character apparently had the strength of the backwoods, a type almost forgotten on Earth. Adjust? I looked back at the ship longingly. This was no place for me. Whoever had had me shipped out here must have known what Mars was really like.

In the confusion, several spacemen got hit, one of them stabbed with his own bayonet, another trampled by angry, or indifferent, spectators. Sheffield's men had to carry that comrade back to the lines.

"Ruffians! Barbarians! Swine! Fools!" the Captain raged on almost as loud as the rest of the crowd. No one paid any attention to him.

Ultimately, the victor struggled free of his captors, to be lifted onto a human platform. Raising a cry for silence, he uttered a towering challenge toward Wentworth. "I...am... Garrigan!" he bellowed. "I speak for Mars."

"I will not tolerate this!" Wentworth snapped. "Where is your Governor? Let me speak with him."

A thin voice shouted out of the faceless mob. "He's hiding, in town!" Calls and rough snickers.

"Then we will go to the town."

That was it, the challenge flung. They weren't ready for it. A general outrage welled up, bodies surged forward, all kinds of primitive weapons drawn—pikes, poles, knives, a few handguns. The soldiers wavered, fell back a few paces.

"Rifles at the ready!" Sheffield called out. "Every second man to the west line." Troops began to move purposefully under his orders.

The Captain, meanwhile, had stepped a few meters behind the lines, his own pistol drawn. Sheffield waited for further instructions. Wentworth gave a signal.

"At ten paces, shoot!" Sheffield shouted.

A wild tongue-rattling cry went up from the women in the mob. They had all spread out now, along a good part of the perimeter. Their racket all but drowned out rationality.

The great beast had been awakened at last.

Carson, I suddenly noticed, was stepping right through the lines opposite Garrigan, his jacket open to display a very unmilitary shirt, red-checked and ruffled. He shoved aside the rifles of the surprised spacemen as if they were swinging doors in a saloon. Then he dramatically raised his arms high to show that he was carrying no weapons.

"Carson! Come back here, you fool," the Captain yelled.

Carson turned in mid-stride to show his back to the mob, and his face to the soldiers. Emblazoned on his shirt was a sign I didn't recognize, an orange disk with a serpentine streak of green.

When he turned again, Garrigan held up his arms too, though he still clutched a gun in one hand and an eyeball in the other—this perhaps his new insignia of office. The two large men stepped with equal even steps until they were only a few paces apart.

The war whoop died, and there was utter stillness. I strained my ears to hear, then my credulity. He was talking reason to this madman, and the madman was listening!

At first, a whisper, lost to the wind. Then Carson said audibly, pointing to the landing mechanism of the spaceship, "Someone here has caused harm to the ship that feeds this planet. If this ship does not go, then perhaps there will be no more. Someone thinks little of living long. Is that you, Garrigan?"

"No!" the big man protested.

"I accept your word." Hastily, it seemed. He'd already tricked the Martian into accepting his authority, when in fact he had none at all. "Who then damaged the source of all supplies? Was it you?" pointing at a man nearby.

"No!"

Carson held up one palm. "I believe what you say," A sigh of relief from the man. "But I ask again, is there anyone here who damaged the ship?"

A thunderous "No!" came back at him.

"I believe all of you who answered!" Carson yelled. Mutters of approval. What kind of trick was this? Absolution?

"But yet the ship was damaged. I saw no one leave. There must be someone who has caused this damage."

A pause, no one spoke. I didn't see the point, but he did have the mob under control. Momentarily.

"I repeat," he said, "Someone must be responsible. Garrigan??"

The new leader of the Martians hesitated. Then apparently something clicked in his brain, perhaps from that first whispered exchange. Yes, the staging was right; it was his chance to show leadership ability.

"Oh. Aha, hmm, perhaps it was...mm...Petten. Yes? Perhaps?" His face showed considerable doubt on the subject.

A few men near the two conferees took up the cry when they understood what was happening. "Petten! Petten! Perhaps Petten!" And it wasn't very long at all before a smallish fellow was thrust forward, to stand uncertainly in front of the two—Garrigan with a sudden flush of righteous anger focused on the knave who would dare to damage the ship—Carson, coolly calculating the possibilities.

Carson began the inquiry. Wentworth, meanwhile, was dumb.

The troops scarcely relaxed a muscle, yet it was clear to all of us that we might just get out of this alive.

"...hurt the ship?"

"No, no, I did not."

"You dare to say no? I say Yes!" Garrigan insisted.

"No, no, not I! Please." He cowered to his knees, clutching at Garrigan's legs for mercy, Garrigan loving it. The belted man pushed him away into the sand with an imperious gesture.

Carson halted the emboldened giant with a hand gesture. The mob quieted again, pushing to see what he would say.

"Stand up, Petten," he said, in a gentle tone, gentler than I had ever heard him.

"My friend Garrigan and I are looking for the person who damaged the ship. Perhaps you can help us."

"Yes, yes," the poor man said, unsteadily. His eyes saw a way out, though he didn't quite see how.

"Perhaps you did no damage to the ship. Is that right?"

"Yes, yes, it is so."

"But on the other hand, perhaps you did. We shall see." He faced the crowd now—those who had been pushing forward now fell back— "I ask once more. Did any of you commit this harm to the food ship?"

"No!!" resounded again.

"And you Petten, do you know of anyone else who did this damage?"

The thin man wavered. He looked at the dark faces staring at him, all energy focused on him, ready to let loose at the slightest sign of weakness.

"I saw..." Petten hesitated as Garrigan leaned forward, glanced rapidly back and forth, back and forth, looking for some clue to the correct response. Carson's face was impassive, blank. "...no one."

"Ah!" said Carson turning triumphantly to Garrigan. "We have many Nos and a Maybe. What is your decision? We..." he swept his arm back to indicate the line of rifles still trained on them "...are waiting for your answer."

Petten, however, didn't wait. He saw too clearly what was planned for him, and he ran for it, down the alley open between the two lines. He didn't make it five meters before guns on both sides cut him down. For a second, his body shook back and forth under the impact of the pellets, making dust puffs from his desert clothing. Those who fired were as surprised as he.

And that was that. A question settled, a diversionary question, but what had been established was a rapport that Wentworth's tactics had utterly failed to make, that Wentworth himself barely understood. A compact made on the body of a man. Had Petten's death been necessary? Even now, I don't know the answer to that. Is history necessary?

When Carson finally came back from his parley with the mob leader, he had a settlement under his belt. The crew would be allowed to go into town; I understood that things were apt to be saner, relatively speaking, despite the fact that most of the people we had already seen here were themselves town-dwellers. The governor, it appeared, did have some powers within the compound, and some, but not much, respect, along with a tiny militia and juridical authority...over those who agreed to be ruled.

Safety was guaranteed for the time being; but tomorrow, the same crowd would be back at the ship. Garrigan, along with the other leaders would have a "leading" role in the discussions of how the supplies were to be divvied up. It was no spontaneous rebellion—this, apparently, had happened before.

And that was only the beginning.

‹‹‹14. DISCOVERED‹‹‹

I almost didn't make it back. It was our overconfidence that tripped us up. The early a.m. had been free time for Billy and me, a time when only one officer was awake... young Rogers, who spent most of his time at another terminal playing games with the ship's computer. He had written a chess program, and was refining it, Billy said, by playing game after game, night after night, in the other end of the craft. Occasionally he'd come in to check on Billy, make sure he wasn't asleep, or picking his toes. On those few occasions, Rogers would poke his head in briefly...with a simple warning circuit, we always knew when he was coming by a blinking red light...while I crouched under the desk. He'd report his progress in the variations of the Sicilian Defense, how many times the machine had beaten him with original moves that night, etc.

One night, something was bothering him, and Billy offered a seat. Half an hour later, we knew how awful his mother had been to him, and was he too young to be married, and what did Billy think about women. The alarm bell rang. That did it. A stray asteroid, uncharted, within sensor range, and close enough to collision course to take a look.

Billy scrunched himself in behind the desk, hooking one leg casually over my rear end, the other locking my chest.

I hoped he looked comfortable above-desk. I sure wasn't.

The control room flooded with sleep-roused personnel, mainly junior officers, I gathered from the frantic chatter, when I wasn't too petrified to listen. As far as they knew, I was dead, and rightfully so.

And then Wentworth stormed in. "Shut that damned thing off. What's the trouble?"

Three voices answered at once. I could have described them… eager beavers, one of them sporting a Wentworth-type mustache, the others not quite so obvious. Wentworth ignored them. The protégés loved him the more for it. New-hatched ducklings attach themselves to the nearest "mother"…be it duck, human…or Wentworth. The adaptability of human beings staggered me.

"Sheffield!"

"Yes, sir?"

"What's going on, man? Short circuit, most likely. It's the middle of the night."

"Debris, sir. Apt to be a big one. Calculated minimum proximity at 0651, distance 500 kilometers."

"So? Ignore it. Everybody back to bed."

One of the lieutenants spoke again. "Sir, there's a variation reading on projected course. Apparently 300 km is close enough to affect our course. Request permission to correct immediately, sir."

"Denied. Sheffield, get to work. Tell me about it in the morning."

"Yes, sir."

The departure of Wentworth did nothing to lessen the hubbub and milling legs visible from my perspective. If anything, the argument increased. Not once did I hear Sheffield's voice until he uttered softly, "Check this, will you, Rogers? (Click, buzz) Right, then plug this sequence in, and notify Earth Tracking. Good night, gentlemen. Three more months, eh?"

A mixture of groans and cheers, and then it was broken

off. Rogers stayed, to carry out the program, and one of his buddies lingered interminably, until Billy eased his legs out, grabbed the guitar, and began to play:

So long, goodbye, farewell,

I'll see you when I get to hell...

But as the door went closed, forming a soundproof vibration-free seal from the rest of the ship, Billy let out an irrepressible laugh, and in the slight gravity-sim fell back on his tailbone with a yelp, Rogers jumped up, ran over to help him up, and for an instant, he froze, bent over the man on the floor, my eyes looking straight into his. The sudden blankness in his face turned to fear. He recognized me.

By the time I had managed to extricate myself, Billy had bounded to his feet, and landed the officer with a gracefully slow flying tackle. I tested my legs briefly, and raced over to bend Rogers' fingers away from the audio circuit switch.

Ten minutes later, Billy was talking to the bound Rogers, explaining patiently that we didn't want to hurt him, that I wasn't a mad killer, that Carson wasn't a god, or even a savior, that what was happening had serious consequences, personal consequences upon the ship's return to Earth proximity, that the ship might never reach Earth again, that the Moon was the real destination...but Rogers wasn't ready for that just yet. Neither was I.

"What are you talking about, Billy?"

"I thought you knew, Sandy. Why else'd you come aboard this deathtrap?"

"Deathtrap? That's what I left in Marsville. With the place surrounded, and everybody, I mean everybody, out to get the reward on my head... "preferably dead" was the way Carson put it...there was only one way to disappear in full view of everybody...the ship. But I hadn't a clue that it wasn't all on the up and up. So Wentworth is really in it, eh?"

"The Cap'n's a clever bastard. I just put two'n'two together, only they added up queer. You can check it out yourself. The course we're on is Earth-bound, all right, but about the time we reach Moon-orbit, so's the Moon. Real close. Wouldn't take too much to dock it down on the Far Side.

Rogers broke in. "That's preposterous. You're making it up. Earth Control would know immediately what happened.

"Oh, Wenty thought of that, too. In my spare time here, I found a little prize. Le'me run a program for you. Pretty interesting, for Earth, but they'll get it later, I guess."

Billy punched a few buttons on the terminal, read the spool, punched again, flicked a switch, sat back. I jumped when Wentworth's voice boomed out of the speakers; Billy edged forward to down the volume, and, with just that act, made me accept it as the electronic reality it was. Rogers, I noticed, was fascinated.

"Captain to Control. Captain to Control. Sheffield, what's wrong? What's happened? Is Earth channel open?"

"Yes sir, but we're not receiving. Communications must be damaged. Port engines faulty, we're off course, sir, danger-ously close to Luna orbit."

A hubbub of excited voices rose in the background, but from where I was sitting, it sounded more like what I suspected it was, someone turning up a knob on previously recorded material. With that in mind, I searched the screen.

"Video, man, are we hooked up?" The screen flickered into color. Wentworth's head appeared from the side. A regular little playlet! I glanced over at Rogers, open-mouthed, utter disbelief and surprise on his face. He inched his body around for a better look.

"Yes, sir."

"Earth Control! Earth Control! This is Fleetship *Fledermaus*, Captain Wentworth speaking. We're in trouble. Repeat, trouble at lunar orbit. Do you read me? Need help."

The head dodged away, the crowd noises grew louder...I recognized it this time, it was on our arrival, when the more anxious Martians had begun chipping away at the ship before we'd even stepped out. Billy's deep resonance, Carson's harsh prompting, even Wentworth himself, just barely audible.

Would they notice that discrepancy on Earth? Wentworth's mother might, but she wasn't at the switchboard at Control.

Wentworth came back on, his hair ruffled, standing along his forehead like a cock's comb, in greasy black jagged clumps.

"We're going to crash! Earth-Control. Read us an orbiting sequence, without use of port engines, quickly. Beam all channels; you're not getting through. Sheffield, how long to impact?"

The muffled voice of the veteran Britisher came back. "Aye to half an hour, sir. There's na mistake. We're doon for, sir." Was this someone imitating him?

"Keep an SOS to Earth, and keep all channels open. We've not got much time. Switching off." The screen went dead. From the rest of the ship, the quiet inescapable hum of electricity, a strange silence.

"Well," said Billy finally, "that's it."

"I don't believe it," Rogers said. "I just don't believe it."

"But what's it mean, Billy? And why didn't you show me this before?"

"Like I say, Sandy, I thought you knowed."

"I'm not prescient! Sorry."

"It's not true, you made it up! The two of you!" Rogers struggled against his bonds.

"Sure, sure, we dubbed the voices and wore masks. Right, Billy?"

"Das right, 'N we did it jus' b'fore you came in yere."

"Look, Rogers, I don't know what this...this fraud is all about, but I'm going to find out. Are you with us, or not?"

The youth stared ahead to a point one meter in front of him, thoughts flashing across his forehead...Sunday School, the Pledge of Allegiance, his teachers bending over him for a moral lesson...his brows drew down into a little bridge over his eyes. He looked up sharply, judging us. "What if I do? Will you let me go?"

We would have to, sooner or later. At least he wouldn't be quite so ready to summon the Captain. "Sure. All right with you, Billy?"

"It's fine with me. It's your life."

As I unwrapped him, I could see the deep grooves the electrical cables had made in Rogers' wrists. His determination was strong; he would make a worthy ally.

We talked, then, and agreed to do nothing until we would meet again the next night. If all went well in Rogers' head, I'd have free run of the ship at night...with precautions— and if Rogers gave it away, then I'd be done for, no matter what, and Billy, despite his optimism, would get no better treatment. But there was no point in bringing that up just yet. Perhaps the eternal cold of space, sans suit. Wentworth had no one to answer to, in space. Or did he?

Something struck me. The show we had seen, it had its own reality in the middle of falsehood, as all lies have their truth. And if that was so, then it might hold a clue for us.

"Hey Billy, run that back a minute."

"Sure, Sandy. What's up?"

"I've got an idea. Back it to the beginning, yes, about here. Notice that background stuff?"

"It's obviously faked," Rogers said petulantly.

"Yes, now listen. There, where it quiets down. Someone turned a knob. Right?"

"So what?"

"So that means there must be a third person who's in on this. Right?"

"Wrong, Sandy," Billy said. "Look again. See, it's just at the right time, see the Cap'n bending down to the board?"

"Wait!" cried Rogers. "We should be able to see that. Run it again."

Billy reeled it back once more. I caught on this time, to the reason why it felt like there was someone else there.

"So. All right, Billy, there wasn't a third person running the sound effects. But there was someone running the camera."

"Who?" We looked at each other. "Carson?"

>>>15. CUSTOMS>>>

(debarking on Mars)

We barely made it to town before Martian darkness enclosed us. Tagging along, as usual, I was the last one in the gate, a double-door affair, really a primitive airlock I was told later, open at the top. Sand had crept into the hinges, but then Marsville had been here for more than ten years. The metal walls bore the scars of battering, no telling how recent. I remembered this very scene, a picture in the Space Agency recruitment flyer, captioned with "The Future."

Once inside, two spacemen stepped out of the line to shoulder me aside. "Captain's orders," they said. "All passengers must be cleared through Customs."

"Nothing else seems to require formalities. Why this?"

"Move."

I was led to a large building marked "Administration," not far from the gate. A few brief glimpses down the streets indicated that the town planners had had a high old time of it, but sand swept along unimpeded by any visible signs of maintenance. Piles of garbage sat outside doors or windows like forgotten corpses. Kingston's shanty town had more style, and certainly more color.

I don't know what got into me, but all of a sudden I felt an overpowering urge to run, I didn't know where. The depressing sight of the major city and capital of Mars... endless twisting streets with closed doors on every house, a thick gloom pierced by blades of light. Sand leaked into my shoes; tiny gusts threw up dust devils at the corners, and at my sides, two armed men whom I hardly knew, one of them motioning me into the Administration Building.

We entered, passed a little office, a desk set squarely by the side like a sentinel. Two feet removed themselves from the desk top, two hands gripped the paper I handed over. "Room Three." My guards fell in before and behind me down the long corridor. Walls were flimsy, the floor creaked. If they'd shipped all this from Earth, why did they choose lousy lumber?

Then a door opened, and I was ushered in; the door clicked, clicked again. I was alone.

A chair sat in the corner, but there was no other furniture. One dim bulb shone down from the center of the room. This was the waiting room, apparently. I stuffed my things under the chair, and sat, arms folded, tapping with my foot.

Before long, two men entered, advanced toward me. One of them, the larger, hauled me to my feet, and slapped me across the face a couple of times.

"Hey, wait a minute. There must be some mistake."

"You're Castle, right?"

"Right," I admitted.

"There's no mistake. We're the Indoctrination Team." The other man pinned my arms behind my back, while the first continued hitting me in the stomach, in the head, beating me all over with a short stick. I lashed out with my feet to try to trip him, but that threw me off balance, and I was thrown roughly to the floor. The beating continued. The edge of my mask cut into my face a bit.

And they left me there, huddled in the corner, bruised, temporarily beaten, and very confused.

No one else came that night. I slept on the floor of that unheated building, covering myself with as many clothes as I had, for what little warmth they could offer. The bulb remained on.

In the morning, a hand shoved a tray of food through the door, then closed it quickly. Apparently they weren't out to kill me, or they would have done that already, so I ate with relish the nondescript items on the tray. Once used to the artificial fare of space, I could swallow anything. With food in my belly, I started planning.

The only thing Billy had said about the government on Mars had been "Stay away." Well, I'd taken the wrong choice already. I knew who my enemies were, but I didn't know why, and until I found that out, I didn't know where to start finding friends. Perhaps none at all. Except for Billy.

Where was he now?

About ten o'clock, I was rousted out, brought before a man dressed in tight-fitting clothes, a uniform of sorts. The man who brought me remained in the room, in case of trouble. And a single piece of paper lay on the desk.

"I'm the Customs Officer," he said bluntly. "You'd better pass this form, or you'll have a rough time here." As if that hadn't happened already. "What's going on here?" I demanded.

"Sit down," he said. "I'm asking the questions. Name? Occupation? Intended length of stay? Purpose of visit?…"

He was right, I might have trouble passing this one. I gave the cover story, all the things that, so far as anybody else knew, I was or intended to be. I was writing a novel about Mars, and I wanted the true flavor of the experience.

He looked up with unbelieving eyes, but wrote down what I said. "Well, then," he said when it was finished. "I'll give you my OK, but you'll have to see the Governor. But remember, don't get in any trouble. You're on your own responsibility."

I didn't realize what he meant by those words "on your own responsibility." What it meant was that I wasn't on anybody's payroll, didn't belong to anybody, nobody was going to take care of me, in sum, that I would have to forage for myself wherever possible. And on this planet, that was an unattractive prospect. But for the moment, I was satisfied. Freedom had always been what I'd wanted, and he gave it to me, but good.

>>>16. WELCOME >>>

What the Governor wanted I didn't know, but I soon found out.

A guard led me to another room, only slightly larger, and a man behind another desk only slightly better-looking. The Governor stood, advanced toward me with his hand out-stretched, a smile strung across his face like beads.

"Welcome to Mars," he said. "I hope your visit is a pleasant one." I looked down at him, for he was half a head shorter than me.

"Like last night, you mean?"

"Last night? Oh, I'm sorry, I wasn't here to greet you. We must have missed each other coming back from the ship."

"Your boys didn't miss," I said, pointing at my eye, which was half-closed from swelling up.

"Oh, well, I'm glad someone was here to introduce you to things. I hope they weren't...abrupt."

"They went quite to the point," I snapped. "But 'welcome' isn't quite the word they used."

"I told them, and I told them. My dear Mr. Castle, I hope you don't get the wrong impression of things. We must make do with what we have to work with. Things are always difficult here, you see."

"Yes."

"I see that you are an intelligent man, Mr. Castle. Perhaps

we may be of some use to you in the future."

"I hope not."

"Please," he said "It pains me to see you act this way. Ah, I have it! I insist that you dine with me tomorrow night? Yes, tomorrow night, for dinner. Do you have formal wear?"

I held up the bundle of clothes. "Not very."

"Well, that's all right. My wife will be pleased to meet you, and we can talk of the great things in the future of Mars, eh?"

What was there to lose? He was harmless, and apparently not very powerful. But he was still the Governor. His side of things might not be very realistic, but at least he would be in touch with some things.

"All right. I'll be there."

He leaned on the corner of his desk. "We all get along with each other here," he said. "I hope you will understand that. And if you are ever in any trouble, don't hesitate to call on me. And now, you must have many things to do. But a word of warning to the wise speaks volumes," he said. "There is much disrespect here, and I hope you will understand that the civilizing mission we have ahead of us still has a long way to go. We are a young planet, and in many ways still dependent on the mercies of Earth. But you must understand that Earth is 50 million km. away, and all the things of Earth, when they are transplanted here, grow like a tropical greenhouse, in strange shapes and forms. I wish I could talk with you more, but other matters need my attention. Paul, will you show him out, please."

The guard said nothing, but opened the door for me, and walked behind me past the front desk, with its feet still propped, and he stood in the doorway as I stepped down onto the street.

So here I was, in the metropolis without a name, the capital of the planet whose inhabitants numbered in the hundreds, perhaps thousands.

I decided to follow the energy, and see where people went and what they did, and how they lived here. I shortly discovered that the Administration Building was on a side street, off the main course, which was only a few hundred meters away.

The people I saw glanced up at me briefly and then looked down at the ground in front of them, and hurried on their way. I saw very few women here, one group of three gabbling at each other, until they saw me noticing them, and passed, and gabbled again.

The small windows of the buildings seemed to fit with the isolating coldness of the inhabitants. In ten minutes I had covered most of the town, found no public buildings, few names on buildings, and was no better off than when I started. But the best part of the day was still ahead, and the sun shown down, friendly but small, its weak rays gathering in open spaces, while coolness hid in the shadows.

I stopped at one building, which bore the title Radio. At least these would be comrades of a sort, in terms of communication.

Perhaps I could offer them assistance. I went up to the door, which was locked, and knocked. A face appeared in one of the small panes of glass, and I heard a ruffled voice say "Who is it?"

"I'd like to talk with the radiomen," I said.

After a moment, the door was unlocked and I was let in, by a man with a drawn gun. I raised my hands hesitantly, and backed against the wall. He rapidly patted my pockets, then stood back waiting.

"My name's Castle," I said. "I'm a writer."

He waited.

"I'd like to see what you have, and talk to somebody about radio." The excuse seemed flimsy, even to me, but in truth, I had no other intention. There must be some way of getting to know people.

A couple of men entered the room, talking to each other, but when they saw me, with my back to the wall, they asked the man at the door what was happening.

"Don't know," he said. "Queer fellow. No weapons, and I've never seen him before."

"Neither have I," said the second man. "What's your business. Who sent you?"

"Nobody sent me. I'm a writer."

"Writer, eh? What do you do here?"

"I don't do anything," I said.

"Who do you belong to?"

"I'm on my own responsibility."

"Oh, yeah," he grinned. "That's just too bad."

The three crowded in on me, and I was beaten again, opening up the sores from last night with more cuts. Somehow, the second time around, it seemed more natural, more bearable, even though the pain made me feel intensely every new bruise.

When I came to, I found that they had tied me to a rack in what appeared to be a shed, very cold. Then I realized I was upside-down, my knees hung over a bar of some sort, and my hands tied on a crossbeam near the floor.

My clothes lay in a heap in the corner and the rest of the

things I had been carrying were gone. My money, though, which had been sewn, on the advice of Marco Polo, into the lining of my jacket, was still intact.

What they intended to do with me, I don't know. I intended to get out, if at all possible. But it didn't seem possible.

My legs from the knees down were numb, from the pressure on the bar. And my hands, though apparently tight when they tired me, now had a bit of slack. I must have stretched while I was unconscious, just a bit, just enough to reach my fingers back to my wrist, and catch in one of the loops. I worked at this for half an hour, catching it and losing it again, until one hand was free, then the other. No one was in sight, though I could hear voices from the other room, and the crackle of radio reception.

During this time, I listened to hear what I could, and discover what manner of operation this was. "*Crackle*—fifteen hundred—*pop*—The men—*crack*—and tired. Send help—*zit*—Governor Daniels—*whine*—too late. Can't hold—*crack*—than a couple of hours."

The men in the room laughed, but sardonically. "All right, Mostro," one of them said, "You game to take this to HQ?"

"Bad news?" said the other. "You kidding? Maybe I'll mail it to them. Ha ha."

By this time I was struggling to hoist myself up and relieve the pressure on my legs, rubbing them, to get the circulation going again, before I chanced a drop to the thin floor.

"Starduster, Starduster," the radioman said, "Message relayed. Governor says no help. Sorry."

Then I heard Mostro say, "Hey, let's have some more fun with Nudie-boy."

My legs were about ready now, but before I could get down, the door opened, and one of them stepped through. I leaped instinctively at him, and managed to smash into the door, slamming it in the face of the second man, and apparently knocking him cold. But the man I had toppled was drawing his gun. I leaped on top of him, grabbed his gun hand and smashed it onto the floor. The gun went flying; he kicked me in the groin. I jumped off him, in the direction of the weapon. He pulled me down again, but not before I had cold steel in my hand. And by the time he was read to lunge, it was aimed at his chest. He stopped. Backed off. Hands held high. "No, don't do it," he said, "We was only joking."

I motioned him across the room so that I could put on my clothes while watching him and the door at the same time. I'd managed on my pants and shirt, and had my shoes in my hands when Mostro came in from another direction, surprising me. I knelt and fired. He ducked and fired—but didn't duck quick enough. He lay moaning on the floor, clutching his right shoulder, while I collected the gun he dropped, and motioned the other over by him.

I tossed on my jacket, kicked open the door from which he'd come, saw no one, and dashed through, firing a shot indiscriminately into the equipment. Then, I was out the door, my shoes still in my hand, and running, running, until I was sure that they weren't following me.

With no one in sight, I leaned my back against the town wall, and began to put on my shoes. One gun lay exposed beside me. But while I was intent on the laces, a small dark figure darted by, kicked the gun away with a quick soccer kick, and still running, picked it up off the carom, rounded another corner, and disappeared.

I finished tying my shoes leisurely, and walked in that direction. At least I had the other gun. Nothing. Nobody.

Darker, deeper shadows now. And suddenly, as I had just passed one dark doorway, I felt a fine shock at the back of my head. And fell.

>>>17. QUARTERS >>>

I woke in the early afternoon, indoors. The uniforms and men's voices shocked me into alertness, reaching for the gun that wasn't there. Then a familiarity with the scene, a coziness that disarmed me. These were spacemen, men who'd shared the Great Voyage with me.

"Take it easy," said a young lad whose name I've forgotten. "You've had a nasty bump."

"Ah-oooo."

"Maybe you'd best go back to the ship. Bargaining's over.

Plenty of room now; man, you should have seen them clean it out. Why don't you ask the Captain, he'd..."

"No! Unh, thanks, but can you tell me where we are?"

"They're putting us up here for the time being. Used to be one of the first buildings. Sure is cold, though."

"Yeah." The carpentry looked amateur, with cracks so wide that I was amazed the roof didn't fall in on our heads that instant. But with one-third Earth-gravity, it might last another hour.

Through a door, I saw a crowd of younger spacemen sitting in a circle, eagerly listening. I got up and walked over to see what was happening.

There could be no mistaking Carson's booming voice, and I steeled myself for the encounter. But in the room, he was holding a bevy of listeners rapt with his speech... the glories of the future as he saw it.

"We're going to get together, I mean, really get together, and there's going to be no way that we can fail."

The men with him, I noticed, were familiar faces, but now they were dressed in civvies. There was no mistaking however, the upright postures and rigid attitudes of men accustomed to taking orders and giving them.

"Oh, hello, Castle. Come in, join us."

It wasn't Carson's normal tone of voice, and I assumed that it was as much for the benefit of the men there as for me.

"We were just talking about the way things are here, and it looks like Hell. The Governor," he said, "is a fraud, there's no respect for law or rules, and something's got to be done about it. Cadet Brown—your friend, isn't he, Castle?—is AWOL, and the rest of the crew is suffering from loss of morale."

I nodded. So far, it was all true, but I feared what conclusions he might draw, knowing Carson's background. I was right.

"We need a revolution," he said. "Want to join us?"

"Join what?"

"The revolution, of course. What do you think we've been talking about?"

"Games," I said. "What are you planning?"

"Are you with us or not" he snapped. "God damn it, Castle, I can't ever tell what you're thinking."

I think you're a bastard, Carson. "I think a lot of things."

"Well, what about this situation?" he insisted. "From what I hear, it hasn't been any better since the first ship lost a man through carelessness."

"You're forgetting about the Russians."

"Oh, who cares about them? They all died, didn't they? I'm talking about right now. You walk down the street, and somebody might decide to shoot you."

It was true. I'd run into the same paranoia everywhere I went. Strange how, in a situation where men must depend on each other simply to survive, that so much uncontrolled violence seemed to rule.

Carson turned back to his audience. "We went through a lot to get here, didn't we? We deserve better than this, and so do the people out there. This could be quite a profitable enterprise, if things were run right."

"Who do you have in mind to run things?"

"We'll decide that later," Carson rebutted. "What's important is that something be done, and quickly. Did you know the ship is in danger? Now, I'm not blaming the Governor, he's a fool; they just keep him as a front to run things their own way. But there's been trouble between the crew and the Planetary Guards."

"That's right," one of the officers said. "We were on post around the ship about dusk, when a troop of about a dozen came up to me and said they had orders to take back more supplies, would I let them on the ship. I told them that I had no authority to let them aboard and the supplies were gone, just enough for the crew. They broke rank to try to force their way past me, when the other guards of the ship came up, weapons at the ready. If it hadn't been for Carson here, we would have been goners."

"I was checking with the Captain," Carson said, "heard the noise and went back out. Good thing I did."

"In any case," the officer continued, "He talked them out of it, but it won't be the last time."

"We've doubled the guard," Carson said, "but there's only

so much crew. They want to dismantle the thing for parts, as if the supplies weren't enough."

"I reckon they're right, Carson. These houses weren't built to last forever."

"But they have no right," protested another officer. "How do you think we're going to get back to Earth?"

Hm, maybe I wasn't the only one with that particular problem.

"Look, Castle, if you have something useful to say, then we'll count you in, right? But there's no time to lose."

"I don't like being forced into decisions, Carson. I've made too many bad ones in my life."

"Perhaps then," he said, "you'd better leave."

"All right with me."

On the way to the Governor's house, I pondered these quick developments. Carson was making a grab pretty early. How he knew which way the dust blew so quickly was a mystery to me. Unless, of course, there was something else, not on the surface. Why had Carson come here? It might have been that Earth was getting tight for him—there had been reverses in his career, as well as successes. I even had a part to play in that, indirectly, in the power book. The geothermal plants in Columbia apparently were built and run with rather loose standards for protection of the heat balance. But I had done no more than collect information already public, pointing the finger, as it were, that certain Congressional committees followed with a considerable amount of political revenge in their eyes. Yes, he had no particular reason to think me a friend. Perhaps he, like the unknown party on Earth, simply wanted me out of the way when it came to clinches.

And yet he had offered help. He even offered to hire me...

the surest way to silence a writer...yes, that would have been an interesting job. Perhaps I would have ended up as Secretary of Communications in his cabinet. But no, that's one place that I wouldn't want to be...under his thumb.

Where Carson called the shots, no one was safe.

>>>18. GOVERNOR>>>

The Governor himself answered the door when I arrived, and he showed me in as if I were an old war buddy.

"Come, Martha," he said, "And meet Mr. Castle. He's a famous man."

Whenever anybody gave me that kind of introduction, I ducked my ego out of sight.

"Oh, hello, Mr. Castle, how do you do? I'm so pleased that you could come."

So was I.

"It's lovely here. Nobody to talk to. Perhaps after we finish dinner, I could read you some of my poetry."

"Delighted," I said humbly.

After small talk, we went in to eat. The Governor and his wife had a long beautiful table of dark wood with a lace tablecloth and dainty napkins, and a full china service—all the pieces not on the table were displayed proudly against a mirrored buffet. The house, though not large, was decorated with taste—about 1940, I'd say. But I reminded myself, this is Mars. Only the slight bounce I felt in walking reminded me of that fact.

The meal was simple—canned goods rather than dried—centered by a true delicacy: chicken. We ate at leisure, while the Governor regaled me with stories of his rise through the halls of the upper civil service under five administrators, until it last, he was , so to speak, kicked upstairs. He didn't say what his particular crime had been, but seemed to glory in this fitting pinnacle of his humdrum career.

His wife, on the other hand, expressed old resentments at men younger than her husband being passed over his head, time and again, despite his breeding, his Harvard degree, and his neatly trimmed goatee.

I stifled a yawn when the meal was over, and accepted a proffered cigar.

"Oh, it's perfectly all right," he said. "The oxygen here is regulated on a separate system, and, God knows, we never open the windows."

God knows, I wished they had. The cigar, while not of the worst, only added to the stifling atmosphere.

Te-dium, te-dium, hum-a-ho-hum. The conversation was boring to the point of nod, hum, and oh? and I spent my time examining the feeling of security that these faded walls exuded. Yes, perhaps it was the best way. At least here, cracks on the head must be much less frequent.

After dinner, we eased up the strain of formal talk to stretch. Martha disappeared with the dishes. Yes, water, too, was a luxury provided to the First Citizen and the First Lady of Mars.

"A word of warning, Mr. Castle."

I jerked slightly. I had been looking out the window into the darkness, into the heart of something unguessable, perhaps unknowable. The words shook me out of reverie.

"Don't think that I don't know what's going on out there." He spoke in low tones so his wife wouldn't hear. "It's been hard, oh, you don't know how hard. They call me Governor to my face, but as soon as my back is turned, they call me much worse. Shadows, Castle, it's like fighting shadows. Nothing you can ever put your finger on, nothing specific. You walk the streets in dread? —How do you think I feel, the only visible figure of power in town? It's a wonder I'm still alive. Every day, I think to myself, Harry, you're living on borrowed time. Don't tell Martha that I told you this, she'd be scared stiff. No, it's better to keep up the pretense at least for now. Oh God. Without our dreams, where would we be? Dream on, Mars, god of war. Dream on!"

>>>19. NIGHT>>>

I rounded the corner of the Governor's "mansion" and...
bop!

It was getting monotonous.

>>>20. COTTAGERS>>>

On my third morning on Mars, my unexpected host, a rough-hewn cottager named Lawrence, introduced me to "General" Wilkes, a boastful man with a self-generated reputation for making deals; of special interest to me were the expeditions he organized... or so I was given to understand by Wilkes... between the main mining camp and the settlement. I couldn't care less about the mine... though a chapter was ready for it, in the book I planned to write. But Wilkes was my only chance, I thought... the caravans were about the only organized thrusts into the interior, and I had to see the Outside for myself.

At the back of my mind, I still had hopes of finding Jim Weston; the lost leader of the First Mars Expedition... on the road with his thumb hanging out, perhaps. Two difficulties stood in the way: 1) there was no road... the shifting sands changed the landscape daily. And 2) Jim Weston was dead... so countless people told me with almost religious conviction (we were both wrong).

General Wilkes had his "office" in one of the squares; he stood, cane in hand, at the center of settlement street life, and the doings of the colony that were not entered on the official records stood a good chance of going through his hands. He had a way about him that was akin to a magician's power. A few words in the right place, a little pressure, and the deed was accomplished. So it had been for my passage on one of the departing trucks.

He had two messengers who came and went at his command: Abdu and Arthur. One of them kept him supplied with food, information, or other necessaries, while the other, Abdu, could be entrusted on money errands. Abdu's floppy cap became a familiar sight in the few days I spent there before I left the settlement.

I talked with Wilkes, and made perhaps a bad bargain moneywise to satisfy my insatiable curiosity about this strange planet, but I got exactly what I asked for, which turned out to be more than I was prepared to handle. Money... normally Earth currency had no relevance to these people, yet that was my ticket. On Earth, I was a rich man; here, the only place money replaced raw power was in the black market, and General Wilkes was the main buyer.

Wilkes proved worldly wise, though... out of that useless paper, he manufactured power, as another man makes chairs and tables. He set me up for the day after tomorrow.

Lawrence and his wife Sadie knew no more than absolutely necessary about the doings of General Wilkes; when I pressed them for details, they changed the subject. Obviously, their lives had touched this sensitive area infrequently, and as a last resort. I, on the other hand, had nothing to lose from Wilkes, and a fat contract to fulfill (pretty naive thoughts, but that's what was in my mind).

The cottagers and I ate our last meal in silence...I would leave them in the early morning... but something had not been said. "I'm very grateful," I offered, after the dishes were cleared, "for everything you've done for me... starting with saving my life."

"Tush," Sadie said. The dim light made her strain to see the knitting in her lap; her bent back reminded me of Millet's "The Gleaners." Perhaps the tiny network of filaments reminded her, now and then, of the once-important degree in electronics engineering...little use for that here. The only use it had ever been, she told me, was to get her a berth on a Mars-bound ship. Had she planned to stay? No, well, maybe. And then there was being a woman, and then Harry, with his dogged determination to make a go of it on a planet that was barely able to support the elements of life.

The tiny flame of their oil-can lamp symbolized the cottagers' spirit of individualism... at least they had no debts to the company store. Yet they hadn't staked their claim very far from town, and the influence of the settlement shaped their lives more than they would admit to themselves. .

The choices they faced were hard ones...go it alone, and struggle; or live with others, and be ruled. The cottagers prized their independence above everything, but even then it seemed to me that that independence had been built on compromises. Did it always have to be that way? And what would happen if the politics of the town changed...à la Carson? Suppose their land was pre-empted? Their trading licensed? Better not to upset them now. Good feelings, that's what was needed in this gloom.

"Hey, I'm going to see more of this planet than you."

"Mmm," nodded Lawrence. "Keep your eyes open," he blinked, "for Martians."

"I've already met quite a few...you mean, aborigines?"

He uttered a formal laugh. "Sure, sure."

"I'm practically one myself...I'm living here, aren't I?"

The shadows in his face deepened as he turned down the lamp until the flame threatened to go out. "Listen," he said. "You don't know all."

"No, of course not. That's what I'm going out there to see."

"There are creatures, and things no one has seen. But I have seen..."

"What have you seen?"

"And heard," he said. "Stars blacked out. Things falling." He stared at me hard. "And the shadows of huge birds. People disappear in the middle of the night. And the tracks... Yes, you shake your head, but I know what I know. I wouldn't go out there on one of Wilkes' trucks. I'll stay home with my Sadie."

"Why, what's wrong with Wilkes?"

"Oh, well, that's another story. He's a chiseler, a swindler, a... but at least he's human."

"What's the matter, Lawrence? Snap out of it. You graduated from, where was it UNU? And you..."

"Stanford," he said. "Now look here, Castle, you have no right to accuse me of anything. This is my home, built with my own two hands, and I'm in perfect command of my faculties. You, you come in here with your big important story, and you think you own the planet. Well, you don't own me, Mr. Big Shot. You've been here three days, and you haven't seen anything. Sure, you're going Out There, and I'm sitting here, and you'll see more. You'll see more than you'll ever care to see—if you live."

"Is that a threat?"

"A warning." His voice stopped short. Then he continued in patronizing tones. "Sit down, Castle. I'm sorry I was so abrupt. But you don't understand, do you? You think I jump at shadows, and run from noises. You think all it takes is balls—sorry, Sadie—and all creation will bow before the mighty pen of Alexander Castle. But let me tell you again—nobody has caught the Martians in any book. They don't belong to anything of Earth. This is their world, still. We're just interlopers."

"Harry, don't say that." Sadie crossed herself; Lawrence did the same, automatic gesture.

"So, you are superstitious."

Lawrence grinned sheepishly. "I guess we get that way, out here. It's different in town. We got reason. Let me show you something." He beckoned me over to a low shelf. His wife's eyes glinted in the faint light, surrounded by worry, as if an old sad tale were about to begin.

"Out there," he began, "the desert calls. I have heard it, it's like a blind urge, or an itch in your mind. Know what I mean? Something about this planet. Well, other men have heard it, and followed. How or where they went, I don't know. The cold—it is cold here, yes, but Out There," his voice lowered to a whisper, "This world is inhabited by ghosts." I looked for a sign that this was a joke, but he didn't smile at my irrepressible laugh.

"You can call us superstitious, all right. One night a month, we leave food on the doorstep. In the morning, it's gone. No man can walk abroad in the night wind, no living man. And there are no tracks, just a scuffle in the sand, could be anything. Except for these." He pulled down a fist-sized rock from the wall, and handed it to me. It was heavy for a Martian rock. The edges were jagged, crystalline. I sniffed it, felt it, ran my tongue over it—a faint tingling taste, almost familiar.

"Have you taken this to the Lab?"

He smiled indulgently. "Let me explain about the town, Mr. Castle. About why we moved out. I came here as a trained monkey out of school, thought I'd take this job here because the pay was good, and the promises—well, the pamphlets in those days put stars in your eyes. But then, you come here, you get sand—not stars—in your eyes, in your food, in your bed. When I came, the town wasn't built, and we all lived together in the ship. Went out in the morning and

108

dug, sweated, we did, worked in our shirtsleeves in the cold, with oxygen tanks on our backs good for half an hour. Jackson Miller ran the show then, a tough man but not very... he couldn't keep on top of things... I guess maybe nobody could, after..." He threw up his hands in helplessness, then tilted his head down, a very tired man.

"What, after what, Harry?"

"After, I don't know what it was exactly. We were a good group, people from all sorts of places—Dallas, Maine, California, PONY—and we were making a go of it, but..."

"Wait a minute. I thought it was supposed to be easy after stabilizing the ozone layer. "How come it fell apart?"

His red eyes turned to me with a pitying look. "I'll tell you. It's no secret. Some of us just... got here faster. You know what I mean?"

"No, I don't."

"A few—say, Jim Weston, he's a good example. He just started living here as if that's all there was to it—it's not as simple as that, from what I've heard, but..."

"What do you know about Jim Weston?" Weston, that was my lead, the enigmatic character who was either the only authentic hero Mars had produced, or the worst traitor since B. Arnold. Weston... the man who had turned his back on the space program. Maybe I could track him down, if he were still alive. He must be... fifty?

"Weston came in one day, let me tell you this story before I go on. Maybe it'll answer some of your queries.

"Anyway, we were still digging at the time... now this is true... digging holes in the ground, to live below the surface, below the permafrost. The engineer should have known better, but it didn't seem like there was anything else to do for shelter. And we didn't have any idea of what better to do.

So, he came in... I was working that shift, one of the first to see him. He was wearing a tattered old space-suit with a kind of hood and short cape. His hair was flying, a great beard covered his face, except for a mass of friendly wrinkles surrounding his two blue eyes. He walked up to us... we must have stood with our mouths hanging open for five minutes or more... and you know what he said? Just like he was visiting some new neighbors down the road, he said, "Howdy. Welcome to Mars. Been here long?" It must have seemed strange to him, seeing human beings again, after five years of silence.

I don't remember what any of us said. Just that "Welcome to Mars" struck me funny. Then he laid down his pack, and started digging with us, with his hands... black hands, hard as slabs, and he could dig with the best of us. Didn't say anything much, but there was work to be done.

Finally, Willard, our section chief, called for a rest. We put on our coats, huddled together in the work tent with a small electric stove. Weston plants himself outside, right in front, and you could see his eyes go off in the distance, thinking.

I decided to talk to him—it wasn't just anybody out there, but we weren't exactly sure who he was. So, he told me. And then he asked what it was we were doing.

"Digging for shelter," I told him.

That seemed all right to him, and then he looked around, took in the landscape—this was where the town is now, right in the middle of Craterland, the south part of Meridian, and we were moling into the soil of a huge flat-bottomed crater. "Lost any men yet?" he said.

"One, and a couple of injuries. We haven't hit bedrock yet."

He stood up, peered at the warm ridge about 5 km away. His eye followed on down, slowly, as if he was using X-ray vision.

"You sure this is where you want to dig?"

"It's near the ship," I protested. But I looked out at the crater wall, and down at the hole we had spend all our time digging. Like a chip out of a bowl of jelly. A piece of crust cracked off behind the support wall, and a few chunks tumbled down the incline. The sheet of metal groaned under the strain.

Then he looked around, pointed to the ship. "You going back?" he said.

"Not on that crate. We're here to set up a permanent station."

"Not going to use the ship, huh?" And then he looked back at the small excavation.

Well, to make a long story short, we got the hint, from that and a few other details we really hadn't worked out. See, we'd brought everything you needed to set up a Moonbase... on Mars.

Jim Weston stayed with us for two months, taught us a lot, enough to make sense out of things, and get used to the idea that our heads weren't just to plug up a hole between our shoulders. Before he left, we were dismantling the ship itself to build the town wall. We had ox-boxes aplenty—but no one had ever thought you could just set one up in the open. See, with a wall, it isn't really open, it's more like a fishtank. The wind whips some froth off the top, but all you do is pump out some more. The winds here are really in distinct layers, despite the thinness of the air, so it all works somehow.

Anyhow, one day he just packed up, thanked us for the

hospitality and the food, and left. Didn't say where he was going, or how he lived. I guess, thinking about it now, maybe he made the right choice. I've always regretted that I didn't go with him."

"Harry!" Sadie burst out. "You never said that. I hope you don't mean it."

"Of course not, dear... after all, I might never have met you."

"But what happened to him?" I said, interrupting the family routine. "Is he alive?"

"Nobody knows, Mr. Castle. God, I hope so." Lawrence rested his eyes, as if the memories came too close. "Yes, he knew when to get out. I battled it out for more than a year, and then me and Sadie sort of—we just moved our stuff out here and started again from scratch. And this is it; this is our home."

The cold stones piled into walls scarcely seemed habitable, but the warmth of these two people... Sadie, who didn't say much, but who had picked me up off the street with a pure and open heart... Harry, who talked my ear off after a little priming... they made the little cave a home. Every rock could fall, and sand cover the spot, but I had been at home here. All of the stereotypes of sod shanties and dirt farmers came into sharper focus... these were not important people who had climbed up from nothing; the Lawrences were technically educated, sophisticated people, who had arrived at simplicity after struggle. My respect for them grew every minute I was with them.

But at the time, I had my mind set on some other things. "When was he last seen?" I insisted.

"Who? Oh, Weston? Lord knows. I think the last I heard of him was from a fellow, not a very nice fellow, so I wouldn't trust him too far, but his name is Dalton Arley. Radioman.

He was mixed up in the scandal over water rights—but that hardly matters now."

"Weston?"

"No, Arley. But stay away from him. He's bad medicine. And don't tell him you know me."

"He has something against you, then I assume."

"And vice versa. I wouldn't have mentioned, but you asked."

"But you talked with him, didn't you?"

"He was boasting," Harry said, sullenly. "I couldn't help but overhear."

"All right, I'll bite. What did he say?"

Harry grinned. "I'm sorry if it takes me a long time to get to the point, Castle. I'm not used to talking at all. My jaw is beginning to ache."

"Then it's something you don't want to tell me. For God's sake, don't keep me in suspense. What is it, man?"

"All right," he muttered. "Arley said that Weston had joined the Adventurers."

§

Some time later, I bumped my elbow on the rock that Lawrence had handed me. "Hey, what about this rock? Did you get it analyzed?"

From his corner, Lawrence looked up. His voice was bitter. "Who am I to ask the Lab people for anything? A miner? A geologist? Or a fool? They owe me nothing. But I have run a few tests of my own, given the circumstances. A semi-metal. Oxide of something. pH about 6. Nothing unusual,

I expect, Out There."

"But then why does whoever it is leave these?" I demanded.

"A kind of exchange, perhaps. We can afford it, one day out of fifty-six. We can't afford not to, now. I don't think it's men that come, or if it is, I don't think they come unaided."

"What do you mean?"

"Harry, please," Sadie interrupted.

"It's all right, Sadie. Castle ought to know. He's going Out There." His wife lapsed back to her knitting with an audible sigh.

"Wait a minute," I said. "You've been out there. You said so yourself."

"Yes," he said slowly. "Yes, I have. During the daylight. But at night... I tell you, Castle, there is not much we know about this world, and much that we don't know." A scurry of wind shot through the chinks, and I felt the cold like a creeping thing. The atmosphere of Lawrence's dread was getting to me. I wanted to switch on blazing lights and banish all spirits of darkness. But, of course, they would live beyond the Wall, out of reach of electric power, for their precious independence.

"Where's your freedom, Harry? Is this what you wanted, this... gloom? Maybe I'd better stay the night in town."

"No, no, please, Mister Castle," Sadie said. "That's worse."

"What's worse about it? Better that than ghosts and goblins."

Lawrence stood, and pushed me back down. He looked at me for a moment, then said, "I apologize. I didn't intend to scare you, but..."

"But nothing. I'm in perfect control of my emotions. Apologies accepted. I'm edgy, that's all. What I really need is a good night's sleep. Without dreams."

"I understand. Sadie, are you ready?"

She hastily bunched the yarn together in a small box. "Yes, dear. Now, you can sleep over here, Mr. Castle; Harry and I will sleep on the bench." Her simple domesticity smoothed out my concerns... the polite conventions ruled this household, and I quickly settled into position. The lamp was extinguished, and the tiny howls of the wind through the rocks mingled with my own tired thoughts, and I drifted off to sleep.

>>>21. HERMAN>>>

"He might not have done it, but nobody else was that crazy. It's just too much of a coincidence that the ox-box broke down just when he disappeared. We might have died. That Weston is a menace to life, I tell you. Good thing they outlawed him. Sooner or later, he'll die, one way or another. No, don't talk to me about him, I don't want to hear."

The man speaking was a neighbor of Lawrence's, by the unlikely name of Herman. He wore a pair of bib overalls and a straw hat—that must have taken up a goodly portion of his free luggage. 10 kg was all they allowed me, and things must have been tighter then.

"Lawrence said he was a bloody gentleman."

"Gentle? He was strong. Did he tell you about the fight he had with old Rousebones Jones? He whupped that fellow right around the ring and back again. Don't know if it was karate or what, but Jones couldn't keep on his feet. Bam! He was down again. Could have killed him, but that wasn't his way. He was a rough one, though. Skinny legs and arms, but he sure knew how to use them."

"Who did he talk to? Did he have any friends?"

"Yeah, sure, he fooled lots of them. Quite a few folks thought he was some tough shit. But you'd have a hard time finding them now."

"Why is that?"

"I guess they're mostly dead by now. Or missing. You never know what happens, one day, they aren't there. The call of the desert, maybe, just wandering off. No telling. Yup, the trouble really started after he left."

"Lawrence didn't mention that."

"Not surprised. Not surprised at all. You see, we had a big meeting after Weston was gone. Rousebones ran it... Big Jack didn't count... and the upshot was that Weston was declared osterized from the camp. It might not have been his fault, but when he was around, there was trouble. That's all there was to it. Morale, we needed morale, stick together and get the job done. But it was too late, the damage had been done. That's when the killing started. First there was a purge... now I'm not justifying Rousebones, may he rest in peace... and then there was secret murders. I formed a compact with two of the fellows I could trust... for protection. But when I came home one night and found them both dead, well, I didn't stay one more night in that town. Lawrence put me up until I built this heap here."

Lawrence halloed us from a distance. It was time to go.

"One last word, Mister. Don't dig up old griefs. The dead deserve their rest. Understand?" He looked at me to be sure I understood. Then he hoisted his scumming gear to join Lawrence.

"See you at dusk, Castle. Sadie will take care of you. But don't mess with my woman. Y'hear?"

I grinned back.

"I'm just passing through. Don't worry."

Even in the light gravity, I was still barely able to stand. I gave one last wave, but they were already engrossed in country talk.

As I wandered back to Lawrence's hut, an Earth song ran through my head.

In the pines, in the pines
Where the sun never shines,
Where did you sleep last night?

‹‹‹22. DREAM‹‹‹

I had a dream last night.

Pyotr, or my father, was in a large chamber, Bible in hand, shouting across the room.

"May it please the court to enter this document into the official record. It bears on the accused and it is in the hand of the deceased, Alexander Castle. The papers were found on his person just a few hours after his return to Earth. The Court of Inquiry will find it revealing (Sees All! Tells All!)."

"Permission granted. Proceed." The Governor, in periwig, spoke from a high bench. Beside him the local policemen from my home town, Socrates, and a few old presidents.

A shadowy figure, probably Carson, melting into the symbol of United Power, interrupted. "Objection, your Honor. This paper is nothing but a trashy piece of fiction, to be sold on drugstore racks. It's irrelevant and impertinent."

"Counsel?"

"Impertinent, shall we say, in the common, not the legal, sense...yes, and this is half its value for us today. Irrelevant? No. The account in this hook is narrative, it is true, though not fiction...no more fiction than the story we already heard today from the counsel for the defense. Unfortunately, we do not have the author here to testify..."

 (I struggled to open my jaw, shout my existence)

"...his book must speak for him."

At this point I woke from noise. Billy says he had to cover

for all the clatter I was making by himself bumping into some expensive equipment. I could hear the Captain tear into him about incompetence, insubordination, etc., etc. It nearly broke me up.

>>>23. SADIE>>>

Lunch of moss soup and a close relative to hardtack gave me energy, but Sadie insisted that I go back to bed and rest.

She had plenty to do, she said, besides looking after me...

I watched her, hour after hour at the rough spinning wheel, her fingers gifted with quickness, her mind focused on the work.

In the early afternoon, she came over to me without saying anything, sat on the side of the bed. Something was wrong, I didn't know what. And for no reason, she started looking weepy, holding back, keeping tight.

I extended my hand to hers like a good father. "What's the matter, Sadie?" in a voice as gentle as I could manage.

She looked at me, and those eyes just filled with water, and then I was holding her to my chest, not knowing any more, and she unable to speak through the tears. I held her close, felt her hot cheek on mine, moist, flushed.

"Sadie," softly. "What is it? Anything I can help with?"

Sobbing, she shook her head, and her whole chest heaved. She clung to me all the tighter, as if I were her last hope.

"Come on, crybaby. Tell Daddy all about it." I sat up, forcing her apart from me, and her eyes just stared at me as if I should know something, do something.

"S...Sandy. I...you..." I gave a stern deadpan face, expressionless, though I felt a warmth for the closeness to a

121

woman. And even her attractiveness, though in this situation, it didn't make any difference.

I leaned my forehead against hers; our noses touched. She broke again, clutched my head with both hands, held me, her face in my neck. I placed a kiss on her neck lightly, and her arms tightened, her breath seemed to let up. Another peck. And then I felt the same on my neck, and a whispered "Sandy!" in my ear. I felt weak all of a sudden, and lay back down. She moved half onto the bed this time, her hands lightly touching my hairs, my head. With one arm, I raised up, rolled her mouth down to meet mine, our lips touched, and the pain in her eyes vanished like vapor.

The words came later. I was still really weak, and it might have been moral weakness as well. My life hadn't prepared me to follow an ethical path. She was there, wanted me. I was there, and hadn't been with a woman for nearly a year. I'd forgotten how basic our human instincts were.

Ten minutes later, she was in bed with me. Strong and sudden, like the winds, soft as fur, the delicate body hairs reaching out for ecstasy. And it happened, just as Lawrence had warned me. He knew.

It was a good fuck, a real good fuck. The female body did wonders for my health. I felt really exhausted, but really a man again.

And Sadie did not want to put her clothes back on, though the chill in the air fastened right onto the fine sweat on our bodies.

We lay there side by side for an hour.

"What will you tell Harry?"

She rolled over and looked me in the eyes. "I don't know. Nothing."

"Nothing? Well, yes, nothing happened, really. Did it?"

"No, it's not true. But...Harry isn't part of it." She shifted position. "Sandy, I can't stay here. I don't know what I'll do, but I can't stay with Harry. Oh, I love him, though."

"Do you have any choice?"

"No," she admitted. "But maybe..."

"Not with me, Sadie. Get that straight. It's been a nice lay. You got your kicks and I got mine, and Harry won't ever know a thing. But I came here to do a job, and that's what keeps me together. I like you, Sadie. You saved my life, and you're a good woman. But a good woman for Harry."

"Yes," she mumbled tiredly. "But not forever. You'll come back, I know you will."

"Maybe." At that moment, I felt the twinge of twisted emotions clashing inside. She was writing me a big part in her script, but it was a small-town production and her imagination didn't offer me what I already had. It was her dream, not mine.

"Of course I can wait."

"Sadie..." It was no use. She had been here too long, out of touch with other possibilities, and when I came along, I was the way out of there.

"When does Harry get back?"

The tears came back. She stood, naked, and as each piece of clothing went back on, so did the slope to her shoulders, the worn look of her features, the psychic scars of a life-time of not getting what she wanted.

"I'm sorry, Sadie. It isn't right. You'd hate yourself."

"Ha. Like hell I would. Harry can make it alone. He's strong." But flickers of doubt at her own words burbled in from another part of her mind. She would stay, I felt certain of that. The heart was too big. And it wasn't hate for Harry; she'd said as much. It was the restlessness that brought her here in the first place.

When Harry finally did come back, I was lying down, Sadie was spinning and a dark space hung between us, a gap with a slender thread across it, a filament of having touched and been touched, of having known for a moment the intimate details of someone's mind or heart, knowing that that tenuous tie would not break before the rocks we sat on, though it might dangle on between circumstances indefinitely. That's what I thought then. I dreamed of Sadie, not that night, but later, and always she was love itself coming to me. Love and strength of desire. Could it have been? Yes, easily. But I loved Harry, broad Harry with his problems and speculations, with his common sense and stubborn ways. I fucked your wife, Harry. Will you throw me out to freeze? No, he wouldn't. I hated him and loved him for that alternately. What kind of man, what kind of life is this?

Mars, he would answer. This is Mars.

>>>24. CARAVAN>>>

Abdu woke me while the Lawrences slept. "Come," and a beckoning hand, was all I needed.

My pack was ready by the door, and Abdu heaved it up on one thin shoulder. I looked back once. There was no point in waking the cottagers... my thanks had been said, and there was really nothing else to say, until I returned.

The sky was still dark: starshine cast a faint glow on the exterior of the smooth city wall. Once inside, we walked along narrow streets toward a part of the settlement I had not seen before.

Abdu led me to an old quonset building, not far from the main gate.

Inside, a single light bulb pulsed brightly... aside from the main ox-box, power would be strictly rationed.

"General" Wilkes stood talking to a swarthy man with heavy mustache, bushy muttonchops. They started whispering as soon as they saw me, but their gestures and expressions showed that there was an argument in progress.

Finally, Wilkes reached into his pocket, turned sideways with his back toward me, and something changed hands, for the mustache nodded without another word, retreated to one of three huge trucks standing by, and swung aboard. Wilkes came over to me.

"Ready, man?" he said. He poked my belly with his cane. "Y'eaten?"

I shook my head, and knocked away the intruding instrument.

"Arthur!" he bellowed. The second boy crept out of a nook, rubbing sleep from his eyes. "Some grunts for the gentleman here. Step to it, you've got ten minutes maximum." A crack from the cane caught the boy's calf as he started obediently toward the door.

He winced, but did not cry out.

The interior of the shed—grease-spattered floor, dingy walls, the corrugated iron rusting from oxidation—probably had not been cleaned in fifteen years. Aside from a tiny office, likewise filthy, a workbench, and some scattered scrap parts, only the three beefy dump-trucks occupied the building. Two men sat in each cab, except for the last one, the one with Mustache.

"So, what's the plan?" I said.

"Plan? That's up t'you, man. You want Out, that's my business— I get you Out. After that, you're on your own."

"But where do I stay? In the mine?"

"Sure, good place. Below the frost. Ain't no hotel, but that's what there is. 'Course, you make the arrangements. Got your wherewithal?" he rubbed thumb and forefinger.

"I've got everything I came with. Typo, notebooks..."

"Spare me the inventory, chum. Ah, vits!" The boy, Arthur, returned carrying a tray. Wilkes snatched out a hot biscuit and popped it in his mouth. "Mm-mmh! Hot! Eat, eat!"

The great door opened, to a gray-tawny sky. The first truck rubbed noiselessly forward, and out into the deserted street. I grabbed biscuits, started chewing, as the boy moved me closer to the third vehicle. The rest I jammed in my pocket, patted him on the head, and leaned up to the cab door. The driver didn't bother to look; all he said was "Shut the fucking door," and we were off.

Just before we reached the double-gate of the town, a bobbing head appeared on my side of the truck. It was Abdu, trying to attract my attention. I fumbled at the door. "Slow down a minute, will you?" I said to Mustache. How do you open this window?"

He glared at me, pointed to a little release button. I jabbed at it, just in time. Abdu, panting, tossed me a package; he waved as the first of the airlock gates closed behind us. I waved back.

As we drove out, the landscape lay before us, no longer a cheap vid-postcard shot, but the real thing. This was Mars, the spectacular features of a growing planet on every side. A few bright stars still clung overhead, though the sun was already climbing. Like the deserts of Earth, morning comes swiftly here, the pastels shading into a grand partial rainbow of reds, oranges, yellows, and a tinge of greenish yellow highlighting the edge of a cloud-mass. We rode out on sand and barely-covered rocks, with a gentle sway from the enormous balloon tires and free-floating suspension. Without a load in the back, the cab sat high above the ground.

The morning air was so clear, dust apparently settling out at night, that we could see as far as the horizon would permit. To the left, an expanse that showed the curve of the planet... Lawrence had mentioned the Zipper, which lay in that direction, a gulf three miles deep and sixty miles wide. No one had crossed it yet, though the site of the downed Soviet expedition was probably on the other side.

To our right, a valley, rough-cut between two mountain ranges, crooked around a bend, but by our present course we would miss both valley and mountains. We were headed straight across a barren plain, occasional outcroppings abruptly interrupting the smooth surface with fantastic wind-carved shapes.

In the distance, a low rim arced around on both sides. I looked back to verify the formation as an ancient crater, meteoric or volcanic. The settlement would be about in the middle of it.

A yellow bank of clouds floated peacefully on our far left. Endless reaches of pink and green and orange colored the buff earth... even the dust trails of the two vehicles in front of us could not obscure the wonder I felt that morning, high over the sand in a whispering electric tank that bounced and leaped like a dune buggy. A gentle spray of sand formed enormous wakes behind our trio; it felt like flying.

Mustache stared straight ahead. I offered him a biscuit. He glanced at it, sniffed it, and ate. Apparently a ride out was all I was going to get. His scowl was etched in, and his black greasy hair hung down in ragged clumps.

By limitation of space, however, we were in intimate companionship for the duration. The tiny cab almost forced us into each other's lap. No expenses had been squandered on these knockabout vehicles.

The seats had no cushions; instead, they offered only a slightly yielding plastic molded surface. Windows were scratched and dirty, the shift knob was held in place with black tape, and the interior felt like it had been designed by malevolent midgets.

A steady hiss behind our heads annoyed me at first, but I quickly realized that this was oxygen. A bare minimum system; crude, but it seemed to serve. Anyway, the truck would get me there, and that was all I cared about.

About mid-morning, I suddenly remembered the parcel. Perhaps it was food. The dark handkerchief it was wrapped in looked used ... but then, laundry would be an expensive process. Wilkes probably didn't make use of it too often. But what could he have sent me?

The main piece in the bundle was a webbed belt with a large soft plastic buckle. Nice, but what for? A talisman of the space age?

"Mm," remarked the driver, glancing at the short belt. He did not elucidate.

There was no food in the package however, except for a much-handled candy bar of an inferior brand. Save it for later, Sandy. You'll need it later; this is going to be a long trip. Still, my stomach needed settling.

As if in answer to my unasked question, Mustache pulled out a shallow can with a "Copenhagen" label. That was why I kept whiffing tobacco.

But what was it the customs man had said when he confiscated my cigarettes? "No smoking, anywhere, ever. You want to blow us all sky-high? No fires of any kind." No fire, no water, no air. But sand, now, plenty of sand... in food, in bed, in clothes.

And tobacco. That explained the peculiar coloration of Mustache's mustache... tobacco juice.

"Can I have a little of that?" I said. No harm in asking.

His fingers closed around it, and he moved it toward his pocket without opening it.

"Wait." I fumbled in my pockets, searching for an exchange item.

Subway tokens, cheese, a crumpled dollar bill, keys to a Manhattan hotel suite, a book of matches from a Chinese restaurant... how did Customs overlook these?

He reached over, snatched up the red and gold matchbook,

flipped it open... green heads on wide black cardboard. He closed it again, looked at me, and waited.

"Something else?" I asked, reaching in another pocket.

"No. This," he hissed, thrusting the can at me. Before I could say another word, the matches had disappeared into one of the zippers of his suit.

I gingerly lifted the lid, smelled the rich black substance. Ah, my nicotine fit would be over. Smelly breath? Well, I had that already. So did my companion.

Half an hour later, I was still chewing. The other trucks were on either side of us, keeping about the same pace as before. Suddenly, we lurched to one side. Mustache peered intently off to the right.

I looked in that direction, but saw nothing, just a low yellow cloud.

Nevertheless, all three trucks now angled away from it, at a speed I hadn't thought possible in the ungainly vehicles. Nothing seemed unusual about the formation at first... after all, Martian weather had a reputation for unreliability. Now, a little sandstorm like that... what harm could it cause? We were completely enclosed, with our own air supply; and it would take a mountain of dust to bury us.

But Mustache tromped harder on the accelerator, as if we had an appointment with the Prime. Every now and then, he'd glance up malevolently at the cloud, which was visibly growing by now, but surely no larger than the spray we were leaving behind us.

The wind apparently swept it off the floor of the planet, though a crater wall stood between us and the peculiarly shaped dust cloud. It struck me, about the time the yellow swirl reached the ridge, that perhaps what I was watching was no natural occurrence.

And then appeared, on the distant cliff, a tiny row of dots. In a moment, the cloud began to disperse. A tiny whine disappeared at the same time... it had been barely noticeable through all the wind whistles and sand patter around the truck. Those specks must be machines.

Abruptly, the whine started again. I couldn't believe my eyes; at this distance, the cliff must have been hundreds of feet high, yet those black dots were racing, falling down its face at incredible speeds. Puffs of cloud began again more than halfway down.

"Hey, who are they?" I shouted into Mustache's ear.

"Adventurers," he said, drawing a gas-gun from under the dashboard.

"Who?"

"Death, friend. That's death coming." He hadn't spoken so many words in one breath before.

Then I recalled Lawrence's warnings... were these the creatures he meant? I hadn't anticipated technological monsters.

They were well past the ridge now, faint black specks at the head of a cone of billowing gold. Whatever they were traveling on, they came incredibly fast.

As I watched, fascinated by the spectacle, Mustache maneuvered us closer to the other two trucks. There was no doubt that the yellow would overtake us. The question was when? And how?

We pulled alongside one of the other trucks: the frightened face of the man beside the driver stared out... his face, and the barrel of a gun. Mustache made a move to get around them, but by now we were getting clogged in our own dust. The other driver pulled ahead, then turned sharply to the left in front of us. Then I caught a glimpse of the third truck, cutting across our wake in the opposite direction. Like rabbits in the chase, they'd gone crazy from fear! Yet Mustache seemed, if not calm, at least intent on what he was doing.

On the second pass, the complex operation began to make sense to me. This was backfield in motion creating a cloud of confusion, in our case, a thick soup of a cloud. The strategy was to confuse the opposition, but not ourselves... as long as we remained perilously close to each other, the plan stood a chance of succeeding. But I, for one, couldn't see a thing.

The dust collected on the windshield in tiny splotchules now, their ticks sounded like gentle rain. The unlit interior of the cab grew darker; bristles of the driver's mustache stood out in silhouette against the yellow screen of flying sand behind him. Sudden shifts in direction tossed us against each other; there was precious little to hang onto.

The maneuvers of the trucks became more erratic, and at moments it seemed as if we were going to ram each other. Finally, we were racing after the truck in front of us, just barely visible through the dense yellow fog. And the weight pushing me against the door let me know that we were traveling in a circle, a tight little circle, throwing up immense quantities of sand particles. Just in the middle, I could see through Mustache's window, a clearing area, like the eye of a hurricane.

How long did they expect to keep up this delaying action? And where was the rescue squad going to come from this time? The adventurers' speedy vehicles may have been more vulnerable to the onslaught of the sand artillery than the trucks were. I'd had only glimpses of the approaching band, not sufficient to identify the distinct shape of the adventurers' carriers; mainly vertical, but it was nothing I'd seen before.

All of a sudden, a black shape hurtled into the inner, less dense sphere and I could make out one of the riders. He was seated in the open, on a huge wheel, or rather inside it, so that the wheel, which resembled the back tire of a tractor more than anything, very wide and big, moved around his body. The wheel was more sensitive to the sand; the rider slid back and forth in his seat in fits and starts, fighting for control. But he knew where he was, and he sprang for the truck right ahead of us. A shot rang out of the truck; Mustache rolled down the window just a peek, fired, and hit the great tire, which wobbled into our path. There was no way of telling whether the crunch and bump under our tires was the vehicle or the man.

Mustache scarcely glanced at me. He stared into the thickness ahead, to keep the square figure of the truck in front in view. Suddenly, the weight shifted in the other direction again, throwing me momentarily into Mustache's lap. Now, we were apparently the third of a line, headed more or less straight for what appeared to be a low spot on the ridge. Once there, the landscape might afford some protection other than the clouds of sand, and the trucks.

And now we three were in what appeared to be Contingency Plan C... the zigzag. Truck Two, the one ahead of us, oscillated from side to side, and from the swirls of dust further ahead, the first truck was presumably oscillating on an opposite course, corresponding to our own dodging pattern, the three of us thus creating a wide cloud sprayed far on each side. And yet that first truck must have been unprotected in front. We must be close, or he would not have chosen to ride point.

A terrific crunching sound startled me. As we sped on, I saw the wreckage of the second truck, its wheels still spinning, half-lofted onto a low rock outcropping.

"Poor bastard," Mustache said. One down, that left two of

us. That peculiar high-pitched whine from the Wheels now permeated the yellow atmosphere, and etched an indelible neural groove down my backbone.

Before I knew it, a man's head materialized out of the fog, right outside my window, and the Wheel spinning around him was almost as high as the truck. "Look," I yelped.

"Shoot him," Mustache said, and thrust the gas gun into my left hand.

I don't know whether aggression is inborn in human nature, and only put to sleep in the last few centuries of arguing against having wars at all, but the natural movement of my own hands surprised me… window open a crack, muzzle out, aimed at the face of the man on the Wheel, who might or might not have killed me… every second sticks in my memory. But it was that face, blown apart, that burned into my brain. That, and the thonk of the Wheel, wobbling wildly now, crashing against the side of the truck, and then spinning off into invisibility. Nonviolence, compromise, truce… these had no reality here. They were merely petty Earth luxuries. And eagerly, I looked around for another target.

Another one popped up, coming almost straight at us, playing chicken, a black vertical shape, spraying sand over its head like a hood. But before I could angle around for a shot, Mustache had run him down, squashed him like a bug, the tremendous weight of the truck coming down on him. We leaped into the air like a colt, landing almost straight; a dangerous swerve to maintain balance, and we were back on the track, behind the leading truck.

I looked down. My palms were sweaty, I could hardly hold the gun. It wouldn't have done much good; there were too many of them now, coming on all sides. Pellets splatted against the body of the truck. The window by my side suddenly broke into a spiderweb pattern, and a tiny hiss of oxygen escaped through the hole.

"Give me that," Mustache ordered, and I handed over the gun. I felt helpless, a passenger on a doomed journey, wishing I had never forced my way on this expedition, wishing I had never been handed this assignment, which at the time had been so like a plum, but was proving to be a rotten apple.

Mustache rolled his window halfway down. The whoosh of sand almost blinded me instantly. He put his whole arm out, the other hand on the steering wheel, maneuvering the truck like a polo pony between the great Wheels of the adventurers. And they were down, one, two, and then his arm went limp. He leaned over me to haul it in, but the truck spun out of control; one of the tires must have been hit. And we rolled, once, one and a half times, and for a brief moment, all I heard was the whistle of the sand, the spinning of tires in the air, and the whine. A whoop of victory went up from a dozen gruff throats. Now there was one truck, and it must have been still going, because the Wheels made a cursory inspection of us, then chased on after the remaining quarry, seeing that the turtle would never walk again.

I may have been unconscious for a few moments, for when I looked up, Mustache was putting a belt buckle like mine over his face, fastening it with his good arm roughly behind his head like a bandit, and crawling, his left arm still limp, across my legs to push open the door on my side and crawl out.

A shot. I felt his body jerk, then slump against me. He had made it halfway out the door. I froze at the roar of a lone Wheel spinning sand, and rich black laughter that faded into the distance. There I lay, pinned, more or less upside down. The door was clogged with what I had to assume now was a dead body.

The dry air sucked at my lungs. I was gulping at the thin air before I realized that I'd better get out of there. With a desperate effort, I twisted myself around to gain footing, and shoved manfully at Mustache to heave him all the way out. I followed fast. As he crumpled on the sand, I thought I detected a twitch, a last twitch, but when I crouched down beside him, sheltered by the truck from the view of the adventurers, it was glazed eyes I saw, and a noise from his throat I heard. The fingers of his left hand grew lax and let loose the gas gun. I grabbed this, and looked around for shelter. The empty bed of the truck, now upside down in the sand, was almost completely enclosed. It was the "almost" that caught my eye... a corner of it stuck up, just behind a tiny sand ridge. If there was refuge, that would have to be it.

I left Mustache then, and crawled, squeezed myself under the truck, until I was wholly inside the cavity, dug sand with my hands and my feet, pushed it frantically toward the opening, until it was completely closed and I was in darkness.

Just in time. For I could hear, as if very distantly, the sounds of the whine, then men talking or shouting near me. They must have gotten the third truck. And there were other sounds. When I rested my head against the cold metal, I could hear them messing with the truck; not content with the occupants, they were desecrating the machinery, too. Tearing out wires, unscrewing bolts, they were like metal mice all over the carcass.

If they did look under the bed of the truck... and it seemed inconceivable to me that they wouldn't sniff me out... then they had better not find me here. Fighting it out with the gas gun would be suicide. It was time to start digging again.

I felt around in the dark until I was approximately in the

middle, and dug a long shallow trench, big enough to lie down in. Then, I covered up my legs, and my feet, and my belly, and my chest, till there was nothing showing except the gray tip of my hood.

I was blacking out from lack of air, almost belly-laughing at the grave I had just dug for myself, when a last rational thought wandered by... it wasn't lack of air in this closed space that made me gasp, it was not enough oxygen on Mars. What was it Mustache had done, the last thing before climbing out? Put a belt across his nose? I stifled a chuckle, and tried the same thing, uprooting one arm to do it. It fit my nose perfectly, and instantly I felt what seemed like fresh air. I barely had time to fasten it, when a chorus of human grunting interrupted my new discovery... a great slice of sky cut into my consciousness. I let my free hand fall, and squinted one more time to see, not sky, but a slash of light across the metal box of the truck. Plato's shadows! Whoever was looking in would see perhaps nothing... the top of my hood covered with sand, my arm hidden by the mound I had made over my body.

Would it work?

One man crawled into the space. His breath, the huge bellows effect steaming through his nostrils, sounded like a charging bull.

Terrified, I looked up; one eye stared directly down into my two... a harsh, ugly, cruel face, distorted into gigantic features by its proximity. I lay petrified, unable to move or scream. He glanced quickly over his shoulder, then looked down at me, pinched my exposed arm, and grinned. Half his teeth were missing.

He then backed out without a word, and the band of light closed down like a clam shutting its mouth, leaving only a thin sliver of brightness. I could make out the voices much clearer now, and his voice among the others. "Neets," he shouted. "Nyeh zayetih." The accent placed him as Eastern European, though it scarcely mattered.

No further efforts were made to overturn the truck. I didn't know what to think.

The voices seemed to he concerned with the body of Mustache, and the mechanical or electrical innards of the truck. They were apparently taking the wheels and whatever came away loose in their hands.

There must have been twenty of them. The leader had a gravelly voice and a way of commanding that suggested pirates. They spoke in an Earth language, though I understood a word only now and then ...a polyglot tongue of English, perhaps Spanish or Portuguese, German, some Slavic components, and here and there I caught the rhythm of darker speakers, perhaps Indians or West Indians, with the peculiar lilt they give to English. "Sava Sava," I heard. "Raust ermano."

Then they were quarreling about something. The big man... the one who had saved me... apparently, pushed to the front of the crowd, and bellowed a challenge to the leader. While this noise was going on, I surreptitiously covered my remaining arm with sand as best I could, leaving as little of me as possible above the ground, as before.

The argument was so vociferous that no one but me paid any attention when a few scattered shots rang out in the distance, with that peculiar slow-traveling sound of the Martian atmosphere.

Perhaps they were not dead in the other trucks, but merely surrounded. And I, who had just killed a man without even thinking about it, had removed myself from the action like a coward, leaving them to die as the jackals closed in for the kill. But no, I put myself in this hopeless position, and now I could do no more than to try to breathe air into my lungs as shallowly as possible so that the sand above my chest would not fall away. Why had I been spared at all? I did not trust my benefactor; he didn't seem the type. If he had saved me from discovery, perhaps he was saving me for himself.

Amid the shouting of the crowd outside my truck, a pair of men were sporting and panting mightily. In a few minutes, the sudden groan of one of them, and the cheering of the rest, marked the end of the loser, that was clear. From the sounds that followed, all sorts of horrible things seemed to be going on, but, not having witnessed any of it directly, I have to attribute to imagination all except the ferocity with which they pursued their savageries.

Through the shell of my hood, and the greater shell of the bed of the truck, and the high wind that now and then sent a spray of fine dust over me, the group outside sounded like a surrealistic tribe of cannibals after a hunting spree. I wasn't far wrong.

I recognized the hiss of an acetylene torch, and there was no mistaking the acrid smell of burned flesh, or the tearing and chewing sounds, lip-smacking, grunts and belches, of a feast. With a shock, I mentally checked out all background reading on the red planet, subdivision "Life on Mars: Edible Animals," and with an involuntary shiver of horror down my spine, it struck me—the main course of a meal for twenty must either be the man who had sat beside me in the truck, or the loser of the combat. Mustache would be too stringy for this kind of enjoyment. I pictured my leg being roasted over an open fire, my torso spitted and turned—but of course such niceties of cookery were luxuries of an oxygen-rich climate. I shrank my body into insignificance, almost gagging on the odors and the thought of what or who was out there, and what they were doing. I didn't dare make a sound.

After an interminable while, the gang suddenly leaped to their feet.

"O passaro, passaro!" one of them shouted. "Avio!" another replied.

And suddenly, they were running every which way. One of them, I could see by his movement across the bright line of light in front of me, had laid his belly across the opening of the little cavity where I lay hidden. His vulnerable belly must have been no more than three feet from my head and it would have been a simple matter for me to have aimed the gas gun, fired, and had revenge for my companion, for civilization, for whatever values I had been brought up to hold dear that hadn't been ground away already by the experience of the last few days.

But I did not. Out of fear, perhaps. Or because I didn't know what was happening outside. A new, more vicious group? There were shots, and shots returned, from what seemed indiscriminate directions.

A pellet clanged against the empty truck bed, and for a moment, I couldn't hear anything else. Then, the unpleasant sound of the little motors on the Wheels started up. The gang was making a run for it.

I took a chance. The man against the truck was still in the same position, clinging to the truck for protection. I twisted about, aimed just at the sand line, end shot him right in the middle.

The clamor of my gun deafened me, but in the confusion, no one else seemed to notice it.

But then, peering through the slit, I saw one of them coming back, yes, the one-eyed man, who had drooled over me. He scooped up the body, and he must have seen the hole in the stomach of the corpse, for he purposefully kicked sand at me, catching me in the eyes. I sat up abruptly, bumped my head, tried to wipe my eyes with my mittens, which were also covered with sand. When I could see again, the Wheels were riding off, scattered across the plain, but generally headed for the mountains near the spot we had first sighted them.

I lay back, petrified, not knowing what to think. Any second now, the rival gang would be here. Whoever had chased these monsters away must be tough. I had to assume that they were human, but at the moment, that was no redeeming feature. I heard no other vehicles than the Wheels but I waited.

I waited for an hour. Finally, hearing nothing except the wind and my own breathing, I slowly pulled my numbed legs out of the sand, turned myself over to a crawl position, and peeked out. Nothing but sand. And in the distance, there was the third truck, rolled onto its side. I dug a crawlspace out, next to where the adventurer had lain, poked my head out, then my shoulders, and wriggled the rest of myself outside. Crouching, then standing, I blinked rapidly to adjust my eyes to what was now overwhelming brightness. Nothing moved across the entire horizon. I looked in every direction. Nothing. A light thin cloud, apparently natural, swept across high above my head.

I climbed up to the top of the truck, near the front wheels, stood balancing myself, eyes shielded. The low ridge that we were trying to achieve looked too smooth, too open... it would have afforded no protection to the trucks.

The serpentine trails of the escaping Wheels, gone an hour before, were almost entirely overblown by the shifting sands.

And then, for a moment, I thought I saw, on the far side of the truck, a few specks above the land. Adventurers coming back? I squeezed my eyes, looked again, but was not sure. The mirage had gone; it was too far. I was alone, standing on the overturned truck like a hunter on his behemoth trophy, victor by cowardice against death.

I climbed down again to where Mustache had been, and in a shallow depression in the sand, the corner of a book of matches peeked out. I fondled it, then put it in my pocket. I felt sorry for him... he wasn't likable, but he was a good bloke. He had saved my life in trying to save his own. Now there was nothing left of him but Chinese matches. I promised to light one for him when I safely could. Not even his bones were left... God, what did they do with the bones?

The scuffle marks of a large group still surrounded the truck. And the motor lay naked on the ground, sand whirling about its parts, at one point forming a tiny waterspout, or windspout, the particles dancing in a tiny column in the air. Beside it, half-covered, a wrench; its handle read "Government Property."

The sun sank now into early afternoon, and I busied myself with the task of picking up the pieces... finding as much equipment as I might want to carry with me. Inside the cab of the truck, under the seat, was my pack. And all the toiletries and accoutrements for a weekend in a motel... except, there wasn't any motel. No wonder they had left this behind. I was certainly not well-equipped. This wasn't in the guidebooks.

It suddenly occurred to me that perhaps I hadn't been the only survivor... perhaps someone needed help. I ran outside to look for other members of the expedition. The rock-wrecked truck was closer.

I could see immediately why they didn't just drive it away immediately. It had cracked an axle on a protruding rock; one wheel was entirely separated from the chassis. No bodies, again.

The scavengers seemed to be as interested in frame parts as

they were in the power system; they must have had clever mechanics to have created the Wheels at all. I had never seen their ingenious design before; perhaps some Segway technology to build machines so intimately responsive to human movement.

My own scavenging was to a different purpose. Or rather, in order to learn what others considered essential—besides the nose mask which I had mistaken for a gewgaw. The gas gun, of course, really a pellet machine, because explosives, even bullets, require oxygen, of which there is little freely available. High pressure, though, suddenly released—that can send a pellet wickedly into flesh.

Nope, no nosemasks, no gas guns. No food. I did pick up some plasticized pieces of clothing, though, and a belt with pockets... now that might be very handy, so I strapped it on.

As I continued rummaging, I ran across an arrow, plastic or glass. I felt a scratch and jerked my hand back. No apparent injury, but as I looked down at my finger, I noticed that a dark blue bubble had formed. What was that?

I stared at the glass rod and at my finger, wondering what mysterious chemistry produced this. I held my finger up to suck it, for I felt a slight throb of pain now, but as I stared, a little tinge of red formed around the drop, and I recognized it as my own blood. Breath apparently gave it the oxygen necessary to clot, and form scabs.

Was this, then, hemophilia for everybody out here, where there was not enough oxygen to stop blood flowing? I hastily ran down an inventory of toenails, fingernails, anything sharp that might penetrate my skin. The suit I was wearing seemed to he designed with this danger in mind. Even the zippers were plastic.

But an arrow? Out here? Where did it come from? The angle it stuck into the earth was a high one, indicating either someone was on top of the truck firing downward, or... above that. Had I seen dots in the sky? Indian spirits? I quickly glanced around again. Nothing.

A faint high cloud haze in the distance, and the tops of what looked like a double string of mountains over the ridge. It must have been there that the adventurers had gone. I loped back to my truck, gathered the pack on my back, and trekked off again, for the last truck, the one that had been the last to go.

Silence and wide open space swallowed me up; each step seemed the same, only a very gradual change in the relationships of landmarks was noticeable, even at a fast pace. I was insignificant in that landscape, a mere speck of human reality in the midst of an alien planet.

Again, at the third truck, nothing. No bodies. Apparently the marauders had carried them off even in their haste. For these, I surmised, must have formed a regular part of their food supply. And perhaps those grisly meals reinforced the aggressiveness of hunting carnivores that set them apart from human society. Predators, nomads, perhaps. And certainly monsters.

The cab of the third truck, though on its side, had no broken windows, and the little oxygen valve was still operative, still the life-giving gas. I sucked at it briefly, and felt human again. It was time to reconnoiter.

The small sun was now creeping toward the horizon, and the air had an extra chill. Here, then, I would spend the night, and pray that no man walked abroad, as Lawrence had said, in the Martian midnight.

And as I lay crouched at the bottom of that cab, around the bent steering wheel, I remembered the song that Sadie had sung, that had lulled me to sleep on my first restless night outside the wall.

Two moons over red sand
Catch a star in your eye
Walk on, this is your land
Your sand, your sky

Lift up your burden
And carry it away
Make your home in the red, red rock
Your night, your day

Two moons over red sand
Nobody to tell you how
No one to tell you anything
Right here, right now.

Except for the marauders, dear Sadie. Adventurers, whatever they are. The dark fears of Lawrence and his wife made sense now, and I shivered equally from cold and from fear.

‹ ‹ ‹ 25. BILLY ‹ ‹ ‹

(back on the ship)

"Man, it was somethin'. You shoulda seen me highsteppin' in between the po-lice and the spacers, with nothing in the middle but dumb luck."

Billy was telling his story, and it didn't look like I'd have much to say. I leaned back and lit a forbidden cigarette.

"Gettin' shuck of the uniform was easy, 'cept I was gettin' skinned but good by a fellow by the name of Wilkes. Ever run across him?"

I nodded.

"He promised me a room and three squares a day for work. Now you know me, I don't cotton to no work, but this was going to be easy, he said. Burglaring, now, I done that before, when I was a young militant... climb in them windows, pick a lock.

"But we was...he had us carrying and toting pianos, least that's what it felt like, and we couldn't make no noise. The boys he had did a helluva job, and licked his boots for the chance, but they was still just kids, you know. I got the heavy end of things. Wilkes, he didn't lift a finger. Most likely he wasn't even there. Like when we got spotted, chased all over hell, come in draggin' our tails, and Wilkes says 'What? Are you crazy? Go. Begone! Come back in the morning.'"

"It didn't take me long to figure out who had the brains, and it wasn't me. But I'd learned the ropes the hard way, so it wasn't but just another step to set myself up. First I found an open space under a heated house. Turned out a widow lady lived there, real elegant, real kind. Anyhow, one day I went up and knocked on her door, told her the whole bit, who I was, what I was doing...all except about crime; I didn't reckon she'd approve. All she said was, eyes aglittering, 'I wish I was a man.'

"Next day, she knocks on the loose panel on her own house, peeks in, and says, 'Billy? Can you come up?'

"'Sure,' I says. 'Wait 'til I'm decent.' Boy, I thought she'd fell for me and just couldn't wait. So I dandied up a bit and comes up with a pretty gold bracelet I'd found. But I walk in the door, and there's three of 'em. Lord A'mighty, I damn near dropped my pants. These was respectable society, and I still had one foot in the underworld. My scalp starts itching, but I wasn't going to scratch, no sir, not in front of them.

"'This is Billy, girls. You should hear the stories he's told me.' And they giggled, couldn't believe it, like what she called 'em, girls. Anyway, didn't take long before they was telling me back what I did, or what I said I did, 'cause, you know, I'd had to sort of fill in the holes.

"And then they scoped it. They weren't just friends, they were a committee, and they wanted some action. Clean up the streets, stop crime dead in its tracks, bolster confidence in the doddering old Governor, make things 'like they used to be.'

"'Well, Billy?' said the lady of the house, name of Wilma.

"'Well, well,' I says.

"'Well, what do you think?'

"'Sure is a lot of good stuff you want to do. Can't argue with it. Can't argue at all.'

"'Good,' they all said at once, pouncing on me like I was the last jelly bean in the bowl. 'When can you start?'

"'Start what?' I said, but I shoulda known better. I was supposed to be the one to do it all. I didn't want to disappoint them, but to show my face anywhere around the govament folks, and I'd be dead, or whupped, whichever was worse, so I thought fast.

"It'd be a good month since I jumped ship. Only folks that knew me for sure was the spacers, and half of them because of my complexion. And even the ones who knew Billy, well, was they gonna be the ones to turn me in? The police, they musta gotten my spec sheet; maybe it'd be better to pull a smoothie, and put myself real outa the way, at least for a while.

"It was pure inspiration, man. I tol' 'em I was a secret agent on a very important mission, and I had to report to the Gov'nor right away. You shoulda seen the stars in their eyes, man, it just sopped over them like molasses on a stack of pancakes.

"Trouble was, it backfired. Got me out of their clutches, but they insisted on walking me over, just for protection, all the way, and stood watching while I tromped up the Gov'nor's steps.

"Man, I thought I was a goner. What was I gonna do, sell him shoe polish? So I thought some more. What was I gonna say when...

"He opens the door, as surprised as I was, this little old man with Esquire mustache drooping over his mouth, vest, slippers, I couldn't help myself, I swear to God. 'Cadet Bright reporting as ordered, sir,' and a snappy salute.

"'Ordered? Whose orders?'

"'From Earth, sir. I'm to be your attendant.'

" 'Oh, goodness. Why, it must be General Perkins, God bless you. Come in. Martha!'

"He was an all-right old duffer, quite a bit on the slow side, which suited me just fine. He and his wife were the ace and deuce of hearts to me, fed me right, bought me cigars and duds, and I did the Rochester bit to a T. Only, it was too good to last. Captain Wentworth came to dinner one night.

"I feigned sick, but listened to every word. And while the Governor raved about me, I chewed a pillow. Wentworth denied knowing who I was, and that was that. When I heard them tromping across the wooden floor together, I'd already grabbed a coat and was halfway out the window."

"And there I was again, on the street."

"Billy," I interrupted. "You're prevaricating. Lying through your teeth. I don't believe a word you say."

"Sandy, now just listen here. I been sittin', night after night, and you're tellin' me about killing people, and weird folk that live without oxygen, and people flying, and shit readers, and three moons, you tell me all that, and did I once question your honesty and honorability as a gentleman?

"No, I did not. Did I say, 'That ain't so' even once? Sandy, I'm disappointed, truly disappointed that you would sit there and to my very face call me a liar. Well, if it ain't so, then you tell me what I did all this time. Go ahead, what'd I do?"

"I'm sorry, Billy. I meant, it sounded like you added a bit here and there."

"Oh, well," he grinned, "that ain't lying, that's making a good story better. No harm in that, is there?"

"No."

"So, where was I? Oh, yeah, running like a purse-snatcher, this was late, see, and I just knew that Cap'n Wentworth would take it as a personal insult... he holds a long grudge, that man... that's why I get the graveyard shift every night, it's the closest thing to solitary and still get work out of me..."

>>>26. OUTSIDERS>>>

The next fear of my life marked a transformation in me that is difficult to talk about. A jumble of individual memories from that time is the best that I can offer for an understanding of the Martians themselves, I believe that they have earned a better claim on the planet, though with less power, than anyone else I met...including the cottagers. On Earth, their very existence is an unsubstantiated rumor, but to me they are kings and queens. I evoke the Exology Statement on their behalf:

> ...The integrity of human cultures or societies
> shall be respected, preserved, and protected in all
> circumstances and for all time...

I shall render these accounts, therefore, as nearly as I can to their actuality.

"Allo camarade. Comment allez-vous?"
"Hello, friend.   How are you?"
"Bien. Et vous?" The figure that had motioned me over
"Good. And you?"

leaned against the rock wall with the nonchalance of a younger man.

His neatly-trimmed mustache, the cut of his short jacket, the spirited tone of his voice...it must be, it couldn't be...

"Pierre Lemoine?"

"Oui, oui. Vous me connaissez?"

"Yes, yes. Do you know me?"

"Pierre Lemoine, de *La Victoire*, n'est-ce pas?"

"Pierre Lemoine, of *La Victoire*, isn't that so?"

"Oui, mais *La Victoire* est morte, une fichue. C'est dommage.

"Yes, I am, but La Victoire   is dead,   what a damned shame.

Elle a été belle, si belle, et capriceuse comme une femme.

She was a beauty, so beautiful— and as fickle   as a woman.

Savez-vous?"

You know?"

The memory moved him deeply, as well it might. I'd been watching the spaceshow on the vid when *La Victoire* blasted off. Three people had been killed by inadvertent spillover of the liquid hydrogen-liquid oxygen... a high wind had blown it right across the flat concrete pad on Nukuhiva in the Marquesas. The French newscaster made it seem that their deaths in some way contributed to the greater glory of France. An unfortunate consequence, and possibly one of the factors that led to the ultimate failure of the mission, came with a strike by aerospace workers in Nantes. Old Fondutel was replaced by Carignac, and a full-scale "investigation" resulted in an overturn in the power structure of the space department... which Lechay and Lemoine, now in flight, refused to accept. By the time they had passed the Moon, the two intrepid spacemen cut off all communications with the French department until Fondutel was restored. Which never happened. Pride, Gallic pride that built an empire now made its spacemen outcasts.

In an unprecedented move, absolutely unique in space annals, Lemoine's brother Jacques, with the aid of the self-exiled and bitter Fondutel, arranged an international syndicalized program... which became very popular in the former French colonies, and eventually throughout the Third World...of the adventures of the Free Frenchmen, Pierre and Albert, in space, intermixed with some hastily drawn animation sequences... the later versions employed professional computer-corrected scenes... and produced by one of France's hottest independent filmmakers, Rene Landou. I mention Landou because he became prominent in the New Push for Space that began about ten (has it really been that long?) years ago.

"La belle *Victoire*. Où est *La Victoire* maintenant?" If the
"The beautiful *Victoire*.   Where is *La Victoire* now?"

wreckage were nearby, I might get a chance to see it.

"Ici," he said, drawing a knife. The back of my neck tingled.
"Here,"

He offered it to me, handle foremost. "Bon, eh? Voyez
"Good, eh? Look at

comme le titane maintient un bord tranchant."
how the   titanium   keeps   a   sharp edge."

"Bien sûr. Merveilleux. Est-ce cela *La Victoire*? Comment?"
"For sure. Marvellous. Is this all there is of *La Victoire*? How can that be?"

"Simplement. Ce banc-là, c'est *La Victoire* aussi. Et les
"It's obvious.   This bench over there, that's *La Victoire* too.   And these

lumières? Oui, La Victoire. Mais le plus important... allons."
lights? Yes, that's *La Victoire*. But the most important... come with me."

He led me into still another chamber, where about twenty people were busy at various tasks relating to a large steel box, which stood off the floor on stilts...possibly the original landing gear. About ten meters cubed, the shell of *La Victoire* still retained an elegance unmatched by the ungainly American or Russian craft, whose designs always showed many hands and many compromises.

"Voilà. Ah, ma belle, mon coeur." The effusive Frenchman
"Behold.   Ah, my sweet,   my heart."

put his arms and his cheek on the shell, kissed it lightly.

"S'il vous plaît, Pierre..."
"If you please, Pierre..."

"Ah, oui. Vous ne sentez la puissance de cette fusée comme
"Ah, yes. You cannot feel   the power   of this rocket   as

moi? Pardon mon effusion. Mais, c'est une affaire. Au
I do? Excuse my emotionality. But, this is a love affair. On the

contraire, Lechay a perdu sa santé le deuxième mois dans
other hand, Lechay had lost his mind in the second month in

l'espace déjà. Et maintenant, il est une bête entière. Ptah!"
space, already. And now, he is totally a beast. Ptui!"

"Que voulez-vous dire?"
"What are you trying to say?"

"C'est-a-dire, il a rejoint les aventures. Merde au Lechay."
That is, he had joined fantasyland. Shit on Lechay."

"Comment est-il possible?"
"How is that possible?"

"Il a la tête em choux. Trop de radiation."
"He had a head of cabbage. Too much radiation."

"Mais, tout le monde reçoit le même dosage...les pierres
"But everyone receives the same amount... rocks

aussi..."
too..."

"Non, non, non...Albert, il devient fou; il a travaillé dans
"No, no, no... Albert, he went mad; he was working in

la salle d'engins sans protection, il fait des choses stupide. Et
the engine room without protection, he did stupid things. And

maintenant, s'il est aussi vivant, il va mourir bientôt."
now, if he were still alive, he would die quickly."

"Pourquoi?"
"Why?"

"Je le tuerai moi-même." He turned away, indicating that I
"I will kill him myself."

should follow. "Pas un autre mot."
"Not another word."

§

On another occasion, Lemoine sought me out. It was just before the night raid on the town. He bustled in as I was bedding down.

"Mon ami, mon ami, vous êtes notre chroniqueur? Un
"My friend, my friend, you are our chronicler? A

écrivain bientôt?"
real writer?"

"Oui," I admitted. "Ainsi?"
"Yes," "So what?"

"Pardon, c'est ma négligence de venir si tard...mais, Pyotr et
"Please excuse me, it was my fault to come so late... but Pyotr and

Simon m'ont dit que je devrais vous confier. Oui. Écoutez
Simon have told me that I ought to confide in you. Yes. Listen

bien. Je vous dirai tout l'histoire de *La Victoire* et après."
well. I will tell you the whole history of *La Victoire* and afterwards."

I made notes of the following story, which is reconstructed as exactly as I was told. Lemoine, alas, will not be able to correct it.

"Bien. Nous...Lechay et moi...nous avons osé, et nous
"Very well. We... Lechay and I... we have dared, and we

avons gagné. Ici commence-t-il l'histoire des deux Français
have won. Here commences the history of the two French

valliants..."
heroes..."

I interrupted. "Au point, s'il vous plaît."
"To the point, if you please."

"Si, si," he said, noticing my blank page in the dim light.
"Yes, yes,"

"Au point."
"Get to the point."

"Je suis né au bord de la mer Mediterranée, et comme ma
I was born near the coast of the Mediterranean see, and with my very

première parole, j'ai rêvé des etoiles. Nuit par nuit, j'allais
first words, I was dreaming of the stars. Night after night, I would go

dans l'abîme de la noirceur avec mon teléscope. Pour ces
into the abyss of the blackness with my telescope. For those

années, c'était mon plaisir, observer le ciel. J'ai eu mon
years, this was my pursuit, to watch the heavens. I had my very

propre planétarium sur un petit monticule derrière la
own planetarium on a little mound behind the

maison, sur une pierre plate je m'asseyais et je cherchais
house, on a flat rock I would sit and would search

les constellations pour un message. Mon père et ma mère
the constellations for a message. My father and my mother

etaient en peine de savoir quoi faire avec leur fils. Jusqu'à
were at pains to know what to do with their son. Until

ce qu'un jour, j'ai lus que les astronautes trainent comme
one day, I had read that astronauts trained themselves like

chevaux de cirque. Après, j'ai mangé beaucoup viandes et
circus horses. After that, I would eat plenty of meat and

légumes, j'ai fais des tractions et pompes et le cours chaque
beans, I exercised with traction and pumped, and ran a course every

jour. Ainsi, j'étais bien le premier astronaute de France.
day. Thus, I became easily the best-prepared astronaut of France.

Lechay était le deuxième.
Lechay was the second-best.

"L'agence d'espace, merde, plus de politique. Lechay et moi,
The space agency was mired in shit, full of politics. Lechay and I,

nous étions prêts à ce moment exact quand Fondutel avait
we were prepared at the precise moment when Fondutel was

besoin d'un spectacle. Nous étions prêts à quitter... une
in need of a publicity stunt.   We were about to quit...   one

fois plus... la bureaucratie me dégoûte trop... et, Fondutel
more time...   the bureaucracy totally disgusted me...   and we

nous appelle.
appealed to Fondutel

" 'Venez,' il dit. 'Vous êtes les deux les plus promissants
" 'Go," he said. ' You are the two most promising daredevils

puisque Blériot. Le wagon n'est pas sûr, mais la fenêtre est
since Blériot.   The vehicle is not safety-checked, but the window is

ouverte maintenant. Si nous attendions, les russes, les
open right now.   If we wait, the Russians,   the

italiens— toussaient— les Swahiles se préparent de lancer
Italians — (coughing) —   the Swahilis are ready   to launch

ce mois. Camarades, pour la gloire maximum de France...
this month.   Comrades,   for the   greatest glory of France...

qu'est-ce que vous dites?'
What do you say?' "

"Fondutel était comme un grand, vieux, un père... un
"Fondutel was like   a grand old man,   a father... a

grand-père de l'espace de la France. Mais il sénilisait avec
grandfather of space in France.   But he was becoming senile with

années passantes... il était peut-être un peu comme un
the passing years...   he was perhaps   a little like a

bouffon. Les politiciens ont crié sur lui parce que le pro-
buffoon. The politicans shouted at him   because the program

gramme avait prie du retard. Cela était sa dernière chance.
had requested a delay.   This moment was their last chance.

Pauvre Fondutel! Une fois, il était mon idole, mon hèroe. Sa
Poor Fondutel!   Once, he was my idol,   my hero.   His

bataille pour le droit d'aller dans l'espace pendant plusieurs
struggle   for the right to go   into space   over a number of

années, Il se bat seul...cela a rendu possible le voile de La
years, he fought alone...   this had made possible the veil of

Victoire, le voyage inaugural d'un vaisseau de France dans
La Victoire, the very first voyage of a spaceship of France into

l'espace profond. Sans equipage, sans argent, mais avec
deep space.   Without equipment, without money, but with

une volonté féroce, Fondutel France poussé là-haut, ici. Et
a ferocious will,   Fondutel pushed France up there, here. And

maintenant, il est en disgrâce. Dîtes-moi, est-il mort?"
now,   he is in disgrace.   Tell me, is he dead?"

I told him I didn't know.

"Peut-être. Promettez une simple chose... si vous le voyez,
"Perhaps. Promise me one simple thing...   if you see him,

dites lui bonjour pour moi et pour Albert. Okeh?" (He
tell him hello   for me and for Albert.   Okay?"

paused). "Comme je réfléchis, en réalité, Fondutel était
                "As I think back,   really,   Fondutel was

comme un vieil avare. N'importe, probablement, il ne me
like an old miser.   No matter, probably, he wouldn't

reconnaissait de toute façon. Et" (he paused), "personne ne
remember me in any case. And,"   "no one is

rentre sur Terre aujourd'hui." (He looked at me keenly).
going back to Earth today."

"Non, je ne reviendrai pas."
"No, I will not."

"Quand même, nous envolons à dix heures un quart. Quelle
"Still,   we fly away at a quarter past ten.   What a

catastrophe!"
catastrophe!"

>>>27. EATING >>>

"Traumatic pneumothorax. Stick your hand over that; we'll carry him back"

I was getting sick looking at the chest ripped, blood no longer gushing and the ragged edges of skin flapping open... and he plunged my hand down, onto the mess: I couldn't look.

"Vomit if you want to waste food, but keep your hand there. He might die, you understand? Die!"

I obeyed blindly, clutched my fingers together... his heart would be just under there, its rhythmic beat pulsing under my palm. I swallowed and held on as they arranged a rough litter out of cloaks and poles. When it was time to rise, my knees rebelled, but I couldn't let them down... or the man on the stretcher. Twenty minutes we walked in lockstep back to the camp.

"You can go now," the doctor said, "He's dead."

In misery and shame, I stumbled back to my little place. Marta rushed out.

"Sandy! What happened?"

The shock waves rushed over me again, and this time, of all times, I let loose. People turned their heads, then looked away. I sat back heavily, stomach churning, throat gasping, desperately alone. Marta re-emerged from her tent with a basin full of water, and took my hand ever so gently to bathe it in the cool precious liquid. She went finger by finger until my hand was cleaned of the blood.

"But... you're not wounded! Where did the blood come from?

"That man... that body," I gasped.

She turned to see them carry the corpse down past the mess. When she looked at me again, that quizzical face was drawn into exasperation.

"I didn't kill him! We were attacked. I tried to help!"

She rose, the red-filled basin in her hands, and walked off in a stately manner, an aloofness that I could never penetrate or understand, the bowl held before her like an offering.

Across the path a voice called. "Come here. You. Yes."

It was Pablo, a man with strong Indian features that I had met just a few days before.

"What do you want?" I demanded.

"What you make for her to usar el agua, eh? Es por beber, for to drink, señor."

"I... but there's water, plenty of it."

"In las cavernas, si, righto. Cuanto lagos, lakes and rivers you see, eh? Quanto mares, eh, señor?"

He was right. I nodded slowly, and hung my head.

When Marta came back, she said nothing, and I imagined that she reviled me in her heart. Why should it hurt so? She was another man's wife, and that man my friend. I tried to cast aside my feelings and think of her as a human being, one who had sacrificed so much for me already... it was no use. I dreamt of her at night, coveting her, despising Pyotr for having such great good fortune.

"Marta..."

"Shush, you rest. You'll feel better after supper. Zabweet,

Do not remember until after."

"After what?"

"After we eat myaso. Feel gooder."

"Better."

"Da. Feel butter."

When finally we marched down, plates in hands, to the mess, the rich aroma of cooking food saturated the air, but I had my mind on other things. Marta and I sat a bit apart from the others after we got out helpings, the regulation green dough made. I was told, from moss flour.

Halfway through, as I was turning over in my mind various apologies, I noticed chunks of pinkish brown tough pieces in the dark mess on my plate. "What is this?"

"Myaso. How dya say? Meat," she said between mouthfuls.

I stopped swallowing, a half-chewed portion in my mouth. Marta continued shoveling it in.

"What meat?"

She stopped also, noted my whiteness around the gills. "Meat. You know." She pinched my arm, as if testing its tenderness.

"Don't do that!"

"I thank this come from here," she said, patting her thigh. Don' worry. Ev'body get same."

Without realizing it, I swallowed the rest of what was in my mouth, and my barbaric tongue was searching out stray bits of flesh from between my teeth. My throat, however, refused to loosen. My lips quivered, and a drop of saliva slid down its own substance to my lap. Marta quickly set down her plate and whipped off a shoulderbag... the kind that Pyotr carried for traveling in the desert.

"No!" I exclaimed, and started gagging. She opened it in front of me, and motioned over some of the men. My eyes went wide... if anything was going to bring my dinner up, it was the smell of several days' shit. I turned to avoid it, but someone grabbed my arms, and Marta, the lovely Marta, forced my head into the bag. It was too much... my body racked convulsively forward, emptying my stomach, heave by heave, until I was too dizzy to stand, too weak to speak. And Marta wiped my face with a tiny piece of cloth, then tossed that, too, into the infernal bag. I could do nothing but lie back on the rocks, swallowing air, gasping for relief. One more time it came... but even the bag couldn't force more out of me. The dry heaves passed, and I collapsed.

Everyone, even Marta, left me alone, then, but I could hear them talking... such a fool I was being, such a spectacle. But deep within was an utter revulsion of what was happening. How could civilized human beings stoop to such depth ...people I called my friends, who had saved my life, taught me how to survive in the desert, accepted my hostility with love...how could they have become cannibals?

A mixture of disgust, fearfulness, and alertness had settled over me by the time one of them approached the spot where I was lying. I didn't know him, and therefore didn't trust him, but when he said "Come with me," no one seemed to expect anything unusual. The little crowd watched the two of us depart, eyes mildly curious, a detached interest but no tension. We headed for a large rock thirty meters away.

As we neared our goal, my escort stepped aside to let me pass. And there, practically underneath the base of the rock was a weathered little man, smiling into the sun, his face splotched with dark red irregular patches. Beneath his hairy brows, two intelligent eyes peered out. He motioned me to sit. The guide disappeared.

"What do you want?" I said.

"Why are you suspicious, my son? I will do you no harm."

"You're one of them. Why should you be any different from the rest?"

He positively twinkled: "I am not. Are you?"

"I don't know if I want to be like them," I snapped.

"What do you know, then?"

"I know the value of human life. I'm a humanist, I've written books on it." The books. Yes, many books by now, and each one filled with doubts. He saw right through me, or allowed me to see myself. That calm of his shook me until I was trembling again, not from weakness, but anger, frustration boiled up in me, assaulting the peace he held in his heart. I couldn't see, and knew as the words left my mouth that it wasn't the real me speaking, no, that was a voice I hadn't dared use, except to myself in moments of extreme despair.

"Teach me, then," he said, and I felt that he meant just that, no more and no less. "What is the value of human life?"

"It's the greatest thing there is, in the whole galaxy," the hogwash tumbled out, sounding falser and falser. I plumbed down for what I really believed. "Nothing compares with it. 'What a piece of work is man.' All else is extra." I stopped. "How can I teach you? Don't you know already?"

"I did, once." He blinked directly at the sun.

"And then?"

"And then I died."

"But how...could you be sitting here, talking to me?" I sputtered.

"I don't know. But here I am. Perhaps it was a vision. Perhaps you can teach me its meaning."

"Well, I'll try."

The old man immediately bellowed out a note...startled me... so pure and even that I was astounded that his small body would fill so much air. The single note sustained and slowly died away until its echoes mingled with it... the rocks themselves seeming to resonate with him.

And without appearing to take a breath, he launched into a song. This is as much as I can remember.

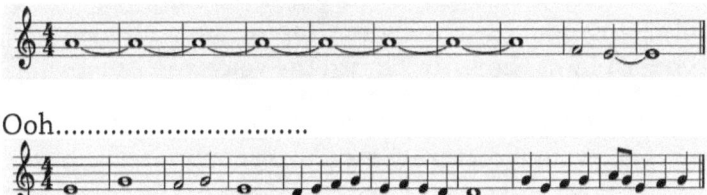

Ooh.................................

I died, I died. Heart and lungs stopped. I was alone.
Hand would not grasp, Eye would not see.

Food in my stomach, Air in my lungs, Blood in my veins, Hair on my head, Nails on my fingers, Spit in my mouth

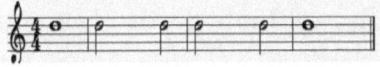

Not mine, not mine, no longer mine. A blackness.
A blackness. All was dark. All was dark.

And I saw an Angel.

And the music, somehow, continued, though he spoke directly to me!

And the Angel said: You are dead, dust with the dust, fragments again, a food for the hungry, a rest for the tired, a piece of eternal whirling atoms. A space between spaces, a juggle of dice by the Master Time. Give over your body, your mind, your soul, your secrets, your dreams to the greater-than-thou harmony of peace.

Sleep, and give up sleeping...see and give up seeing. Surrender to the abyss. Surrender to the abyss.

And I was sleeping and I was seeing, and there was sleeping and seeing. And then no more sleeping, no more seeing, a stubborn I was there. And heard the voice once more:

Welcome stranger, to your home, and know this...your bones and your blood are the walls of your house. Your feet walk on flesh and you are that, too. The rock in your hand is your heart, to build and rejoice, to live and be glad in your living. Wake up.

I woke to feel the sun again, its warmth on my face the last reminder of what had been. I have been dead, without doubt, and I am alive.

Can you tell me now, about life?

The last sentence glided smoothly out of the chant as he turned his face toward mine, his eyes staring directly at my left ear. He was blind! This smiling serene man, this prophet, could not see my face

"I don't know," I said inanely. "Sounds like a nightmare."

"I woke up from my nightmare," he said. "We welcome life, and celebrate it, here. We also celebrate death. Have you seen our kitchen?"

The creepy-crawlies grabbed my throat again. I choked on "No."

"It is an altar for offerings, the most priceless of which is the human flesh which you have such difficulty receiving. Our cooks do not understand how they may please you. The man who brought you here was tonight's food priest. He is ashamed, and you can help him overcome his disgrace."

"I can't...eat..."

"We are lonely here, we humans. No dogs, chickens, goats. cows, fish or lobsters to keep us company and trade back and forth the complex molecules of higher life-forms. When a man lives, we value him above all things for being with us, helping us to stay alive, and much more. He gives what he can, and that is always more than enough."

It was true. The selflessness of these people made me feel small and mean inside. I had suspected that a source for this goodness came from some one person... this old shrunken body shunted off to the side may be the one. I didn't for one minute believe that he had died... but at the same time I understood that he believed it. Perhaps that's all that mattered. But this business of cannibalism... I'd had a close scrape with that one already, and I didn't propose to be on either end of the fork, thank you, no.

"I'm going back down," I announced. "See you later."

He didn't protest, he didn't say anything. When I looked back for the last time, he'd turned once more to the last rays of the sun fall full on his piebald face, oblivious to any other thing.

‹ ‹ ‹ 28. BILLY AGAIN‹ ‹ ‹

On those lonesome evenings, Billy told me the whole story, and sometimes, I'd nod my head forward. not really listening, but keeping time to a melody in my head. And then I'd listen:

"...keep on runnin' 'til my head was ready to bust. Slim was right beside me, and we..."

Then I'd dream off again, thinking of Manhattan, not for the first time homesick for the dirty streets and tired people, but. perhaps, who knows, it might be the last time. Maggie and me...but it wouldn't have lasted. Either I would be off to do another show, or she'd fly to Europe or Australia, the "white countries," as she called them. I detested that quirk in her, the old-fashioned attitudes that she clung to because she couldn't face the future...and yet was such a creature of it. It wasn't the future that interested me then, it wasn't the past: I needed constant stimulation, physical, mental, moral, style-wise. Maggie was quite enough stimulation, a real challenge because she was real, with all her fantasies and neuroticisms. In the midst of a whirl of phonies, I needed that challenge just to keep alive my own dreams.

"...ducked into a cave, where we didn't know if anybody lived, and man, it was dark, I couldn't see my hand in front of my face."

"You'd blend into a sunset, Billy, sort of between orange and brown."

"Sass, that's all I get from you. Anyhoo, we crawled down a

side passage, Slim goin' first on account of he was so thin, see, and..."

Maggie. Wonder if she knew. It was me that called her up, but maybe George guessed that. Sure, send a man to the next planet, you'd expect he'd call up his old lady. Would she trust him? Could she keep a secret? How much did George know? My guess is, they bought him off with money. Nothing else would satisfy that monster ego: he measured his self-esteem by his bank account. Just as well; I had nothing but scars to show for the last few years, most of them emotional, where it really hurts. No, they'd let him know where to cash the check. He must have believed that story, or he never could have convinced me.

"...backed out of there so fast, Slim jammed his ass against my face, and we..."

The shadowy figures behind the operation... it's hard to believe that orders to kill me originated at a board meeting of the power monopoly group. True, they had reason, but no legal recourse after I fought them and won in the courts. Campbell? No, he would never allow anyone else to do it, and he couldn't stomach doing it himself. Unless..

"...all our hollering had brought on the 'Ventures, and he had to creep back in deep, and hope they'd get tired or the dinner bell'd ring. and they'd go home. But we hadn't figured on..."

Campbell, now there was an interesting figure. He'd turned down the Republican nomination twice, because he felt the job he'd made for himself was more important, possibly more powerful. Self-sacrificing?

There was that fifty million-a-year cushion in his contract. And he was right, both times. The Republicans were swamped, their vote split right down the middle between the Staters and the New Americans.

And while the now unwieldy Democratic regime washed away the last of the Roberts Court, Jeremy Campbell stood like a single pinnacle, a rock, an institution. Innovative technologically, nimble politically, his views were almost timeless, relying more on Plato than on Info. Yet he moved in and breathed the air of management and government as easily as a bee in a garden. Campbell? No, he'd sooner defend me so that he could revile me. But death? Exile, now, that'd be closer to it. OK, suppose that was his idea. He had the contacts.

"...belly ripped open, bug-eyed, staring at the sky like he warn't going to admit it. Served him right. But the rest of them..."

Then, if it wasn't Campbell, it'd have to be someone strong enough, or crafty enough to change the orders. I'd read the files on every executive in Power above Grade 7...not one of them had the gumption, and/or would have been anywhere near the action. Carson had said it was a man of consequence... wait a minute, how does Carson know so much about it? He must be in on it, some way or other. It was hard to tell the difference, come to think of it, between the threat from the spacers and from Carson's men.

But there must be a link, a missing piece, that held together the Mars plot and the plot to kill me. Something connecting Carson and the Power magnates. Both were right-wing, but that didn't mean anything. Something Carson had said, what was it?

"...took me up with him to his little place in the rocks. In the morning, I was near froze, but he sat, with his little solar oven, makin' swill...that's what he called it...for breakfast. We..."

"For a greater purpose than you can guess, Castle. You think I'd do this merely for personal ambition? You underestimate me. When a man's destiny is clearly written in the stars, how can he help himself? You're a disbeliever, Castle, a cynic. History will sweep you aside like so much mud-crusted garbage, don't you know that?"

"The tide crashes on the shore, Carson, and dribbles down to foam, and then to nothing. Nothing!" Nothing. That's how he started out, a real nothing. What drove the man? Maybe he had the equivalent of my imp, or Socrates' daimon...a twisted power-hungry elf, hardly human at all, yet understanding how to exploit human weaknesses, because he had so many himself.

>>>29. BREATHING>>>

I had been with the group for a month already. For all I knew, the rocket might be headed for Earth by now—I didn't care. I was happy, as I had never been happy before, not since childhood. Marta and Pyotr were my constant companions. I could hunt the barbels as well as most. And there was Chidnaq, a girl of great beauty, full of life, an Eskimo girl. Besides myself, she was the newest member of the clan. She spoke no English that I didn't teach her—and she was very mysterious about how she got to Mars. From what I gathered, she didn't really know herself.

Pyotr said one day that it was time for both of us to learn breathing —"And no more mask. You be like us."

But I couldn't get any more out of him except "Wait to see, Sasha."

Our teacher would be the little old man I had encountered on the rocks. Without warning, he came into the tent and beckoned us to follow. Chidnaq and I went out as we were, expecting to go to another part of the camp to have our lessons. But as we neared the last tent, he gave no sign of stopping.

"Is it far?"

No reply. Chidnaq looked at me and shrugged. The old man set a good pace, he must have had some other sense to replace his glazed eyes, for he was leaping from rock to rock. It seemed like we were always going up, but when I looked back, it was hard to tell any difference. The camp disappeared from view sporadically.

After about half an hour, and we still hadn't reached the spot—wherever that may be—I began to worry. The indicator on my filter read low.

"Hey!" I called up the slope; he was a few hundred yards ahead by now. "Slow down! We'd better turn back!"

He appeared not to hear me. I raced up ahead of Chidnaq, and it took every ounce of effort to catch up with the old man.

"Stop. We can't go on. Look at the readings."

He turned toward me with very sad blind eyes. I was huffing and puffing through the mask to get enough oxygen into my system. As soon as I could speak again, I called down to Chidnaq.

"Don't come up, we're going back."

We had come to the crest of the ridge, but I hadn't had time to look around when the old man grabbed me with incredible strength and whirled me around and around until I fell down from dizziness. When I looked up again, he was doing the same to Chidnaq.

"Hey, buddy, what's the matter with you>"

But then I realized that was an intentional act, without apparent motive. This was how we were going to learn to breathe? I was more concerned with getting back to camp before our oxygen supply ran out, and the filters would be working on nothing but CO_2.

But then I calmed down. Chidnaq was by my side, and we waited for a word from the master. He made no move, but sat perched on a rock.

"Well? Take us back."

I shouted, "Our oxygen! It's running out!" I removed the

little filter mechanism and showed it to him. "See? The grains are turning black."

He took it from my hand, felt it curiously, and tossed the tiny element over his shoulder casually. I scrambled into the rocks, holding my breath all the while. I almost choked before I located it down between two rocks. Now I was mad. Chidnaq couldn't restrain me. The man was a raving lunatic, even though he looked calm. Brain rot must have gotten to him.

"Take us back, you bastard! Chidnaq, do something, help me knock some sense into him." Chidnaq stood, scared of us both, wild me in a wild place. "Chidnaq, snap out of it. It's the oxygen. Do you hear me?"

She nodded, but she was swaying on her feet.

"Come on, let's go. He can find his own way back."

"Yes, Sasha. Air..."

I caught her, steadied her. The old man sat still, like the rock he was perched on. He almost took delight in our pain, which surprised me, since it was very unlike the rest of the camp members. This man was a teacher? Of what? Insolence?

I gave her some mouth-to-mouth resuscitation, and it probably helped more from the stimulation than from the weak air I was breathing. I know it helped me. So we started on down the hill. I took a look around every once in a while to see if I could find a path, but we hadn't used one going up. Down at the bottom, though, on flat ground, it shouldn't be hard to make out the camp.

By the time we reached sand, I was ready to kick in. But then I turned around, and there was the old man, following us. He hadn't made a sound the whole way, and he didn't now. He had a twinkle, though, as if he could see things that we couldn't, as if he knew a secret.

Chidnaq stayed close by me, and we walked out away from the rockpile called a mountain. Still no camp. The sun was setting, and... but isn't that where it came up, from the east?

"Chidnaq! Where are we?"

She gazed at me dumbly, terror in her eyes, her breath in short gasps.

"Sasha!"

"We'll make it. Out further, maybe we can see where we are."

And so it went. Chidnaq and I trek out for a mile or more, but nowhere did we see a sign of the encampment. And the little man followed us, though I tried to chase him away. At one point of desperation, I tried to capture him, force him to show us the way back. It was then that he spoke for the first time.

"There is no way back. There is only the way forward."

Forward to where, he didn't explain, and it was still a long time before we found out. The wind, meanwhile, was puffing gusts of dust into my face. I could scarcely breathe now, and the exertion of running after the madman had exhausted my body reserves, even the myoglobin in the muscles. My lungs ached for oxygen, heaved full and empty, but unrequited. I began to have hallucinations. Chidnaq seemed to sway like a willow tree, but it could just as well have been my eyes unfocusing. My depth perception played tricks, the horizon coming at me, then receding as soon as I tried to get it in focus. The sky seemed solid, threatening, and the gravity felt as if it were changing every second.

Chidnaq must have been faring as badly as I, but I could be of no help to her in my condition. The strength had gone out of my arms and legs, and unconsciousness dodged around with consciousness, fighting over me. I barely noticed the madman creep up, whip off our masks completely, and run off a short distance. I feebly struggled upright to chase him again... he settled down a little ways away, right by a little ridge.

And he laughed. That maddened me, and Chidnaq too had had enough. If it was the last thing we'd do, we'd get those masks back.

Stumbling forward, we mutually supported each other. But now he was stuffing the masks right into the Mar! Chidnaq fell a few feet from the crack in the ground, and I made a pass at the old man, who danced there, just out of my reach, not going too far from the masks.

"Stop, please." Too late. Chidnaq and I both lay down to reach our arms into the hole. A fine vapor rose from it, which felt cool but refreshing. He had really stuck them down in there.

We struggled with better strength, for the vapor seemed to spur us awake. By the time I had wrenched a mask free, I was breathing easier.

"Wait," the old man said.

I hesitated, staring at him. My lungs were calmer, taking deep drafts of air. Air! But the mask was in my hand! And Chidnaq too, I could see in her face, was much more self-assured.

"Sasha, the hole brings air," she said, taking in great lungs-full, and smiling. The old man, too, was smiling, running up to the crack, heaving in air with his nose, and his Adam's apple going like crazy, motioning us to do the same. Chidnaq tried it.

"To the stomach, Sasha."

I tried it, belched loudly. The little man laughed, and let loose the longest burp I had ever heard. His belly went in to nothing. And then he started in again, his throat working away. I tried again, this time to keep that precious air in there.

We had been gone by then for more than three hours, much longer than I had thought possible. But many people at the camp lived without external aids, and it had never struck me that there was anything special about it. I had thought the teacher was a fool, and I still thought he was crazy, but at least he was teaching us, the hard way. Come to think of it, there was probably no other way that he could have gotten me to take off my mask for more than a few seconds. Yes, I was prideful; that must have been obvious to everyone else at the camp. So little egotism among them, so much openness that I always felt uncomfortable before. And now, would it be better? I had learned that air was no longer a bugbear, it can be handled. Had I learned humility?

After this episode, the three of us sat down to a meal, bits of a sweet substance that the old man had brought. I wasn't frightened any more, but Chidnaq and I still had no idea where the others were. And since we had come to learn, I had questions.

"OK, this is fine, but what happens when there isn't any vapor? How do you find them out here?"

He nodded that he understood, but then went into a trance-like state, very peaceful, very quiet. Just to keep the silence, Chidnaq and I imitated him, sitting uncomfortably on the ground, waiting.

Slowly, very slowly, and without seeming to move, his body rotated around until he was facing away from us, about 45° to the left, toward a small rise. I closed my eyes and tried to be aware of my senses. Smell, but not quite smell, it was something like when you are in a chem lab and the mixture is not right, a new faintly familiar combination, a perfume. In that still Martian atmosphere, there was a presence, almost imperceptible whiff of what is described in the books as a colorless odorless gas. And I knew where it was coming from. The old man's body pointed the way. By directing attention, I could sense it.

Chidnaq must have known too, for she had already risen soundlessly; yes, that was the direction she took, straight where the teacher was looking. It hadn't been my imagination, then. "When the body is starved for a food," Pyotr told me later, "It is eager for that food, so eager that the merest presence of it is immediately noticeable."

And so it was.

Other tricks we learned out there that day, and none of them tricks, just good common sense and awareness. The planet was still in the process of evolution, fissures were everywhere, now that I knew that some of them could save my life, and sustain it without the need of man-made devices. Such an adaptation had other effects on me, too, which I will note for scientific curiosity's sake. My blood almost congealed. Days later, accidentally stabbed myself with a needle, in the process of repairing my clothes, and the blood did not flow. I asked about it, and this was indeed one of the observed phenomena of adaptation to this planet. Other changes came more slowly, and more as a result of skill than of biological change in body chemistry. I mean, the increased sensitivity of nose, eye, ear, and even tasting the wind...which is always full of some kind of dust, even on the clear days. Much like the sailors of old Earth, I could now sense a storm coming on, only I did it by sticking out my tongue!

>>>30. JUNKMAN>>>

One day, after hunting with the big Russian Pyotr, I tore the wristwatch from my hand...Earth time was of no use here...it had lost, accurately, thirty-seven and a half minutes every day... now four hours behind in less than a week, its anachronical value utterly ridiculous to me.

"What you doing, Sasha?" Pyotr exclaimed with mock horror.

"Unburdening myself of Earth, Pyotr. Look at it...liquid crystals, beautiful case. It's a pretty toy, eh? You want it?"

"Give. I take to Junkman. He fix."

"Fix? No, that's impossible. All the gears are set wrong."

"Fix, umh..." Pyotr gestured words in the air. "He use. Make good thing. You see."

"Sure, Pyotr."

Almost as soon as we plopped our gear down, Marta came running up to us. Marta, beautiful Marta, though the planet had aged her fast. Her face reflected a radiance that came from inside her, but she was not the only one of the Outsiders who had this inner strength. At first I was uncomfortable with the openness of Marta and the others, the frank expressions, and the constant demand to be honest. Honesty after all, wasn't my business; I was there to get a story, the story about a new world. In other words, as far as I know then, I was sent to capture some of the newness of Mars that Earth needed so badly. Nothing less than words seemed worth their weight in freight over a single planetary step.

But honesty had its points.

Pyotr lay down on his blanket. "You go," he said, closing his eyes. "Marta... you," and with an elaborate hand gesture, he dismissed us.

Marta led me down one of the side passages of the great central cave, without light. I followed, slowly, my hand on her shoulder, the other in front of my head. The air, though damp, grew increasingly colder... at points it was like plunging into a cool bath, so distinct were the changes... down and down, her surefooted confidence taking us quickly away from the sounds of the others. At bottom, we walked across sand, the echo more distant... this would be a largish room, but totally black. On the other side. she hesitated, then found the way again, this time on a steep upgrade, then a long level slope. The air here was considerably warmer, and definitely moist. And we were there.

She took my other hand, placed it on her chest, on one round bare breast, warm to my cold fingers, and with a few shuffles of clothing dropping to her feet, she was naked. I clasped her to me, and felt her busy hands exploring my cloak for a belt. Almost as quickly as she had undressed herself, she peeled off my clothes, and we stood, wordless, touching each other. Her hand caressed my organ, which had swelled upright and had started oozing Cowper's fluid. She rubbed it with the cupped palm of her hand and laughed a woman's laugh. Suddenly, empty space stood in front of me, and to the left I heard a splash, and here squeal of delight. I stepped gingerly out of the puddle of my pants, reached the water, and waded in... right off a ledge. The water was very warm, warmer than I was, and delightful to feel after a week of dust.

She caught me by the waist underwater, and I dove down

to grab her upside down. We tussled, she righted herself, pushed my head under, slipped away again, and I had to swim very quietly to catch the slightest sound. In the blackness, it was impossible to see, but I thought I saw a flash of white flesh. When I reached out to grasp, it was slippery... a fish-like creature!

She caught me from behind; I twisted around until we held our bodies touching full-length in the warmth, melting my organ, finding hers, fusing in the water, pumping and bobbing at the same time, without words, a marriage of bodies on the instant, pure animal enjoyment heightened by the total darkness and the thermal springs.

On the way out, we were laughing and giggling, until at a certain point, she clapped her hand over my mouth, and we trudged silently toward the gradually lightening passageway and the voices.

Back at the tent, Pyotr was still on his back, relaxing. "Ah, mozhno, Marta, moy drustva zhenita. Khorosho, Sasha, eh?"

I flushed, nodded. What he said I didn't want to know, for Marta's easy familiarity with him made it apparent that he and she were, if not married, at least lovers. He poked at her belly and winked... could it be that she was pregnant? I glanced at her anxiously, curiously, but she betrayed no sign of uneasiness. I dug into my pack, mindlessly, for something to do that would not necessitate words.

Fifteen minutes later, my heart pounded. Marta was beckoning me with a grin. Pyotr slept, curled in his blanket.

We re-entered the cave, but this time we took another turn, and arrived at a softly irradiated area. At the side sat a man wearing pockets. Marta handed him the useless watch.

I looked at the Junkman's nimble fingers, the fingernails themselves honed down as tools... a screwdriver, tweezers, punch, putty knife, rake or comb... his speed was amazing. The watch was apart in seconds, its innards sprawled about in five minutes. Wheels and sprockets spread over his apron, drawn tightly over his knees for a table. Marta brought two metal boxes for him, and withdrew the proper implement from the jumble on command without a single slip. He was re-arranging the pieces as if they belonged to a three-dimensional jigsaw puzzle, dropped some back into the boxes, moved the rest around.

An LSI, a mercury tube probably from a thermometer, bits of resin board from a printed circuit, new and old stuff from the last fifty years of electronics, magnetics, and thermionics, it was all there, in his head and appearing in his lap.

And it, whatever it was, appeared in his hands, a shell for it made out of the watch case, sans strap and pins... these went into the scrap boxes for later inspirations, apparently.

"Dere," he said abruptly, brandishing the watch.

"What is it?"

"Vat it is? It's a vat-you-call?" He looked up at Marta. She shrugged her shoulders. "A plutometer."

"Measures Pluto?"

"No, no, you no understand a thing. Tell him, Marta."

"Well," she said. "You know Mars...action. Active. Areology, you say."

"Areology...hmm...like geology?"

"Yes, for Mars. You remember hot springs?" I blanched, but she didn't notice. "And fissures in rocks?"

"Yes."

"All those plutonic...come from under the mar. Plutometer sees before you can very see them."

"Op to three mile," interjected the Junkman smugly.

"So you don't fall into volcanoes?"

"So we find life stuff where vapor collects. Very important. Thank you, Junkman." She pecked at his cheek.

"You velcome." And he stuck his thumb in his mouth, his fat belly showing behind the now disarrayed apron in a broad stripe around his middle where his shirt ended.

>>>31. STORYTELLER>>>

In de morgan zon,	In the morning sun,
In de morgen zon,	In the morning sun,
Denke op uw rood vleesch.	Think on your red flesh.
Drinke de lucht, nu ander	Drink the sky, no other
Veroorlove a jong loven	Permits your young life.
De winter steam lang hier	Winter stays long here
Het ijs oversteke paar heden	The ice crosses to today
De tijd is lang, zeer lang, en	Time is long, very long,
De dag vechte met de nacht.	Day struggles with night
De dag vechte met de nacht.	Day struggles with night

Marta and I were talking, such as we did, those days, about the way things are. And though I acted as the "eager pupil" for the sake of being with her as much as possible, the discussions often led us out into the camp to listen to others. Looking back, now, my education, spotty as it was, gave me a perspective that perhaps none of the campers were quite aware of. And yet, it was only in particular persons at particular times that I came into contact with the feeling of approaching the inner essence of their life. One of these particular people was Hans, the storyteller.

We found him huddled up inside a hut built into the hillside with large flat rocks. Marta introduced me as the New Child, here to learn the stories, and we settled in to listen. His features and accents were certainly Dutch, both wellworn like a sailor, but he had suffered a physical injury to his head that left him helpless as far as common sense. Yet,

Marta said, he was wise as a child is wise, and he saw what had been before, visions that ran like primitive histories, without beginning or end.

"In the old days," he began, his eyes seeming to pierce the wall behind us, "When people were different from now, a great hunter and his friend and both their families were cut off by a storm from their home. The earth breathed fire, and the snow was black. So strong did the wind blow that they were unable to move from their temporary shelter even to relieve themselves for many days.

"When they were finally able to come out, their children had grown taller, and the dogs with them had multiplied. Arriving at the last valley, the hunter cried out 'The mountains have moved!' And nowhere could they find the village that they had left. The two men decided that it would be better for the winter to find them with another people. So they all journeyed south to meet with others before the long night.

"Many marvellous rocks and cliffs they saw, and a great boiling bay across their path where none had been before. The hunter's friend argued that they should turn back to familiar ground, but as they were talking, a great noise frightened the dogs and the children. When the men looked back, the land they had crossed was red and steaming, and cinders began to shower each of them."

Marta's knee nudged mine; the cold was bearable, though my legs were still unused to sitting on the ground. The storyteller lapsed easily into a kind of sing-song pattern, as if the words had taken on the sacred character of tradition by repetition. There were no rhymes, but his body swayed back and forth, back and forth very slightly, his head nodding for emphasis... until I found myself doing the same.

It seemed to make sitting much easier.

"Soon, the families found themselves on an island, while all around them the shores of the land vanished slowly, as if in a dream, until they were in the middle of ocean. Making scarce living, they built stone houses and gathered together all the food they had remaining... a large store, since they had hunted well. But even this great supply became a few mouthfuls before the fishes returned.

"The sons grew into men, and took wives of their sisters and cousins, and no one wore the heavy coats and boots in the everlasting summer. The old people died, and the old ways were forgotten by the young. 'What need to learn sewing and harpooning, when there is nothing to sew, and fish come too small for a heavy stick?' At last the island became too small for the many families, and a grandson of the hunter gathered young men about him to make a journey to see if the world was not just an old man's tale. His group left the island in a dozen boats, provisioned for many days. They sailed between rising and setting sun to the land of the fathers, and did not sight land for two moons. Many died from fighting among themselves... and some turned back. The hunter's grandson held the others to the task, though, until a white land with a dark rocky coast was sighted at last.

"The snow was entirely new to these naked people, and they rose in anger against the hunter's grandson, and slew him. Of those that now remained, only one couple had an idea of how to live in this new land. The rest perished from cold, or hunger, or from each other.

"One day, as the man and his wife were sitting by the shore, a man came to them. By signs, he showed them he was a friend, and had great gifts to give to them. They left their house and followed him, over two hills into a little cove sheltered from the sea. There, other men were standing beside a great kettle. One of them spoke in the words they knew, though as a child. He told them that if they wished, they might again see the land of their fathers. The man said, 'More than anything in the world, it would give us pleasure.'

"The men gathered, and agreed that the couple were indeed worthy, but they must be warned that they might be happier where they were. 'No,' cried the woman. 'My husband can provide, wherever we are.' Thus it was agreed.

"The couple went inside the kettle with the men, and journeyed with them a long time, and learned from them. This, now, is what the teaching was:

"'In a time before Brother Sun and Sister Moon, before even the Earth and Sea and Sky, that-which-was could not be counted, and the people were not yet. In this time before times, was the world before worlds. The Mother had given birth, but not yet suckled the flowers, the fishes, the foxes.

"'But when Time began, and Life struggled with Death in its seasons, the Mother smashed the one world into many worlds, and brothers and sisters were split apart, not to see each other, nor their children, nor the east side of a field would meet the west.

"'And of the many worlds, three were chosen where Life would win more than Death, and the Sun warmed these three more than the others in his pleasure, and they grew strong.

"'But in strength comes not peace, but struggle. The first child grew slowly and small, each day adding just a little. The other two, however, tussled and argued over toys, until the Sun, in his wrath, struck at them violently. As soon as the hand extended from the shoulder, Sun regretted what he had done, for the third child died instantly. Its bones fell apart, so that it could not be buried. The second child grew very sick, and even the first child was affected by this anger.

"'Afterward, the two brothers knew less of each other, and did their separate things. The memory of that time of sadness slowly dissipated, and forgetfulness covered both.'"

The old man's nodding so hypnotized me that it was minutes before I realized that he was not speaking. He had either fallen asleep or into a trance.

Marta motioned me up, and we retreated out of the house on hands and knees, very quietly.

"He is far away, Sand'. We come back later."

"OK with me. What now?"

"You might like to see how we bake, da?"

"Wait a minute. Bake what?"

She pinched my arm. "Oh, ho, ho, no, is not meat. That, later. Here is tent for baking khleb, omelet, kapusta…"

"I'm not going in there until I know what kleb and kapusty is. Omelet, that's omelet, like, with eggs?"

"Come. I show you. No harm. Come."

I let myself be dragged through the closed flaps into the tent. Inside, two women were standing in front of a row of pots, each one steaming around the lid. The atmosphere inside was decidedly thick, and delicious.

"Jambo, Marta. Hamna Pyotr?" a black woman said.

"Hakuna. Habari gani?"

"Nzuri. Who is your friend?"

"Ni Sandikassel. What's cooking?

The other woman answered without looking up. "Makroni-cheeze, stufpeppers, boilcabbidge."

I'd know that Bronx accent anywhere. "You American?"

She looked me straight in the eye. "Use't'be. 'Zit matter?"

"Well, I thought we might know some of the same people."

"We met. So what's the rest of them got t' do with it?"

"Nothing, I guess."

"Right. Hand me that spoon hanging... it's right in front o' yer nose. Yah, thanks."

"My name's Sandy."

"So I heard. I'm Emily. Been here long?"

"A few days." There were so few people here...I had thought that a stranger in their midst must have caused quite a stir. Struck out again. But Emily might be the put-down queen.

"This Anyosisye, Sand'. She best cook for green. Emily good with bread and meal."

"How do you do," Anyosisye said.

"Just fine. Glad to meet you."

"Anye," Marta said, "We get just odin vkus...one taste? For Sand'?"

"Ha. 'Odeen fkoos' coming up. Open!"

She thrust half a ladle-full into my mouth...the steaming hot liquid burned my mouth, but I could neither spit it out nor swallow. I nodded anxiously at her questioning face, and she smiled.

Outside, Marta asked, "You all right, Sand'?"

I motioned at the mouthful. She laughed, the heartless creature. She laughed and laughed until I managed to swallow out of frustration to say something in retaliation. "Fuck off!" was my eloquent outburst, which only made her laugh the harder.

"Are you finished now?" I said.

"Ya. Oh, Sand', you look so fun-ney. was soup good?"

I licked the remains from my teeth and gums. "Hm. Yes. What is it?"

"I don' know. You not ask Anyosisye?"

"I couldn't pronounce her name."

We headed back for the storyteller's hut. He was fast asleep, but woke as soon as we entered, and continued as if somebody had interrupted with a sneeze, and had just finished wiping his nose.

"A hole was made in the forgetting...

"A time for meeting, every ten thousand years, to keep away ignorance, and to share, and to remember the lost sister. That time is now.

"The couple rose from the kettle, thanked the men who had brought them and walked off into the new land, even colder than the one they had left. Few people did they meet, and those few could help them only little, for the land was parched, and the people poor.

"The couple mourned after years of living, for though they had food enough, and a large house, it did not echo with the sounds of children. A neighbor, a good woman, noticed their sadness around her scampering, and she understood.

"'You have given me much.' she said. 'I will give you more.' And she led them to a faraway place, a town where nobody lived, though the houses were fine, and well-repaired. In the largest house, she took them, to a machine. They went inside, and heard the roar of a storm on the ocean, or the fall of water over smooth rock. When they came out, the woman smiled at them.

"And each year after, the man worked harder and longer, for his family grew very large. He worked so hard even in bad times that the time of hunger came only for days, and then left. And his sons grew, his daughters married with the inhabitants until his blood was spread over a large area. People came to live near him, and, though their ways were different, they listened when he spoke.

"His family became known as the Handsome People, whose descendants live even now with the power of survival. A man or woman of this tribe has received the teaching. Others, such as myself, may speak: the people of the Handsome Face know."

The session was over. Hans offered us tea, but he had little to say.

Rather, he seemed to expect me to respond in some way. I left a ring with him and he proffered effusive thanks. Yet when we left, a certain uneasiness hung in the fetid air of his house.

Marta walked on a few paces ahead of me, her head bent forward, so that I couldn't see her expression.

"Well, that was interesting," I said.

She stopped and stared at me, as if she were about to cry.

"You understand nothing! Nothing!" she yelled, and ran back to the tent.

It was some days later I noticed a workman and the old storyteller side by side, lifting stones for a wall. It might have been my imagination, but the thought came and wouldn't go away: that man, perhaps he is of the Handsome People. Certainly not my idea of handsome...he was short and squat, his nose scarcely visible between broad leathery cheeks, his eyes embedded behind folds. His manner, though, and the deference that the old man showed toward him... and was that a glow about his body? No, I decided, the different spectrum here must catch light differently... a thing I had noticed at various times of day.

‹‹‹32. BREAKDOWN ‹‹‹

Toward the fourth month out, Billy and I had already relaxed our vigilance. No one, we thought, except the Captain, would connect me with those faraway events on a planet they all wanted to forget. But our optimism was misplaced. Carson's ambition spun long threads across the empty spaces he had once despised, to find me, since he had failed on Mars.

The call came through on Billy's shift, and I had an impulse to dash in front of the cam to wink at Carson and stick out my tongue.

"Priority. Private message," the unscrambled voice said, "for Captain Wentworth of the Fledermaus, from the Supreme Arbiter of Mars." Then a 5-second pause.

"I always read these," Billy said.

"Winston, I've got a clue on the Castle case. He isn't dead, and he isn't on Mars. That much we know. We have a crew-man here, Shelton, who claims that he was shanghied by a woman, his uniform stolen, and his space suit. Neither has been located. I have a strong reason to believe that Castle may have tried to stow away on the Fledermaus. I want you to conduct a thorough search for him, inside the atomizer, if necessary, but find him. He could ruin every-thing. He's got to be there. When you find him, you know what to do. And I'll want proof that he is no longer with us. Understood?

"Aside from that messy little detail, everything's going much better than anticipated. Order is established up to 50 kilometers from the town walls, and the people are beginning to realize what the grinch harvest is going to mean. Let's get this first shipment unloaded. I leave the details to you. We're depending on you, a whole new nation. Our agreement still stands. You'll be rich, Win, rich." The machine went dead.

"Billy! What'll I do?"

"Do? You ain't got to do shit. Just sit here a minute and collect your cool. That's right, man. Ol' Billy'll get you through." He stuck a pencil in his lips like a cigar, and chewed on the eraser.

"We could destroy the tape."

"No, there's bound to be a follow-up. Carson'll smell the difference."

"All right, don't be so negative. Let's put our brains to work; that's what we humans are for. How about a mutiny?"

"Who's going to mutiny? You?

"A mutiny... or a breakdown. The ship grinds to a halt, too much sand in the engine."

"Be serious, Billy. That can't happen. At this speed, we're coasting anyway. But..."

It struck us at the same time. It was possible to make the ship break down in more ways than one. Credible ways, like communications, or even the unscrambler.

"How about if we dub over a new track?... No, this gear wasn't built for editing. I wonder... we could switch over to this machine... have to do it by hand and eye..."

"Hey, boss, what you doin'? You gonna get us in a helluva mess."

"Relax, Crusty, this is what I was doing before they called

me away on this godawful project. I know media inside and out."

Half an hour later, we sat back to watch.

"Winston, on the Castle case. / He is dead. / Shelton claims he was shanghaied by a woman. / He's got proof that he is / no longer with us. Understood?" And then the rest of the message.

"Ha! So much for the messy detail."

"Man, we're in!" He slapped my knee. "Old Slick-head gonna blow off which way we tell him. Sandy, why didn't you tell me before? We coulda had this ship headed straight for Mars."

"Well, I... Hey! If we did it, add like a minute or so... but where's the video come from?"

"Nah, don't worry 'bout that, there's a whole shelf full of the stuff."

"There's just one teeny weeny flaw, Billy. I think we'd better hold off on this editing job."

"What's eatin' you now, Sandy?"

"You sleep some, right? And loaf some? This middle-of-the-night message was a fluke. We'd better go through with it; no sense in taking that kind of chance."

"Sandy! You know what you're sayin'?"

"Yeah. It means I disappear. Got any ideas along that line?"

"Mmm, hmm. OK, listen to this. They be lookin' all over the inside of the ship... Here, it's simple. They're lookin' for a man and a spacesuit, right? Don't do us no good to hide a man, and they find the suit. How'd it get here, somebody swallow it? So, we just put the man inside the suit, and the suit outside the ship.

"Wait a minute, it's cold out there. Outside, you want me to go outside?"

By 6:30, Billy had stuffed me into Shelton's suit, and shoved me into the airlock. The steady hissing ate into my nerves, and the pressure gauge dropped to within a hair of zero. I stiffened, and began slowly turning the crank to the outside. There wasn't anything to stand on, just emptiness. My legs refused command after command. Skydiving had been easy compared to this; there wasn't any place to fall to.

"Hurry up!" crackled through the headset. I jumped, and had a helluva time getting back to close the door; when I did, it clicked shut. I was alone, with a tiny maneuvering pistol, and a hank of rope.

More or less straight ahead... I must have been traveling hundreds of thousands of kilometers per hour, along with the ship... the twin darlings of the system, one dead, one very much alive, white and blue, bigger than stars, held out a promise, and a threat.

"Find a nice place, and stay there..." he said. "I'll call you into the airlock when it's safe." Sure, Billy.

Meanwhile, I'm floating in the biggest sea of all, the universe, stars swimming by my head, and emptiness all around me.

I wandered around the hull to an area with some protrusions to tie myself to, as the spirit of the vastness looked over my shoulder. Earth was about an inch big, judged by my fingers at arms length, a blue ball flecked with white. My mind refused to accept this picture as anything more than a wall poster drawn by a lonely madman.

Four hours later, I heard crackling on my radio. But it wasn't

Billy! Something must have gone wrong... They'd weaseled a confession out of him, and were coming to get me... No, they were a repair crew. I had nowhere to run, this time, but I hauled myself in, untied the rope, and drifted toward the prow. At least it would be the easiest place to defend. A few more seconds... Did they see me?

No, apparently they weren't looking, for the crew settled in around the maze of retractable instruments I had been attached to.

Half an hour later, they were gone again. Thank God space doesn't carry sound. I'd had to fire my little maneuvering gun more than once to stay out of sight.

I straddled the nose to see how it felt like to ride a rocket ship. It felt cold. My whole body was working to put out the heat lost by radiation, but it was a losing battle. Fingers and toes went numb first. Hurry up, Billy. There's no more oxygen than what I brought, and no food.

I'd passed out, or fallen asleep, by the time Billy roused me. Inside the airlock, I took off my helmet as soon as possible, and lay there, breathing in great gulps of air, foul as it was. If I had left the Earth, instead of thin-atmosphered Mars, I would never have survived the lack of oxygen... as it was, I had to use all the tricks Chidnaq and I had learned in the desert. Strange, even now I called it "desert." Weston hadn't quite sunk in.

And then I was inside. Billy unwrapped me, rubbed my hands and feet to get the circulation going again.

"Man, you crazy. You almost blew it. I thought you was dead man, Sandy."

"Why? What's the matter?"

"Just about everything. But we got away with it. Lord, you was sitting in the middle of the dish; you was sending in signals like a drowning man. You shoulda known better than to hook yourself to the video channels. I could almost see your body on the screen. Lucky for you they called it a malfunction; I wasn't about to tell them different."

"You mean I was seen by everybody?"

"Don't look so astonished. Yes, that's the size of it. But panic's over. This time. Now come on in, we can't stand here. Sshh, now, the first peep, and…"

>>>33. HOMER>>>

He had an eternal tired sag of a face...even for Mars. He'd been through the worst. When he was excited, he'd just prop up the furrows in his forehead with his eyebrows, the thick eyelids perpetually at an awning tilt. He shaved, Godnose with what, but the black stubble refused to yield the field. His wild mop marked him from the rest as a sentimentalist, but the carelessness of his appearance set off the efficiency born of ultimate weariness; he knew his business, even if nobody else did.

Homer Tent, the prophet from Passaic, was perhaps the one person I could talk to at length on the topic that fascinated me most... politics. But chance rolled us together only a few times. I'd filled him in on what I knew, but he was a step ahead of me. Where he got his information, I never found out. Marta said he had power, whatever that meant.

And then I'd see him, and we'd start in again.

"So Carson plans to use the energy resources of Mars...a much smaller planet...to stave off changes on Earth. That won't last long."

"But it'll ruin Mars. And it won't solve a thing. They almost killed the space program by starvation; now they plan to glut themselves until the cupboard is bare."

"The thing he doesn't understand...and for Gods-ache, how long did it take us to see it... is that Earth ecology has nothing to do with the kind of balances on Mars. Pure homocentrism is in his head, and there's no way to budge it." He eased back. "Know what I'm talking about? It's simple. We came here, straight into the middle of a system that had extreme solutions for extreme problems...some of them so delicate that a day without wind, for example, would mean an end to the fluffs, believe it or not."

"But there're so many of them, once you get away from camp."

"You noticed that, too? And there are other creatures to whom our very presence, the merest whiff of Earth life in any form, is a death certificate. Have you ever seen a warfle?"

"No, but..."

"You may never have the chance. Weston described them in detail... one of the most moving entries in his journal...no, sorry, I don't know where it is now... is when he realizes that it was impossible for him even to see one that was not already dying. It was a severe crisis for so gentle a man. But perhaps that marked a new beginning here on Mars. At last it was obvious that, though we could take over another world, we would serve Shiva rather than Vishnu."

"Eh?"

"Shiva... the Destroyer."

>>>34. SMOKESCREEN>>>

With Homer's help, I had been making notes on the culture of the Outsiders, trying to make sense out of the society they had established in the outlands of Mars, hardly using the civilized inventions that had made it possible for them to arrive... on the whole, the Outsiders were as technologically sophisticated as anyone I met here. As Homer pointed out, technician was the lowest class permitted to hop planets, with very few exceptions, like myself. Yet they used devices sparingly, like the old Indians of North and South America, and only when their senses failed them.

The people here are supersensitive to sound, to smell, to touch, and to an understanding of the life of the planet, which is practically invisible to an unpracticed observer such as myself. But not to Homer.

I might have missed the hollow rocks, hollowed out by primitive life that yet have the capability of reproducing themselves, refined to the point that the bacteria on Earth are small in comparison. These tiny creatures come from the rocks and form the rocks, much as coral does. They maintain an existence in conditions that I would have declared impossible for life in any form. Perhaps old Barlee was right! "Life fills in the crevices." Or, as he more eloquently put it: "The possibility of life is a probability."

Like the snail on Earth, the Martian creatures that form the pseudorocks, or rather, are the pseudorocks, create forms of symmetry and patterns of beauty, the beauty of life wherever it is found.

We were engrossed in comparing designs of these minuscule

animals through a handheld 30x lens, and Homer, as usual, had a definitive comment. This time, he never had the chance to finish it.

Marta rushed in, breathless.

"Quick, come quick! Hurry!"

Homer tumbled out first, and we all raced to the mouth of the cave.

Smoke poured out, a white column of billowy puffs. Marta rushed in, us following... it wasn't smoke, but a warm vapor... water!

I could barely make out the disappearing figure ahead of me, and I narrowly missed cracking my skull on the jutting rocks of the ceiling several times. We were going down, down to the great chamber, and past it. The only way I could tell we had gone so far was the sand under my feet.

"Over here!" Marta called. In the dim fog, one or two luminous panels made everything a white blur. I reached out to touch a figure...it was Homer. Marta stood by his side, talking. A faint hiss.

"It comes from there," she said. "The Junkman's corner."

By the time we arrived... I bumped into the halted Homer... the awful hum that made me grit my teeth had stopped. Its source was faintly visible... the fat old Junkman hunched over like a boulder.

"Ummmhummmhummm."

"What the devil! Are you doing this?" Homer fairly yelled at him.

"Aiiee!" We had taken him completely by surprise. He almost fell over backwards. "Vas ist das? Der Donner? Ach, nicht berührte! No touch!" This to Homer, who had advanced a few steps to stop the billowing clouds that were even now rising over the tops of the cliffs.

"Junkman, you're giving us away!" Homer's strained voice rattled out. "The smoke, it's too much."

"Ja? So." He clicked an intricate sequence in his ample aproned lap, and instantly the air around him began to clear. Now we could see the diabolical instrument, which turned out to be no larger than a box of kitchen matches. He held it up for our approval. "Is good," he grinned. "Is de-eye-dra-fon-iktur."

"Is what?" I gasped.

Marta, at my elbow, helped with the translation...her gift at interpreting amazed me again... the device was a dehydrator. Junkman opened a little drawer on the side of it, knocked out a fistful of dust into a jar.

She threw her arms around his fat head, kissed him until we all blushed. "Oh, Junkman, you are so good," she cried. If all it took was a little smoke. I'd make a truckload, just for her.

"What's this all about? Smoke and dust, that's all I see."

"Sasha, not smoke. Vapor. Is water. See? All we need, not from plutons, from rocks. Yes, Junkman?"

"Ja, Look." He aimed a karate chop at the rock he was sitting on, and pieces flew off like baked clay. Marta knelt and handed him one, which he inserted in the drawer.

"Bitte, ein kalt Glas."

The ready-to-please Marta fetched a jar from one of the recessed shelves. A few clicks... I could have sworn it was magic, and yet technology, it seemed, was past parlor tricks forever...and while she held the jar upside down over the box, I saw beads of sweat form in the jar, until it was dripping a mudpuddle at Junkman's feet.

A thin cloud formed in the corner of the cave, but most of it collected on the walls. My clothes felt damp.

"All right, all right. We can lick the floor when we're thirsty."

Homer looked at me disparagingly. "You don't have much imagination, do you? Ever heard of a still?"

"Yes, but..."

"Same principle. Use the condenser coil. Takes some tubing... and half a brain."

I was about to launch into a witty reply when our attention focussed on commotion at the mouth of the cave. A struggle was going on, people yelling at each other. I raced out ahead of the others to reconnoiter.

Moncho was perched up on a rock, shouting instructions. I ignored him and sought out Pyotr by his tent. Together, we dashed into the chaos.

Men I'd never seen before were shouting obscenely and rushing in here and there in an attempt to cause confusion and fright, in which they partially succeeded. Pyotr rallied a few campers nearby into a group armed with whatever was at hand, and stood off an onslaught of the invaders... the campfolk moved as with one mind, though I had seen no military preparations of any sort.

>>>35. ATTACK>>>

Elsewhere in the camp, cries were heard of people dying or wounded, and we rushed, I with Pyotr's group, to where the action was thickest. I found myself in hand-to-hand struggle with a man twice my size, and as he was about to deliver a brutal blow to my vitals, I had fallen, had only the useless defense of lying prone on the ground. Pyotr aimed a shaft that felled him. I regained my feet, and my confidence came back with a deep breath. I leaped on the back of another attacker, who turned to toss me away... but in that second, the fatal loss of attention to his former victim allowed the camper to strike him in the neck, a blow that nearly severed his head from his body.

The struggle went on, and it seemed that there were too many, and yet we fought, knowing that there was no place to run. But, abruptly, a shrill whistle sounded. The attackers backed off into a retreating mass, chased by a few of the younger men for a short distance. We let them go, and stood wondering.

It was time to count losses. Marta entrusted me, since I had paper, to be the official secretary. We had lost thirteen—five men, six women and two children—while the attackers, whom Marta identified as Adventurers, left behind eleven of their own, large men, fully armed, who now stared glassily into the dust.

We gathered their weaponry, their clothes, and a small troop was organized to carry the bodies to a site pointed out by the head cook, where they would be wrapped, I was told, both friends and enemies, and left to freeze, and later to thaw. And their meat, now that I had come to accept reluctantly their crude customs, would be of great value in this barren land. The meat from these twenty-four would serve us food of a high protein variety through most of a Martian winter with little need for the back-breaking, time-consuming labor of scavenging sufficient low-life from the dust and the rocks for our sustenance.

We then reconnoitered the retreat of the Adventurers to make sure that all was safe. The highest climber reported that they had stopped at a distance of about three kilometers, where they had left their vehicles. And now they were assembling in motorized formations to return.

Lemoine called the men together to discuss battle plans, and in the midst of the tents, in that moment, he was selected as leader for the campaign. Immediately drawing plans in the sand, he conferred with one set of men and sent them off in various directions. Another group routed the women and children out of the tents to a safe place in the rocks behind. A third group hid in a tent on the far left side; still another group in a tent on the right side. Those men with good bows were collected in the first tiers of rocks overlooking the camp.

The formation now began to take on a U-shape, one of the classic campaign stratagems as Creasy might have described... the tents flapping in the middle would be the bait. A few campers stationed themselves a little to the rear of the middle of the tents. Yes, it would surely appear that the force was weak and unorganized.

Several of the slighter youths gathered long poles wrapped in cloth, which they carried up the side of the hill, up beyond the archers, and half-hidden by a large rock. From a glimpse, here and there, though they were mostly hidden, I could see that they were assembling something from the poles.

In the midst of these preparations, I noticed out of the corner of my eye, the lovely Marta helping Junkman to a rock outside the cave. But I was too busy to notice further...until later.

The wind by now had shifted to a steady 15 kilometers an hour downslope. We could begin to hear the motorcade making its way toward us. They rounded the last bend and circled in front of the tents whooping and hollering. The defenders held in front of them two great logs as a kind of rough shield or barricade; with which they advanced a few steps, then retreated a few steps.

By the time the leader of the Adventurers gave the order to charge, a vapor cloud had formed in the camp, billowing out from the Junkman's little box. But the machines came two by two, straight at the tents, straight at Pierre's little band, shouting and cursing, a few projectiles exploding amid the empty tents. With no deviation in their paths, the Wheels ripped right through the first tents, and the second, until a shambles on the ground made it more difficult to maneuver the machines. The first pair came straight at Pierre; he did not flinch. He'd taken the precaution of backing the group near to the slope, where a few rocks and then a ledge of boulders gave the advantage to men on foot.

Through the white cloud, I could barely make them out. But now the middle of the barricade had been unhooked, and as the Wheels slowed right in front of them, each log moved in a transverse direction, like scissors opening, then abruptly reversed, they closed like a gate on the Wheels, catching them at an oblique angle, knocking them both together, but now the campers were vulnerable from the side to the second pair. The logs were hoisted over their heads to the other side, just in time, and now, as if at a given signal, the men hidden in tents on both sides rushed out, while the archers above shot their first volley of the glass arrows I had once feared so much.

The formation of machines now began to break in the narrow confines, each struggling to maneuver and maintain balance through tent poles, stones, twisted tent fabrics, and fighting men.

The covering fire from above split the Adventurers into two pieces, one caught within the camp—only a few would escape. The second contingent veered off to the right to reconnoiter, regroup, and attempt to come around behind the foot fighting. But then, out of the puffs of cloud, came giant birds...not birds—they were the youths clinging to cloth wings, dropping explosives into the second group of Wheels beyond the camp. The confusion of smoke and dust and vapor effectively cut off any help to their trapped comrades, now being decimated by the campers. One giant of a man bulled his way out of the closing ring, just in time to catch an outstretched hand from the last Wheel as it spun out in a spray of dust.

A bird had been hit, and it came spiraling down, right over the remaining formation of machines. It was Samuel. I yelled to Pierre's group, now finishing its bloody work. Pierre nodded briefly without looking up, and the archers in the rocks aimed their weapons at that great distance; Samuel emerged through the vapor in a run, straight for the camp, in a path between where the arrows were falling.

I joined the fray in the camp, despite Pierre's warning to stay out, and I fought as hard as the rest to topple the surviving Wheels. The men unwheeled ran rather then fought, but uselessly. Arrows from the hill cut them down, every one of them by the end. Outside, I could see no more than yellow dust and white fog, but the dust now was retreating. And there could have been no more than half a dozen Adventurers remaining in the attack group.

A lightning stroke signaled the beginning of a brief rainshower over all of us: it may have been that that convinced the survivors to abandon their assault, for when it was over, they were far from the camp. Later, Homer told me that it was probably the first water rain on Mars in a million years, for in the thin air, water rarely had a chance to collect at all. The Junkman had done it again.

So, the Adventurers had lost most of their men, most of their machines, and we expected to see no more of them. The rest of that day, we spent recuperating. In the second attack we lost no one, though many were wounded, some seriously, and the cooks had a busy time cleaning the bodies that had been ripped open by explosive pellets.

Marta and I returned to the camp and directed the removal of an additional twenty-six men. The food cache would now be more than sufficient, except in variety—though I had learned to accept the consumption of human flesh in principle, still, I didn't look forward to the same food day after day. The regular change of "food-priests" in the ensuing months continually surprised me with the variety of possibilities for the preparation of flesh. I favored the spicy versions of Anyosisye, particularly roast toe.

At the end of that day, exhausted and yet exhilarated, I might have fallen asleep, if it had not been for a celebration to relieve the tensions of having fought and killed. This procedure, only as common as battles, did a thorough job in its frenzy of cleansing any thought of violence. And in the group dance, I began to feel or suspect that I was now baptized in a sense. In a deeper way than ever before, I had become a part of these people, for I had shared something very strong, an alcohol of the spirit, and had shown myself capable, as with another man, of defending the camp. And yet the flush of victory also left me wondering what was becoming of me. Strange feelings, the source of which I could not locate in my own mind began to take over.

The drumming carried a primitive message and the utter

precision with which the dance steps were taken, even my myself, who did not know the dance, gave me an uneasiness that was not easy to brush aside. And at times, I had the feeling that we weren't private individuals quite. Though each man spoke for himself, yet each man was also all men of his group.

With these thoughts I went to bed, tossed, and had light dreams of being alone and of being many people, a whole parliament or assembly. And each of these people knew everything that was going on in the minds of the others without the need to say anything. Yet one did not act as one but as many.

Every simple action required a vote and a consensus. Every single thought was debated and discussed, and passed on. And the steps of the dance seemed to lift me up to the stars and through them, until my body was filled with the galaxy. And I touched other galaxies who were dancing in the same rhythm, and I felt their smile in my face as if I were looking in a mirror.

I told this dream to Marta the next day. She laughed.

"That is good dream," she said, "You tell it to Stan?"

"Do you think that would do any good?" I said.

"Listen," she said.

I thought she was about to say something; it was perhaps the wind she meant me to hear. But I could hardly concentrate on that, for a strange feeling filled me, as if the answers rose simultaneously with every question, and I felt sure that I knew what the dream meant, though I couldn't say it.

"Listen to what?" I said.

Her smile turned into a little ironic grin. Her eyes sparkled. "You are ready," she said. "Why you not come with us?"

Though her words were Russian, I knew what she had said. "Come? Come where?"

"Come... here," she said. "Is good."

I felt that I had touched something but not quite grasped it. "I don't understand."

"You understand, but you are afraid."

I had scarcely admitted that to myself—could she tell so easily? The uneasiness of last night returned.

"Stan will help," she said.

I waited, but she made no move to introduce me to Stan.

"Tonight," she said, "We will be together. You will come."

"Yes," I said, "I'll come."

"We will be Stan." And then she left.

I passed it out of my mind, and went back to look at the mysterious stones I had collected. But now for some reason my mind was clearer, at peace, and it seemed that I could read the whole history of the planet in these little formations. Nothing was hidden from me. And I knew, without knowing how I knew, of the long and uneven history of the place where I stood.

I thought of Marta, and instantly her face was in my mind, and she seemed to be speaking to me, but I could not hear the words. It was as if a pane of glass still separated us, through which I might look on wonders, and never touch them.

I lay down on the bunk, and tried to sleep. Thoughts crowded in, but I shoved them aside with the stern command: Sleep, sleep, I must sleep. And all was quiet.

I woke gently, perhaps an hour later, and came out of my tent. Saw no one, but then, at almost the same instant, people from all over the camp came out of tents, stood in various postures stretching, as if they had all been asleep. Well, it was time to get some work done, and there was still plenty to do around the camp.

>>>36. YOUNG BLOODS>>>

The young bloods of the tribe carried out their revenge on the remaining Adventurers—tracking them down to their hold in the hills, a place they described as a miasma actually overgrown with the rank Bayta weeds, the source of the bitter brew used by the outlaws before an attack—much like the Berserkers hyped themselves up on whatever-it-was.

Fifteen gliders came silently soaring over us at the same time we rushed out in hasty battle lines against the sound of the Wheels, three of them, but there was no battle; it had been fought already, and won by the Outsiders. The Wheels were ridden by three toughs, including the leader or spokesman for the group, the Martian-born Moncho.

The council was to begin the day after tomorrow; the call had gone out over what network of communication I didn't know, to the chiefs of all outlying groups. Everybody celebrated as soon as the gliders came back, all of them, in formation, like vultures of war. At council, the trophies would generate respect.

While the rest stood cheering, Pyotr shook his head, and put his hand on my shoulder.

"You know, Sasha, tovarishch. Is trudny. Trouble."

"But we won! What's the matter, Pete?"

"You no know? Aih! We see him come, tomorrow we see him talk. To all the come-ers."

"So?"

"You see tomorrow."

And I did.

People began arriving early in the morning, in small groups and large. I hadn't imagined that there could be so many survivors of the Martian desert.

They varied from gypsy-types to stern Germanic warriors, from an all-black klatch to Chinese, Russians... who greeted Pyotr warmly in their language... all manner of Europeans in mixed bunches. Most of them still wore the remains of official uniforms... for there was no native cloth that hadn't required weeks of patient work by the women. But about half had some sort of hat, the variety distinguished by inventiveness rather than style.

I counted over fifty separate groups by late afternoon, when the chiefs were to get together for a preliminary briefing and agenda meeting. Marta sat in as secretary, but no other member of our camp took part, except for the withered old man who had "taught" me breathing.

I sought Pyotr out. He was busy sorting one camp site from another for the comfort of all.

"Who is standing in for us? Surely not the old buzzard."

"Buzzer?"

"You know. Shortie."

"Ah! No worry, Sasha. Haha. No worry." And then he went off again to attend to the problems of arranging the shelters in his diplomatic way.

I wandered among the new arrivals, scanning the faces. Perhaps Billy was here, among them. Most ignored me, but quite a few waved hello or shouted greetings. I responded to each in their manner. All of them bore the signs of stress from living off the land, yet throughout the encampment, the signs of intelligence were clear, in their eyes, in their faces, in the ingenious ways of dress and equipment. It

214

wasn't just the desert, it must have been the ultraviolet too, the powerful rays that soaked into the skin, burning the blue skin brown. Compared with them, I was still a paleface, though cyanosis had turned me blue, and the sunlight baked me tan. Pyotr said that when I was as black as he, then even through my clothes, I would feel warmer.

But I quickly got bored without my friends. The chiefs had retreated into the cave, and that's where the real action was going on. I decided to sniff it out, find out what I could. Everyone else had community affairs on their minds. I still suffered under the delusion that since I had accepted ten million dollars for a book, I ought at least to make an effort to know what was going on. In my mind, at least, I still had a job to do. If nothing else, it would give me the hope that one day I might again stand on the good green earth... even the concrete-block cities would be better than this.

No guard stood at the entrance, so I just casually walked in, being very quiet, taking care not to crunch the sand more than absolutely necessary. As soon as I was inside, a flood of doubt, subconscious warnings, rushed at me out of the darkness.

I should have listened. One of them was a reality. A hand grabbed my arm, and a figure stepped out of the shadows. It was Moncho.

"Where do you think you're going?"

"I was curious about..."

"Shut up. Rause!" He twisted my arm backwards, and yanked to make sure he was understood.

"Wait, you have the wrong idea, I..."

"Later. The Council will decide."

Two other young toughs came over to lend a hand, and I was escorted at a rapid march through the tent grounds.

Fortunately, Pyotr saw me and rushed over.

"What is?" he said. "Sasha! What you done?"

"He was in the cave," Moncho snapped.

"What's wrong with that? Nobody told me anything about..." My arm bent up another notch toward breaking.

Pyotr handed a small amulet from around his neck to the leader of the toughs. "Pledge," he said, softly.

Immediately they let go of my arm and I nearly fell over. "That's better," I said to no one in general. Pyotr and the youths faced one another like ancient enemies peering through a thick glass. Only later did I realize how impenetrable that barrier was.

Pyotr said nothing more, though his downcast eyes told me something was not right. Later I asked Marta about it, when he was out of earshot.

"From his neck" The malchiki stone on a string?"

"Yes, that's the one."

She looked ready to burst into tears. "Oh, Pyotr! Do you know what you done?"

"I? I did nothing."

"Entering the Chamber of the Chiefs... you call nothing that?"

"I didn't get halfway in the door. Besides, why does Moncho have the right to go where I don't?"

"It's privilege of Mars-born, they call it. All not agree. But all obey. You will see at the Council."

"I already have. Can you rub that shoulder a little lighter, Marta, please?"

>>>37. STAN >>>

Marta led me to a low rise near an open area surrounded on half its perimeter by rocky slopes, now peopled by the men/women of the camp and travelers from, I assumed, settlements similar to our own.

The strangers' garb varied from dun or gray camouflage wear... sometimes a movement would startle me until I could make out the human outlines in what had been rock a moment before...to gay and colorful motley, frequently in advanced stages of patchwork rehabilitation to the point where the original, perhaps denim or canvas, had been so thoroughly covered as to be debatable. One woman had gypsy in her blood or her spirit, not only by color of clothes, but in an insistence on the fin-de-siècle revival of voluminous skirts and puffed sleeves; like Indian women of all times, she wore her wealth, though in fabric instead of jewels.

All faces turned toward the center in a hush of silence. I glanced at Marta for instructions; there were none. As if watching an invisible pingpong championship, her eyes were rolling gently from side to side, not focusing on any particular object, but seeming to sweep in those eyes on the opposite bank...which were engaged in exactly the same movements as Marta. Gradually a calm settled me as well, though I was more curious than a squirrel at a picnic, anxious to see what's happening, and to spy out the goodies. However, I let the gentle rhythm of soundlessness lull me into dreams, and thereby missed whatever might have happened...rather, my eyes were open, but the quality, or tenor, of my thoughts were more akin to dream or fantasy than to reality, so I record the following with trepidation.

Whether these visions, or sonsions...to coin a word by paragogy, meaning sound hallucinations...were shared by others, I do not know. I suspect they were, but I must report them as my own mental meandering here, despite the conclusions and discussions afterward. I am not competent, or willing, to make such a judgment, opposed as it is to my own beliefs in the limitations... and magnificences... of the human mind.

At any rate, this is what I heard:

I call my people together. You have come. From your lives, from your families, from your ambitions, fields, dwellings, beds. I have called and you have come, brothers, sisters.

I will share with you what is in me, that we may all be troubled, and that we may together resolve the troubles. I am an old man, nothing but an old man; your respect warms my bones and makes my resolve stronger. Through you I live mightily, and breathe with a thousand breaths at once.

Through you I have seen much lately, and we have been troubled, in larger-than-personal ways. When one dies, we all suffer a death; when one sickens, so do we all. So does the world experience a lessening.

And when the cause of sickness, and the reason for death, and the origin of sadness, when these become known, and become common knowledge to us all, we may act in various ways. One runs with fright, one stands in ignorance, one sits in ambush, one lies down in despair, one fights with animal rage. What one may do by himself many may imitate, and so all die individually. That is the way it has been; your thoughts affirm what I say.

Remember the Stan. (*Here the voice, or chorus, grew louder*) You are Stan, and we are Stan, and Stan is I speaking through you. (*I can only relate here the most prominent of*

218

expressions, for the entire assembly, if that's what was happening, seemed to be shouting together at this point as a pond of bullfrogs open the evening concert by tuning up their throats. The cacophony rose to ever-higher levels of intensity, meanwhile dissolving into mental harmonies and developing counter-rhythms in increasing simplicity and force until, as it were, one leading party subsumed the rest into harmonic variations of itself, a paean of song, bursting with exotic subterranean, subarean, emotion.) Stan! Forever Stan!

Weston-Stan! Together-forever, forever together. Stan lives, Mars lives! *(etc., etc. until the one voice appeared again as if a powerful orator had suddenly raised his hand. I looked at the field… empty. The mouths…all closed.)*

The Great Return is always in process, as an egg hatches, as a plant unfolds, as the borotons form and re-form. Likewise the traveler of planets plunge the Great Deep in isolation, to emerge finally from the nest to a bewildering world of sights and smells and touches that both frighten and beckon. We of a Mind remember, will not be able to forget, that planetary rebirth, and may indeed remember a previous rebirth, and a rebirth before that.

As each is all in Stan, so all is each. The names of leaders and inventors may pass away as unimportant in the vastness of Stan, but not the leading, not the inventions, not the realities and memories, not the cutting short of memories, not the sudden joy of new awakenings by the hairless Earth-sent or winged or wingless originates or partials. *(The tumults here at each named group ranged in depth and volume through a gamut of possibilities I could not have imagined…yet where had these ideas entered my head? Perhaps, like Weston, my mind let loose greater and greater aberrative fantasies in this wild, fantastic setting. Yet his visions were not like my own.)*

But though we know and are all, yet some have not been

touched by Stanhood. Some nestlings have not opened their eyes, do not recognize their Mother, do not know their powers. Huddled together, though insulated from each other, the seed of One has not the chance to grow. The barriers of metal form too strong a pod, and the overgrown chicklings are content to remain warmed and asleep.

These sleeping ones pursue dreams of helplessness, and the accommodations to this helplessness multiply as borning becomes more difficult. Inside the shell, encased in Earth-some square delusions, the unborn know not of the now-named Mars which is their true home. Artificial power, artificial radio, continual overdosage of oxygen... these may not be blamed, though they are causes of process-stoppage. No blame, but yes a great sadness.

Sadness to be suffered, as many events have been suffered...endured for the sake of the completeness of the eventual delivery of new-kindled spirits and their subsequent proper development.

(The voice was interrupted at this point by an impetuous shout that echoed in a new silence, a faster silence it seemed, a silence of awe at the daring boldness of one like Moncho.)

Wait! A mind we are, and all we here/now know what one knows. Listen and learn what one knows, then. The city of steel spawns steel pawns, casts out fast the mad hermits of Mars. Mars, seek revenge! Mars of battles unending lies restless under alien powers, chains of insolence that rankle the heart. Expunge the interlopers, rise as One together to the combat.

Time burns slowly down the fuse of patience until patience is exhausted—and indignation flares. Death will be answered by death, battle by battle, aggression by aggression. No more suffering without reason; if we would suffer, let it be honorably behind the standard of Mars, weapon in hand, with one purpose in mind: the cleansing of rottenness from the surface of our world. Eggs that do not hatch must be tossed into garbage, burned into nothingness. A flower that will not open is not a flower, but a weed. Rank weeds must be pulled out, root and all, and though the gardener gets his hands dirty, yet the garden will thrive.

We who are one may live only by intelligence in the face of rampaging enemies. By speaking our mind we may come to know the appropriate time to strike. These eyes, and others, have seen that time come and go; our best advantage will not come again, and is even now receding into memory, falling away into the oblivion that met the Astran originates who so loved their world that they would ignore the faults and fissures at their feet, and so were blasted apart. We remember from then a debate of as great moment as we now sit debating. And, though names be lost, issues are not. As we are One, let us act as One together, and strike! Strike the stillborn festering in our bosom before the cancer of single-self-ness spreads.

For know this, that plans have been written...these eyes have seen, these ears have heard, these nares have smelled the coming purge of the Outlands, and among the messengers of destruction are included the misbegotten cousins of ours called Adventurers.

(*A massive gasp.*)

Yes, the unbelievable may also share credibility with plain truth. By one inconceivable, by many it is possible to ply the power of false promises, paper values, hidden lies.

(*Yet another voice, very familiar, broke in. If it weren't for the fluency, I might have thought Pyotr had invisibly taken the podium.*)

I call again the Stan, the One-in-All, to hear what one has to say. We are One together by being called together to be One. Let not the One become Two, for the evils of selfness may creep in unnoticed by way of division. One speaks as a timeless force spanning three planets and several species; One also speaks as a being threatened by individual destruction from outside. And we all share both, for we are both...we know the truth of both and feel at the same time the calmness of rock and the passion of survival.

Yet these are not contrarealities within the One. Nor are they paradoxical outside the One, for we know in our midst such a being as we would not harm, yet such a one holds bright promise of eventual transforming that it would be a pity...a crime...to shut him out of the One.

And he stumbled into our midst without any realization... as most of us did, one way or another, in our beginnings. Must there not then be many more who are presently victims of the selfness of others, many more indeed than perpetrators of the mask of self? If we seek to expunge the illness, let us rather deal with it at its source, and not destroy wantonly the lives of these whom we might rather have as friends, allies, or share-brothers.

Let us, on the one side, restrain our anger so that we may see whom we would strike...and whether striking is the proper relation to have with any at all; in other words, let us consider when voting the votes of those who would be here if history had allowed it.

And on the other side, let us in truth feel pain where it hurts, salve wounds already received, and also gird weapons when attacked by Mind-less creatures, beings of alonenesses who scarcely know their individual minds, and certainly know much less of this Mind now speaking. As a sitter may blink dust from his/her eye, so we may act to retain the Unity when blasting and ignorant winds would grind it away.

But further, we may ponder for a moment the course of maximizing, which is a law of all living things, the Stan not excluded. As layers of experience teach us growth in peace and growth in struggle, we may understand that adversity often spurs life to new heights of excellence that, after a period, result in fruitfulness beyond the common sweet grapes of long sun and rich soil.

For let us not easily toss about names, as "Mars of War," or "enemies," or "unhatched chicklings." For truth is in a name, but never the whole of Truth. And, if we would see clearly, we must see with many eyes, and those not alone of the being in which we are One. That is to say, we have, and admit the presence of one who, without the power to speak here, yet has seen what we have not, the inside of the "rotting egg."

(I felt, suddenly, a moment of panic, as if a thousand minds had plunged into my own. Was this real? The vividness of a flood of my own memories of the settlement, from landing to early-morning escape by one of Wilkes' trucks, all jumbled together, things I'd forgotten I knew, made me suspicious of my own doubts about this Mind they kept talking about. In my wildest shows on Earth, I'd never approached the intensity or depth of this dream-experience, more-than-dream but less than reality as I knew it. Every impression, every tingle of sand on skin, every shadow cast forth in frightening boldness...my mind flayed open until I was standing, screaming "Stop! Stop!" though all I could see were the swaying bodies in that natural rock bowl, half-closed eyes still rolling from right to left, right to left. And, abruptly, a whoosh of sudden vacuum, a last few little animal-like scurries out of my mind. Drained, I collapsed in a pile, unable to produce a coherent thought of my own from early childhood, when I had a club in a dark storeroom...utter sensations I couldn't identify as my own. I clung to one image, a time been "initiated" into a treehouse, fright at sounds I couldn't locate, and the blessed relief when the door opened just a crack, and someone's parent saying sternly, "Come out of there.")

By the time I recovered sufficient sanity to be once more aware my surroundings, the third voice was still speaking.)

...as in Japanese chess, a captured piece changes sides, we may hope for an enlargement that may serve to increase the One. The "alien energies" are simple games using the forces of nature in specific ways; we use the same forces, we may even employ the same instruments for an increased harmony of all life. The deleterious effects of certain radio frequencies, for instance, can change to marvellous well-being if tuned to less dissonant wave-lengths.

In short, we have much to gain from the very source that some would have us destroy, others would have us ignore...

(The rest of the meeting, I shall only summarize, for these three positions split the resolve of the group into fragmentary impulses, and re-iteration of similar arguments did nothing but add confusion to dissension. I sensed that the first statement, while respected, lacked the dramatic appeal of a call to action; the second seemed baldly oversimplified and emotional; the third, while reasoned, was less than satisfying to the major-ity. At length, the meeting fell apart without a conclusion being reached. The second speaker declared that he and others would take direct action anyway, and prayed the rest to follow not too far behind... though it sounded more like a threat than a prayer. Then, it was over.

When I opened my eyes, many had already left. Children were chasing each other and some pet monkeys, around the flat open area in the center. Pyotr and Marta were holding each other very tightly.)

>>>38. SCROUNGING>>>

About this time, it hit me. There was everything I wanted out of life here, friends, excitement, a whole new life. And this time it wasn't boredom. Restlessness, maybe that's the word for it.

Anyway, it came to a head at Initiation time. If I went through with this, then it would be pretty hard on everybody if I turned them down. Any way I did it, it was going to be painful.

Pyotr and I had gone out scrounging. That's one English word he used for every description of hunting, harvesting, surveying, ambushing—if it was out in the wilderness, it was scrounging.

So we were scrounging over by the cluster of round rocks, or rockers, loosened from the floor of the desert by temperature changes, and independently mobile in the high winds of summer. Today was calm, though. The dust clouds had settled out in the past few hours, and visibility, well, you could see for miles. You could even see the moons in daylight, and more than just the brightest stars.

Pyotr sniffed, though. "To see, you know, is not with eyes," he'd said to me. "Eyes good for quick look, da, but scrounging, is with whole... whole..."

"Person?" I offered.

"Pirsoon. You glom on the barbel when you don' see him, by nose..."

"Glom?"

"Glom. Is Inglitch word. Homer teach me. See, I learn. Speak good." He grinned.

But now we were entering the danger zone. The smooth boulders, any one of which could have crushed a man, were still, set in the sand like a Japanese rock garden, giant-size. If the weather started up again while we were inside, it might be tricky business to get out alive. Still, that's were the best scrounging was. The barbels, snoots, drinkas, rasties, they all hid here at times. No telling what we'd find. Or, for that matter, what might find us.

We were advancing on the rockers when Pyotr suddenly crouched down and nodded to me to do the same. The hunt had begun.

When I looked around, Pyotr was gone. "Wait," he'd said. "I go for the other side, come through. You make silent. Be still like a stone." He patted one of the rockers, and with that light pressure, it moved. I saw it move.

Then I was alone. An hour passed. I sweated in the cold of late afternoon. The tenseness of keeping still, alive to every tiny noise, keyed me up to a point where any moment, I expected Pyotr to come charging out pursuing a small mobile creature. Any moment, any moment.

But the moment never came. When the sun touched the edge of the desert, I started calling out with all my might. "Pyotr! Pete!" The peculiar acoustics of the rounded surfaces mocked back at me. No reply from Pyotr. He must be lost. Or dead. No, nothing could kill that big lug of a man. He probably fell and bumped his head, or was taking a quick nap. Boy, would Marta have a laugh over that one!

It didn't take more than fifteen minutes to circle the little colony of boulders, though a few of them were scattered apart from the rest, shifting in the wind. I glanced up to catch a last long look at the clouds; from Pyotr's tutelage,

I should be able to tell if a storm were coming. The fleecy high clouds were the ones to watch. Enough of those going fast, and anything could happen. At nightfall, especially, when the temperature dropped over a hundred degrees in little more than an hour, the whole character of the plain would change. And it was coming. Pyotr was nowhere in sight.

I ran back around the rockers to check for footprints. Time and again, my eyes deceived me in the dusky orange light. Could it be that that little depression is a footprint? But the sand was already lightly drifting over it, fine particles falling in and scooping out.

I didn't dare go home alone. Marta would go crazy with grief. The only time you stayed on the desert was when there was no choice, or you had to prove something. In some ways, this group I was living with still had a rather primitive mentality. But no one would tell me the details of the upcoming initiation rituals for the youth. Youth! I had promised to take part this year, but only because of Marta's insistent pleading.

But I had to find Pyotr, and quickly, or face an endless task of dodging boulders all night. As long as the light held, it was easy. They moved like giant billiard balls, knocking against each other, or rolling to a stop. And if Pyotr were lying on the ground, unconscious, one of them would surely crush him. There was only one way to make sure.

I dashed into the thick of it, just as the winds started battling each other in earnest for temporary control of the rolling field. First one way, then another, and it was fine as long as they moved together. But some, more sluggish than others by reason of more weight, would get in the way, and the caroms and ricochets would be entirely unpredictable. At one point, I was knocked unexpectedly from behind, into a second moving stone that spun me around and dropped me to the ground. For a moment, I thought I'd had it. My leg was caught, and it would have been crushed, except that the fickle winds changed again, for once in my favor.

And then I heard him. A moan over to the right, not far away. I raced in that direction, between the boulders, shouting "Pete! Pete! It's me! But when I had gone at least far enough, I found no one. "Where are you, Pyotr? Hallo!"

It seemed that I had heard it, a distinct human cry. Yet what was that? The by now strong winds whistling at me, tricking my imagination to hear what I wanted to hear. The movements of the stones made it impossible to stand still, and my own plodding feet fooled me more than once with echoes combining forces with the muffled quality of aural perception forced on me by my headband, now absolutely necessary against the creeping cold. Tears kept coming from the cold, too, and I'd blink them away, but not fast enough. Not only that, but the pace of the enormous moving rocks was faster than my own darting and dodging. It was hopeless. I'd have to get out.

But almost as soon as I'd decided it was too dangerous, the moan came again, this time a word, or almost a word, from the very center of the "Brownian movement" of the giant boulders. I plunged in after Pyotr again. At least with this strong a wind, every stone would be going in roughly the same direction. All I had to do was watch behind me, work my way sideways to their motion. The violent movement also seemed to separate them; the gaps between allowed me enough room to maneuver.

But still no Pyotr. For fully half an hour more, it seemed, I was in there, getting tireder by the minute, but determined to find my friend before he was done for.

Then, straight through the high whine of air, came laughter, men's voices, a party. Whoever they were, they might be able to help. I ducked toward the sounds, against the current of rolling balls. When I emerged, I could barely make out faces. But they were definitely men from the camp. "Quickly!" I yelled. "Come here! Pyotr's lost!"

A fresh burst of laughter. I was angry now. "He'll die in there! What's the matter with you? Come on!"

"Heard who?" one of them said.

"Pyotr. He's worth more than any of you! Hurry, he's in the middle of the rounders."

"Wait, my friend. How can he be there when he is here? Right, Pyotr?"

"Da. Sasha, do not go any more into the balls for me." There was no mistaking his deep-throated voice. I could have been blown over by a sneeze; all blood seemed to drain out of my brain.

"Pyotr! But you... I thought..."

"OK, tovarishch. We play a little game with you."

"What! Why, I could have been killed in there. But wait, there was someone in there. I heard them moaning!"

"Like this?" said one of them. And he cupped his hands to throw his voice down toward the rocks. It was the exact same moan I'd heard before.

"But why?"

"Sasha!" exclaimed Pyotr in surprise. "Why you angry? Do you not tell Marta and me many times you wish you see initiation?"

"Yes, but that's for youths. I'm 46. I wanted to watch, just to watch."

"But you want to be family, yes? You say so before. And no watch initiation, no, no, must do, then you see."

"Yes, but why the tricks?"

"You eat at our table, you play by our rules," a second man said. By the gravel in the voice, that would be Homer. "It's the way."

"Yass," said a third. "We not afford strangers. To be initiated is not your choice, kamarade. You go, or you stay. But to stay, you be initiate-mensch."

"Now wait!"

Pyotr came up to me, his voice lower than the others. "Oh, Sasha, Sasha, I sorry to see you mad. Don't do like mad person. I think best for you is this. Not even the whole initiation. Not even the flying, you not born for big air," he gestured at his chest. "Need big... lungs. Here now, take this hand of friendness. You pass first day." He visibly winked. "Is also scrounging. See? Find what you not look for."

"Or," boomed Homer Tent, "you might call it snipe hunting. Well? Are you in or not? Don't matter to us either way."

Pyotr's hand in mine ultimately decided me on that question. "Yes, I'm in. Do your worst."

Pyotr laughed. "Worst is over for you, Sasha. Tomorrow is with boys. Children's play. De good. Now come. We go home."

>>>39. THE YOUTHS>>>

They Put me with the oldest of the prospective initiates, a fellow named Wolfgang Kroeder. In the contests, I easily beat him with my weight, experience, and dexterity. But he was a good competitor, and when we were paired up for the final event, a scavenger hunt for the name animals (the bigger the animal you bagged on this day, the grander your tribal name), I was happy to be with him. He was by far the most intelligent of any young person at camp, though I would never have picked him for a leader.

Moncho and Leon took off first. The rest of us spread out in all directions, Wolfgang and I toward the steep-sided wall of the Zipper. Climbing along the stones was time-consuming, and it would be difficult to catch anything...only bare hands were allowed today. But we shared the fond illusion that we'd be able to nab a small crevice animal and quit.

We'd underestimated the little martians. First a dorshter, then a winkle, slipped through our fingers into the cracks. There was no coaxing them out, once they knew what we were after.

What we hadn't counted on was our own clumsiness. Wolfgang slid down to a ledge below, safe enough maneuver on normal days, something he'd done many times before. This time, though, the ledge he chose had a flaw that the erosion of the winds had weakened but not defeated.

The additional weight of such a large animal as a human threw the balance over onto the side of collapse. I could barely make him out in the clatter of rocks tumbling straight down into the valley.

How he kept his head in those circumstances I attribute to destiny, his destiny. When I arrived at his side, much later, he was resting, not in pain, no bones broken, but encased up to his chest in rubble caught in a protruding shelf. I gingerly stepped down on each stone, so as not to repeat the performance, then began digging him out. As we talked, he told me of his plans. Only his self-confidence kept me from laughing. At first.

>>>40. PAMPHLET>>>

From here on it was confusion. The Council was over, but nothing had been decided. The Mars-born, led by Moncho, were determined to seek revenge; about twenty of them, the best of the young warriors, fully armed, went off by themselves to plan their battle strategies, though from the looks of it, it was going to be an extemporaneous affair, guided by the judgment, sometimes rash, of the unpredictable Moncho—Moncho, who had taken over the speaker's rock, and thundered his warning to the assembly, Moncho, the rude symbol of the new Mars... and to my mind, one of the most dangerous people then on the planet.

I was musing in my tent, when Wolfgang came in again with a proposition that startled me for its boldness. Here was a youth who had failed in battle and had been disgraced, yet I knew him to be highly intelligent. What I hadn't reckoned on was his bullheadedness.

And despite the absurd nature of the act that Wolfgang proposed, I was much more attracted to it for political reasons that appealed to my own background in radical politics. First of all, it was nonviolent. Second, it had to be democratic—naïvely so. Third, it just might work.

We were to make up pamphlets for the town, attached to each of which was a ballot. On the ballot was this statement:

> People of Mars, of whatever jurisdiction,
> whether in town or out in the desert, whether
> outlaw or police, whether Marsborn or
> Earthborn, it is now time to be one people of

one planet, and to establish our sovereignty,
our Martian independence, from all control
that does not originate here on Mars. To this
end, I, Wolfgang Kroeder, propose a ballot and
a constitutional assembly, which shall super-
sede all previous authority of whatever sort,
whether Earth-legal, anarchic force, or politick-
ing connivery. The ballot attached herein is
for you to put down the names of three men
whom you select to speak for you. These men
or women will then gather for a constitutional
assembly on the first day of the new year, dat-
ing from Weston's calendar, Year 16. As of this
moment of writing, the Governor is believed
dead, the Vice Governor missing or fled, and
no civil authority exists. The time is now. Cast
your ballot, friend. Vote for the Mars you would
like to see. The Mars of the future. There is only
one way to build a world, and that's to dig in.

Wolfgang Kroeder.

I found the text sophomoric, and yet to the point, understandable to all parties, in one form or another, in fact,
somewhat craftily designed, this whole idea of calling an
assembly, for no group, not even the Adventurers, could
afford to ignore this document completely. And there was
really no way, given the device for casting ballots, that it
could be stopped.

I foresaw that there may be in the proposed assembly the
same tensions that now existed between the groups that
I had seen. Particularly the Adventurers—and I wasn't
too sure of the groups within the town, as to who was on
whose side, and where the power really lay. Perhaps it was
composed of fronts that held only for the moment, for
instance, the radio-cum-police-cum-warehouse group...

what was it that really held them together?

One thing the pamphlet would do, though, was to clarify the issues. And that seemed to me at the time to be more important than the highflown idealism of the document. Wolfgang, of course, was enthusiastic about it, and I could see his dream of the people at the camp, and the people in the town, of all stripes, sitting down to talk.

It was the liberal dream, and it wouldn't have taken too much to overthrow the authorities, unlike America when that independence was gained. Earth would have great trouble to bring any form of coercion upon the red planet, within the time that it would take for a whole civil war to be fought. Wentworth's crew was too small in number to be effective except for protecting their precious ship, and the Captain was bound by his own law not to interfere. After all, there were less people here than there were in Oklahoma or Alaska, when they became states.

By the next morning, Moncho and his group were already gone. Wolfgang gathered a number of youths and myself to distribute the documents. We were to go under cover of darkness, to each and every house or compound in the town, and that was only the first step.

Each individual was to receive one copy and one copy only of this non-reproducible paper ballot, and then we had to encounter the Adventurers on a peaceful basis, which may have be a contradiction in terms—and do the same for them. Another group would go to the mining camp, and others to all the scattered remnants and tribes, and towns that failed; one group to the Soviet settlement, with a large bundle of ballots, some extras for the babies that may have been born in the past year. Those, translated. Pyotr had unwillingly set forth the words. I could recognize his bold handwriting, even in the Cyrillic alphabet, and he signed his name at the bottom underneath Wolfgang's.

The first problem of the assembly would be, in which language to speak, though from what I gathered in my experience at the camp, the languages would be changing, because of the constant need for exchanging and communicating with people on a day-to-day basis. Words would creep in, and already there was a polyglot tongue that I had some difficulty with at first. And yet in the long run, it made much more sense, for it reflected better the people who spoke it. None of them claimed allegiance... nostalgia maybe, but not allegiance... to their native lands on Earth.

In any case, the task must be performed within the next two days, for the assembly was to be called within the week. Rather than have ballot boxes for this procedure, Wolfgang had settled on the ingenious scheme, borrowed from his Earth childhood, no doubt, of boxtop coupons. At the bottom, each ballot had three seals, and the person was to convey each of these seals to the person he had selected. These would then be counted at the convention for entry. At least this would solve the problem of constituting an authoritative body without previous authority. So it went.

Over Pyotr's protest, I talked Marta into joining Wolfgang's team commandos, and we fell in with the group going to the town. I knew the streets almost as well as anyone. Most of them had left before the reconstruction, and had never returned. It was only later that I realized that to some people in the town, I was persona non grata and even shoot-on-sight material. In any case, when the pseudo-police discovered what we were up to, any of the people caught distributing the pamphlets might be shot.

We settled on the plan of entering about dusk. Two or three crept through the gate; the rest of us remained outside until after dark. By the time we'd left camp, most other groups had already gone, except the few brave souls who were bound for the Adventurers. Those volunteers I pitied, for I loved them all, and if their contact with the outrageous hoodlums was anything like mine, they'd be lucky ever to come back.

And so we started off. I got my first taste of the flying machines; with some prompting, I was able to keep up with them much of the way. Marta stayed by me at the tail, to make sure that I didn't falter on the way, in the fitful winds. And once I did ground myself, when there was so much dust that I couldn't see. She brought me up again, against my will, into the winds, and I discovered that above a certain altitude, the dust lessened, and it was possible to go on.

Night had already fallen by the time we swept down toward the walled city. The sight of electric lights there in the desert made me gasp; by their light, I could still distinguish the darker areas a short distance from the wall, where the prebiologic materials could still survive, despite their proximity to the toxic byproducts of human existence. But the lights, the sparkling lights, yes, that was human, and it seemed a friendly haven. Yet we would wait outside in the cold Martian night for one hour, two hours before the signal came from inside, and we went in. One fellow was left to defend the kites, and the rest of us, in pairs, slid the ballots under doors, according to Wolfgang's census count. We prayed that no one had died, no one had been born, no one had moved in the time since that count had been made. In any case, the election was bound to be full of irregularities. Let the representatives establish their own procedures; they'd have a vested interest by the time they sat.

Marta and I were walking on one of the back streets when we ran into a policeman, big fellow, jovial, who could have knocked us both to the ground with one blow, it seemed. He was suspicious at first, but his first word spotted him as an Irishman, and I knew Irish accents well enough to fake a bit of a brogue. I showed him the document, being as forward as I could, without the least hint that he should be upset about it. We stood before him, while he scanned the document with his flashlight. At the last, he looked down at his badge, up to us with a lowering of the eyelids, said "Are you Shuuure?"

Marta nodded, I nodded, as if the whole of righteousness and humanity were behind us. Indeed, Wolfgang had been able to impart that feeling to all of us.

He let us pass, though we had to promise to leave an extra ballot with him, so that he could double his personal vote. Before I handed it over, I asked him who he would vote for.

He winked. "Oh, ho, ho, now. That'd be tellin'. We shall see, at the assembly, shall we not, now?"

I nodded. Yes, he betrayed little awareness of how many voters might cast ballots outside the town. In fact, the town was outnumbered, though not by any one group. And that was part of the problem. No one group dominated, and no one group was that unified. Even among the Outsiders I had lived with, the small semblance of democracy was really an agreement to be anarchic peacefully together. There was no telling to whom the little seals would fall.

The rest of the distribution was more or less uneventful, but once we were outside the wall, I realized that the others didn't seem to be aware of the Cottagers, including the Lawrences, to whom I owed so much. So I insisted that we round the town on all sides to locate each of the huts, and leave the ballots in plain sight. I made my way straight to the Lawrences' to attend to them personally. Peeking in just a bit, I found them asleep, so I left the papers and returned to the rendezvous point.

And then we were back in the air, wafting this way and that, following in formation the youth who was leading us, who could sense even in the night the landmarks by which we would return to our tents.

It was very cold in the air, this time. Yet it was still the time of maximum radiation from the planet's surface into outer space, and the thin atmosphere aided this process. Dead cold would be later, when even these feeble rays were dwindling.

Back at camp, we all snuggled in, and by morning, I'd had a good night's rest. I sought out Wolfgang to ascertain how the other groups had fared. He wasn't around; all groups had returned except his, the one to the Adventurers.

And then, in the first hour of sunlight, we spotted a lone kite flying toward us, from the valley of the outlaws. We feared for him, and rushed out for the news. He landed and amid a rush of words related what had happened:

They had come upon a lookout, who'd sounded the alarm. Wolfgang, who had volunteered for this most difficult task, without which, he thought, the whole democratic equality thing would have been a fraud, had decided upon a daring stratagem, to land directly in the middle of the group, amid the flying pellets and projectiles coming up at him. And it worked. He was, though, shot in the leg, but managed to survive and to talk, incessantly talk, before falling unconscious. Bravely, he held out one hand with the sheaf of ballots, which were obviously not a weapon (but what power it had!). The leader of this band grabbed one up and, before tearing it to shreds—his natural impulse—he read it. He read the first line, laughed; read the second line, snickered; but then he read the rest, while Wolfgang was lying on the ground, clutching at his leg, and his kite was tumbling over and over in the wind.

The look on the leader's face must have been so thoughtful that the others gathered courage. And one by one they walked up to the wounded Wolfgang, each snatching up his own piece of paper to read. A little bit of civilization still clung to them. Anyway, they were talking and arguing and cursing and laughing, but not fighting. The rest of the troop, four others, landed by the edge, folded their kites, walked over to help the wounded lad.

The leader, it appeared, was among the first critics, and then among the first proponents of the plan. He harangued the group with a strong voice, shouting, "I lead you by force, I knock your heads together to make you do. And this boy asks each man to choose who should lead. You lunkheads, I knock your heads because you are stupid, but I know also you are men. Now, this paper says each seal to the man you choose. I knock your heads once more. Each give me one seal from your paper. You keep two seals, and you have a ballot, you have a vote."

The others muttered and argued, but it seemed, for the moment, a reasonable compromise. If these men too were to vote, then they too would bring their ways into the assembly. Wolfgang must have known that, and the offer apparently pleased them that anyone would ever consider them legitimate in any way. For though they had the free life, they didn't have the freedom to walk into town, to trade. They took because they had to, and because they wanted to, and it looked like a glimmer of hope was being held out to them, without giving in to anyone.

Their work accomplished, the pamphleteers made ready to depart again. Two runners were holding Wolfgang steady while another prepared to loft the kite on a cord, the idea being that, once aloft, his useless leg would simply hang idle and the wind would do the work of bringing him back. But they were interrupted.

The leader, now effusive in his gratefulness, prompted them to stay. They did, somewhat reluctantly; it was obvious that they had no choice in the matter. He led the group into a cave mouth where they saw a small emaciated man, dressed in dashing clothes with a scarf at his neck. It was the missing Lechay, the companion of Lemoine on that epic flight the Frenchmen had made years before. Lechay seemed peaceful and calm, not at all concerned about the hubbub around him. When he looked up at the newcomers, his face broke into a wrinkled smile; he nodded hello, his whole body rocking back and forth from the lotus posture.

The leader of the group broke into this silent conversation saying, "Would you like a friend? We have this sluggard here, he does no work, kills no men, and eats food. You have use for him? Take him. He is El Stupido. Knows nothing. You do for us, we do for you. OK?"

Wolfgang weakly nodded. But now there was a logistics problem. Five had come on five kites, and now there were six, one of those wounded, another possibly incompetent, and certainly very weak.

Two could not fly on one kite, but perhaps other arrangements could be made. The other arrangements, as it turned out, were a makeshift rope litter for Wolfgang, another for Lechay, which were lifted by the four kites in conjunction, two to a cargo, which worked to get the adventurous band of pamphleteers away from the Adventurers. But in midcourse, the plan collapsed. The ropes were too few, the arrangement too cumbersome, and the messenger, now, simply asked for men to fly with him with extra kites.

Then I spoke up and said that we had some captured Adventurer vehicles, why not use them?

"No," someone replied, "we don't know how to run them safely."

"The Junkman, the Junkman, he'll know how," someone said. And again the technological wonder emerged to examine the machines, explain its mechanics until several of us were able to operate the vehicles. We took off, brought back Lechay, brought back Wolfgang; and the deed had been done. The pamphlet had been broadcast to every known settlement, including the Soviet camp, and the Chinese reconstructed rocket site.

The next step was to wait. I hoped for the sake of us all, that it would go better than the meeting of the clans, and that we would be able to recall Moncho and his renegades before it was too late, before the ongoing political oppositions petrified into feuds that would never end.

Thinking back on it, I was amazed at how many people Wolfgang had been able to embroil in his project, and the amazing commitment and dedication of the people who had faced all manner of Martians with a piece of paper—nothing more than a promise that could not be kept, except by the Martians themselves. Surely no nation had been born in more chaotic circumstances, but I prayed that all would come off well, and I sensed that others felt the same.

>>>41. KILL>>>

Someone tried to kill me. There was no longer any doubt that it was me in particular that they wanted...yet I was among friends.

Who, then? And why?

I didn't burden Pyotr with my suspicions, and Marta, glorious, giving Marta, no, I had no wish to embroil either of them just yet. I had no proof, no leads. And if it were me they were after, then P. and M. wouldn't be in any particular danger, I hoped.

But it made me angry, too angry to sleep. I had to take a walk, cold as the Martian night was, bitter dry cold that sucked at your bones, cold enough to crack rock to powder. I could have crushed rock myself, but it was all frustration. Until I knew. Perhaps the night would offer a clue.

I unzipped the sealed tent quietly but as quickly as possible. Marta was curled up against Pyotr already... and I didn't want to make them any more uncomfortable than necessary. I poked my head out...a sound, very faint, of running footsteps. The faint glow of the stars had been partially obscured by high-flying layer clouds, not the sort to cause ground weather. When I stood, no one was in sight...yet it had been from the other tents that the sound had come. The rustle of my own clothes against the tent opening? No. I couldn't believe that was all I had heard. It was too dark to see tracks, and they'd be erased by the dawn winds.

I checked my belt... the knife was ready for my right hand. Looking all around first, then cautiously advancing, I made my way toward the tents. Quiet, slow, so as to pick up any sound from any direction... right down to the borderline of imagination.

A shadow seemed to glide away on the other side of one of the tents. I ran toward it, ran through the middle of the camp, and stood on the other side, facing the plain. Nothing. No one.

I whirled at a noise, footsteps crunching heavily.

"Who's there!"

"Moncho. And you?" His tone was surly, grouchy.

"Alex. What are you doing up?"

"I could ask the same of you; you disturbed my rest."

"Did I? I was chasing someone."

"Who?"

"I don't know," I admitted.

"Ahahaha. My friend Alex, now you see ghosts. Was there someone?"

"I'm not sure. I heard a noise; I saw... I'm not sure."

"Well, look again in the morning, eh? Night is cold, to hibernate. To bed."

His youth hung lightly on him when he barked orders. Only a few days before, he had commanded his fellows, had killed men twice his age. And I respected his strength, though the mutations that marked him, I believed, had still not found their bottom. Something strange, though human, touched me deeply, in an unfamiliar spot. Precocious?

Perhaps, but also something else.

"Good night, then."

"Goodnight," he said definitively, and stood until I walked back to the tent.

Had it been he, using a battle trick on me to sneak around and behind? It could have been; he was quick and agile. For all his presence, I doubted it. Honest wasn't the word for him. but straightforward was. If he wanted to kill me, he could have done it then, couldn't he?

That would have been the end of the mystery... the end of me, too. I sought out the zipper to Pyotr's tent, slipped inside, and settled down to sleep.

>>>42. LECHAY >>>

From the way he talked, you could tell there'd been a change in Lechay, but whether it had been of nature or of human will... well, perhaps that isn't such a solid distinction. He had the air about him of a gallant warrior from a medieval romance, to whom nothing wrong could ever happen. And he'd been through the worst... captured by adventurers, but not killed.

He and Lechay had landed La Victoire, and survived. Their ship couldn't have been in worse shape... it had been iffy to start with... But the radio worked. And there was that crazy TV series about two renegade astronauts that Papa had sold to commercial interests in North Africa, Asia and South America. Lechay felt an obligation to keep up the story, real or manufactured, and Lemoine just went along with it, though he ended up being the dupe of most of it.

One episode, the brainchild of one of Lechay's bad nights, apparently involved Lemoine getting lost. Ever one for realism, he managed just that. He did the job so well that Lemoine was left in the desert—the sand of Mars like a sandbox, but with no toys, no people. The biggest sandbox ever.

That wasn't the start of the feud between the two French-men, and it wasn't the end.

§

Lechay came over to me one night, clutching a worn book in his hands. He glanced furtively left and right, thrust the book at me, and disappeared without a word. Marta and Pyotr were absent at the time, and I inferred that Lechay intended it for my eyes only. I went inside the tent to read.

The pages were well-weathered, ink smeared in places, but it didn't take me long to determine that this was the very document I had traveled a hundred million miles to find... Jim Weston's journal. Without pen and paper of my own, I read slowly, picking relevant passages and memorizing as I went along.

For I quickly realized that no other book was as important in the whole of Mars as this beat-up diary. I prized those brief moments spent alone with a man I never met, a man whom half a world fears, the other half reveres. And I know why.

>>>43. ABOUT WESTON<<<

James Prescott Weston, son of Midwest money, was perhaps the man most responsible for the renewed interest in a Mars expedition. His drive sparked the nearly defunct International Space Consortium into life again, and for a brief moment, long enough to sell the idea, partly by means of his own exploits on the Moon—the daring rescue of trapped Russian cosmonauts at the risk of the entire mission—this gave him the leverage needed to rouse world opinion to such a peak that it was done, this impossible task the politicians had been battling over for fifteen years.

Never had such a shining boy been seen since Armstrong. And the choice of Commander had to be Jim Weston, there were no two ways about it. He even handpicked the crew, so the story goes. Mars was in his pocket. It could have been the stepping stone to something really big on Earth. But that's not the way it happened.

When the Mars Expedition returned without him, politicians had a heyday, and the consortium fell apart again. The first interplanetary flight might have been the last. It was five more years before the Russian group, with cooperation from Japan, England, Italy, and the Eastern bloc, launched their ill-fated ship. Space became the playground of the powers—each one fighting for a piece of the action, spending duplicate billions to get there first. Weston's name disappeared almost as soon as the man did. The original team hired out, with little luck. A private corporation took them on as advisers, and only one of them saw space again.

The first ship to make the orbital jump again was the French jalopy, piloted by Lemoine, navigated by Lechay. These two daredevils held their vehicle together with chewing gum and piano wire, and they must have known it was a one-way trip from the beginning. In any event, they landed over a thousand miles from the first site, on the edge of Syrtis Major, a dominant and stable mare-configuration. They radioed back for months, the brief words carrying a soap opera tale of heartbreak and mechanical difficulties. Finally, the broadcasts ceased. The last message read:

Mars, c'est un enigme énorme.

The big riddle gobbled them up in silence.

The second of the national, or pact ships, built by the industrious Swedes, flown by a Common-Market-cum-Third-World team, followed the lead of the Frenchmen, and even located the lost ship. No crewmen were ever found. The relics of this crusade can be seen in the Smithsonian, bought piece by piece from individual crew members and from official sources. One or two spurious items still sit side by side with the true jetsam of space.

The years of loneliness had made Lechay a bit daft, but he talked, and I have no reason to doubt his story; too many details gibe with what is known.

The cross of the Sapphire, that beautiful piece of carving, he says, was not on board, to his knowledge. And his friend, Lemoine, would surely have taken it with him when Weston led them away.

Yes, Weston. He found their ship, God knows how, and brought them out of the tight little artificial Earth-style environment that would have been their tomb—taught them the secrets of the planet, and how to live with it. The mystique of Weston had begun.

>>>44. JOURNAL: AMBITION<<<

This passage from Jim Weston's diary, hereafter called the Journal, speaks for itself. It is from the first pages, in meticulous handwriting on faded paper that almost crumbles at a touch.

I have been called ambitious, in regard to my own efforts in maintaining the space program. This criticism hurts more than the more professional critiques of my work. It is true, but not in a personal sense. How shall I describe this?

When the last moon rocket fired, I was in the next generation of astronauts. If there had been more careful planning, or more money, I would almost certainly have gone then. I wrestled with jealousy all through that flight, but I won. I felt then that it was time to move on to other matters. But the moon project was no more. Apollo was dead, and the spirit of adventure died with it.

The next round of space shots were child's play, tiddlywinks as they were known around Space Central... the satellite-and-shuttle juggling set. Perhaps I expected too much too soon.

No one worked harder than I did, those days... I do not boast for my own glorification, but to make my reasons clear. The rest of the crew would put in a day's work and go home to their wives. I had no wife; I was known as a drudge. But in the process, I learned everything there was to know at that date about space and rockets...very simple gadgets, really, tied to a whole scheme of conservatism and safety engineering. You light the fuse, and then ride on top of an explosion; the rest was all timing.

But the clock-makers in Washington pulled out sprockets and springs and pinions, dollar by dollar. We did the best we could against the primitivism of the money mentality, but there was no way to undate minds programmed to get votes in Arkansas or West Virginia.

Eventually, the time came when I walked in space. By that time, nobody cared about space... it wasn't a headline game any more. I stepped out... I had forty-five minutes...and suddenly, without any transition, I was there, really there, among the stars. I lost all feeling for the task I was to perform...it was utterly unimportant in the face of eternity.

The ship glowed, but not from the sun: I saw another light there, an inner one. Chuck Bramway would be inside, bent over the console, watching needles bounce. Another kind of explorer. Mathematics was his reality.

I felt as if I were swimming in the ether, in contact with everything, space over thousands of miles, in the current of the solar wind, abreast of the magnetosphere, riding a cosmic wave. This sensation was something extraordinary, I knew, when I began to hallucinate.

The stars grew larger, like jewels set in a great music box, and a symphony played for me, just by wishing it. I saw a figure in front of me, where no one could be.

She spoke: "Come, Weston. Across the pool of emptiness, safe to the other side. I have many things to show you." I asked what she meant. "You will see when you return to Mars. You will find me there."

Her beauty, her sureness made me believe every word. I listened for fifteen minutes until my earphone cut in. "For Chrissakes, Jim. what's going on out there? You all right?" Good old hardheaded Chuck. The vision was gone, but not the warmth and joy I felt. I finished the task in three minutes, and floated free a little while longer. She did not come back.

Ever since then. I knew with an utter certainty that I would "return to Mars." The question was, how to get there amid Congressional cutbacks international space politics, and the inner squabbles of NASA itself? I had friends, but also plenty of enemies. And many of them were behind the cancellation of the U.S. Mars Flight in 1987.

I almost killed myself from despair at one point... but I looked up, that night, for one last look at Mars. The eyepiece of my telescope fogged up.. I was pretty close to crying... and when I wiped it off and looked through, it was as if the woman had returned. Something held me there, staring at that red disk, for more than an hour. Dew formed on my shoulders. I resolved that nothing should stop me, if I had to crawl, or stow away, or bribe. I would be on Mars. It was my destiny.

And so it has proved.

>>>45. JOURNAL: LANDING<<<

Speaking of one-way, here's another excerpt from Weston. What gall the man had! But what presence of mind.

We set down in the Martian afternoon in the Meridiani Sinus, very near the prime longitude. The area had been selected for its diverse surface geology, and also to investigate features that had no counterpart in other areas of Mars, in particular, the precisely mapped region called "Little Europe," which had retained its individual characteristics right in the middle of the crater belt.

The two crewmen had been through a lot with me... intensive space preparation schedule, classes, and the two-year trip itself. I would hate to see them go back without me, but I was still determined to do it, if only to prove that it could be done. No Earth-bound narrowmindedness could stand up to a fact like that. And, I had to prove it to myself... beneath all my altruistic superstructure ran a vein of selfish ambition that held it all together.

But when we first looked out on this planet. I was afraid. Alone. As my companions cheered wildly, I sat numb, my mind racing.

The plan was to sleep until the following morning, but they cajoled me into stepping down on the planet. Nothing could be wrong, Bill cried, and Ted was already adjusting his helmet. As captain, it was my right to be first down. It was what I had been planning for, wasn't it? Not quite. But if I didn't go, they wouldn't... that's how loyal they were.

At length, I gave in. For an hour we just romped around like kids... the experiments weren't scheduled until tomorrow. And it gave me a taste of a power I had never feared before, the power of being free from Earth control.

That night, I did some checking. The telemetered data on the reserve tanks I knew to be inaccurate...the trick was now to determine its true value. No, there wouldn't be quite enough... I had planned too well. The extra weight of my pack had taken up just enough so that two men could go back, at least within range of Earth station, or Skyhook... but no more than two could make it that far.

The other problem was psychological. Could Ted and Bill survive each other for two years?

I broached the subject indirectly with them that first night. "What if something happens to one of us?"

Ted: "You don't have to worry about me. Captain. I'm going home, no matter what."

Bill: "Me, too. And even if I busted a leg and you had to shoot me, Houston could drive you down blind. It's easy, just aim at an ocean and dive in."

Ted: "And you could fill in for me. You might have to move fast, but that's never been a problem for you, Jim."

Jim: "And what about me? Suppose you two have to make it back alone?" (My heart sank... neither of them spoke. They looked at each other instead)

Ted: "Jim, you can survive anything. Why, that last day at training..."

Jim: "Not anything. There just might be something I couldn't handle."

Bill: "Well. it's all written down somewhere, isn't it? And the launch window's pretty wide. Sure, I guess we could, don't you think so, Ted?"

Ted: "Sure " (grudgingly)

Jim: "All right, let's log some Z's. We've got some tall work ahead."

During the following month, I chose inconspicuous moments to drag out more gear and stash it away from the rocket. On the last day, I rounded the cache rocks, and almost ran into Ted. He was standing over the pile of equipment.

Ted: "Hello, Jim. I thought there were an awful lot of tracks out here. I hate to ask because I think I know, but...what's all this?"

Jim: "What do you think it is?"

Ted: (poking at the pile with his foot) "Sleeping bag. foam pad, solar cells, stash of food." (he bent over to pick up an object.) "Soap? No, you've got to be kidding, Jim. You can't, not out here. You'll die."

Jim: "Will I, Ted? I'm making a bet, you might say. You know why they delayed sending a manned flight to Mars; no one had been in space that long. Months, yes, but not years. That's bureaucracy, Ted. We've been here a month, and they'll check out every scratch, every sniffle, and it'll be another fifteen years before they send anyone here to stay. If then. You might say I'm impatient. I don't belong on Earth, Ted. You do, and Bill does. Go back, and God be with you."

Ted: "You're crazy, Jim. Look, we came at the best possible time... it's summer, and we're in the balmy days at 15°. But what happens when that sun gets smaller and smaller, and you want your Mama? You'll have to yell mighty loud, and the rescue truck ain't right around the corner, you know."

Jim: "Ted, I don't need hassles. I'll have enough of them

after you leave."

Ted: "No."(he stepped between me and the pile) "I won't let you do it. It's suicide."

Jim: "I admire your loyalty, Ted. But it's no use. I had to pay a price to bring this stuff. In fuel." (Ted started) "There isn't any choice now. If you force me to go back, we won't make it. There's enough for two... but not for three."

Ted: (looking down, tears in his eyes.) "Jim, I wish I could have said 'Don't do it' two years ago." (he brightened, almost choked on a laugh.) "Say, if one can do it, so can two. I'm staying with you. There's enough food on the ship. I'll go and get..."

Jim: "Hold it right there, Ted. Haven't you forgotten about someone? Bill can't run the ship alone...and you know that he couldn't last here, even if he wanted to, which he doesn't. No, there's only one way, Ted. And, I'll admit this, in two years I've had my own doubts, times when I thought I was crazy, too, if that makes you feel any better. Like right now. But there isn't any other way. Believe me."

Ted: "What if I stayed instead of you? That'd be another way. What then?"

Jim: "To what end, Ted? A useless sacrifice out of misplaced loyalty to whom? Yourself? Me? The Space Corps? Do you want to stay here? Look around."

Ted: "Damn it, Jim! Damn you!"

He pummeled my chest with fists, but ended up clenching me tightly, and I held him awkwardly, the emotion of clutching the last man I would see finally getting to me. Then he let go, and stood looking at me. He stuck out his hand stiffly.

Ted: "Well, Jim. Good luck."

Then he turned and walked away. At the edge of the rock, he called back.

Ted: "What, shall I tell Bill, Captain?"

Jim: "Tell him I'll be back later. Stall him for an hour."

Ted: "Is that an order...sir?"

Jim: "No, Ted. You're in charge now. A favor. We're still friends, aren't we?"

Ted: "Sure , Jim. Goodbye ."

Jim: "Goodbye."

In an hour, I was well up in the rocks, where no trail could be traced.

This would be my first night out, In the morning, I'd awake to the rocket blast, and then I'd be alone with Mars at last.

>>46. JOURNAL: INVENTORY<<

The rocket that carried me here lifted off an hour ago. The sky is beautifully clear and crisp. Moisture crept into my sleeping bag from underneath last night, straight out of the rocks. Except for making me numb with cold, it's a good sign. The permafrost reservoir of water, the solid equivalent of a water table, must be everywhere.

Inventory:

- 1 sleeping bag
- 2 blankets
- 1 sleeping pad
- 1 sewing kit, heavy duty
- 1 soft space suit
- 1 tent
- 2 sets thermal underwear
- 2 pair gloves
- 2 pair boots
- 3 pair socks
- 1 denim apron for patches
- 4 weeks' food
- 2 weeks' oxygen at 5 lb. partial pressure
- 10 liters water
- 1 Martian chronometer, waterproof
- 1 collapsible solar oven
- 2 solar cells
- 1 generating flashlight, 3 bulbs
- 1 mirror

50 meters nylon rope
2 knives
1 backpack with frame and extra strap
1 pair pants
1 sweater
1 padded coverall
1 volume Shakespeare
1 notebook, 500 pages
4 ball point pens
1 pencil
1 radiation counter
1 sun shooter
several packets seeds, mixed
1 pair sunglasses
1 floppy widebrimmed hat
1 toothbrush
1 recorder, soprano
1 first aid kit
2 Ace bandages
1 star chart
1 bandanna
1 roll duct tape
extra bolts for pack
assorted small bags
1 roll Saran wrap
1 block salt
pepper
1/2 k. sugar
And down on the plain:
1 dune buggy
assorted scientific experiments
1 memorial plaque

1 slightly charred rocket platform

>>>47. LECHAY 2>>>

The next time I saw Lechay, he ran from me like a guilty child, and it was days later before I cornered him alone.

"Where did you get the book?" I demanded.

He whimpered, but saw that I wasn't going to beat him, and his fear died down until he could talk tearfully. "From the vieille. He leave to me when il est meur' (*died*)."

"I don't believe you." But with the very words coming out of my mouth, I did believe him. Who, after all, was willing to spend time with a dying old man but Lechay? Who had the angelic simplicity not to know how to lie? "I'm sorry, old boy. Of course I believe you."

He softened up a bit, even smiled at me, from the side.

"But why me? Why did you give this to me?"

Then he made a gesture that I didn't understand until later, a shoulder shrug and a brave smile.

"At the time, he give to me. Now it is time. I give to you," and suddenly remembering—"The vieille, ol' man, he know. Il dit, 'the book need a Keeper. Always. Not let book die.'"

Lechay's large eyes looked into mine steadily now. I wanted to convince him that he was wrong, that I was unworthy, that as much as I had hungered for the book, I was in no position to keep it safe. His eyes told me that I might be as poor a choice for the job as himself, yet the choice had been made. And that was that.

"You make copy. See." He tore out a page and crumpled it

like October leaves before I could yank the book away. "Il a besoin (*need*) de... to copy."

The next day, Lechay disappeared from camp. He may have had something to do with the bombs in town... certain things Lawrence's neighbor Herman had said reminded me of Weston's lost cause. If Weston were alive, he might have done the same thing, with cool clear-eyed determination; I pictured poor Lechay, scared out of his wits, but holding onto a faith, being blown to bits for a belief in another man's ideas. Hadn't he survived the Adventurers on such faith? Poor Lechay. Only when he was free of the notebook could he act. And most probably, die. That was why he gave it to me.

Now I'm divulging the book. It's the best way I know of keeping it alive, and keeping active the hope that someday there might be a Mars like the biblical planet that Jim Weston tried to create singlehandedly. Yes, the possibility... strong enough to fight for. Die for it? I might not even have the choice any more. At least it would make sense, this way, spreading the gospel, if I did die.

And is it my turn to die now, after the book leaves my grasp? No matter. That's my business.

<<<48. SCOTCH<<<

Weston may or may not have seen the sights that he describes so meticulously. After all, he was alone for a long time, longer than most ascetics manage before weird things happen to their minds. The fact is, no one else could ever verify some passages.

I thought that once I had the book itself, the mysteries that grew up around the romantic volunteer maroonee would clear up. Instead, they multiply. Is it possible, after all, that the Eskimo tapestry of speculation about an early mystical connection to Mars has a solid root somewhere? Weston may have started it all, but others continued the stories. And there is Chidnaq. There's not a doubt in my mind that she is full-blooded Eskimo, and not at all a technician.

Billy tossed me an idea about it. "Look" he said, "What's all the fuss about? You worry about the wrong things. Point is, what happened to old Jim? Set your mind to that one. Who knows? You might even find the man."

"Not now, Billy. He's got to be dead. And even if he weren't, what good would it do us here?"

A twinkle in his eyes told me that Billy Brown wasn't saying everything. "OK, spill it, Billy."

"Oh, nothing. Just, well... it's not important probably. Besides, you heard enough of my tales."

"Billy!"

"Sure wish we had some of that Scotch right now. Then I could get in the mellowest mood you ever seen."

"Cut the shit, Billy. There isn't any Scotch closer than 50 million kilometers."

He rocked forward to his feet, stretched up behind one of the panels, tugged, and came out with a Johnny Walker. Two swallows sloshed around in the bottom. Billy licked his lips.

"Where on earth did you get that?"

"Borrowed it off a fellow… but it wasn't on Earth, it was on Mars."

"You what? But who would have a bottle of… say, it must be the Governor's. You grabbed it when you ran out."

"Well, not exactly. Of course, it might have been there awhile. I picked it up off a dude named Jim."

"Jim!… Jim Weston?"

"Here," he said, offering the bottle. "Take a swig of this. Then we'll talk."

I tilted up the glass, felt the hot flash of strong liquor hit my unconditioned throat. I barely had time to swallow before the alcohol oozed right through my tongue. Billy did the same, and we both stared straight ahead for a moment. A flood of memories I'd left behind came rushing over my consciousness like a spring storm. Trees whipping in the wind, Emily, school, the vacation coming…

"All right, talk."

Billy snapped out of it. "Yassuh, Massuh." He fondled the jug, took another pull, and sat back laughing. It was five minutes before I had him calm again. "Trouble is, oh, this'll get you, you bugger. It was after I cut my way out of the 'Venturers hideaway, really it was me and this other guy, but I went through the hole first, and he didn't follow, so I high-tailed it…"

"Wait. What's that got to do with Jim Weston?"

Laughs. "Well," he said between breaths, "Maybe something, and maybe nothing. Depends."

"All right," I said. "I'll listen."

"Like the Scotch?" he said.

"I'll listen if you stick to the subject. Yes, the Scotch is fine! It's... well, sort of dry..."

"That Scotch, that wasn't no Scotch. I seen that bottle empty." He raised it to the light. "Like now." He seemed to remember something, his face turned tight, and he started crying, not big sobs, but like a man, tears rolling down his cheek, into his mouth. A quiver played about his lips. " I saw it empty. Sandy, you religious?"

"No, why?"

"I didn't used to be. I saw him, though. He asked me what I wanted, and he gave it to me." His voice now squeaked out. A Johnny Red. I coulda kissed him." He lurched up, steadying himself by clutching my knee unnecessarily hard. "I don't know if it was Jim Weston or not. Honest, I don't know. But if it wasn't, by God, I'd believe anything." He finished in a rush, to get the words out.

Calm him down, get it straight, as straight as Billy told any of his stories, half embellishment, but underneath it all, grounded in some speck of truth. Now, though, it was his evident emotion that shook me.

For the next hour, I piece together the story. He'd been running from the Adventurers, whether they knew it or not was really irrelevant, and on a lonely rock prominence, he'd met a desert wanderer who might be named Jim. He was an old man, and he carried with him a huge pack. In the pack was an empty bottle... and since I had this evidence on the table in front of me, I was inclined to accept its existence. The liquor that we drank, Billy swears, is the best imitation Scotch he's had, even from his roaming days. I tend to agree.

But where it came from, Billy didn't know. First it was empty, sitting on a rock, and ten minutes later, it was full. Billy asked him suavely, "Hey, how'd you do that?" and the man shrugged and said something that Billy didn't understand. Like "wadrflaw." Perhaps a name for a place, or a plant. And that was all he knew.

In the morning, Billy woke to find the man gone, though a bottle still stood amid the rocks, full again after a hard afternoon's drinking. Billy then left, hurriedly, to adventures of his own.

Alcohol, that would be one of the byproducts of living matter, perhaps especially those prelife forms that are almost inorganic. So, this fellow, Weston or not, would have distilled the stuff. Now wait. Scotch, that's the booze that's smoked over peat. My tongue remembered distinctly that tingle, an out-of-doors kind of flavor. The guy must have had fire, too, not just a solar oven—too little oxygen for it. There were only two places to get fire. In the town— and then only under the strictest circumstances. Or right out of a volcano. Incredible. Maybe around the edge, where the mosses burned.

"Billy, draw me a picture of him." I'd seen enough publicity photos of Weston at various stages in his career, before he blew it all. Billy sat at a scratch pad, and this is what he drew:

"Hold it!" Before he'd finished the whiskers, I knew who it was! Not the Weston from old newspapers, it was the crazy old man who taught Chidnaq and I how to breathe! Son of a gun!

There he stood, right on the page, same curious look about the eyes, same open face, big nose, it was the same man! "It must be Weston...but how could it be? Weston'd be at the most a little over 50... Why, this geezer is at least 70. You don't think, no, it couldn't be—but maybe..."

I was confused. Just one more speck of proof, and I was ready to stake my life on it.

"When did you see him, Billy? How long ago?"

"How long? Oh, let's see, could be about... it was before the dragon, and the time I was in a tunnel, being chased by a..."

"Billy!"

"Mmm... maybe three months before we took off."

I did some quick thinking of my own. Three months. I'd have

been at the camp, and the old man had disappeared, or had he? Marta knew. Damn it! It was just after Initiation. That was it! The time I was out of it. It could have been him... I'd blocked those scenes of madness out of my memory as too absurd, too dreamlike. Was it real, then the terrifying moans and screams, hallucinations in color better than video?

"Did he have a tiny scar right here?" I pointed to the corner of my eye.

"You put your finger on it, Sandy," he said.

>>>49. WOLFGANG DIES>>>

One of the Junkman's toys sat in the corner making soft electronic sounds, repeating one phrase over and over in different keys intertwined choruses of "meditation music."

A groan broke the spell; outside, several people had gathered around the crumpled body of Wolfgang. His clothes, tattered and bloodsoaked, told of a terrific beating, and his lips quivered with the rest of the tale. I crowded my way in to kneel by him. Moncho stood, ears pricked, but unbending, over his former opponent. Marta ignored us all to salve his wounds with water and tenderness; a twinge of envy ran through me.

"The town is crazy, crazy," he sputtered. "People don't know what they're doing. The Police shoot at each other, nobody trusts them. The Governor is rumored dead, tied to a post in the center of town, his body... hacked. The young are hiding, couldn't find my contact. Maybe he thought I was too..." he swallowed, "...too old. But it might be the chaos. The Radiomen have taken over five buildings; the Warehousers joined them. The American who came..."

Carson! Suddenly everything was clear. He'd made his bid, perhaps a bit soon, from the sound of it. So he was actually doing it. I underestimated the man. Less than a year, and he had it in his pocket, the whole fucking planet, while I sat on my thumbs in a village, digging native life. And who had gotten into Mars better? Damn. I had forgotten how it went, all those rules of civilized life, from the Magna Carta to the latest UN pronouncement, and every bit of it building up a structure that made sense—on Earth. Carson was still "on Earth," riding white-hatted across the western plain, battling dragons, charging the enemy bunkers with a "Geronimo," the hero rides again, roughshod over the Martians.

And Wolfgang lay dying on the sand.

"I was brought before the American, told him of our dream, and he agreed! He agreed! One friend in that town; he is willing to help us."

Wolfgang, you're so wrong, but arguing might take your strength. There will be time enough for that. Later.

"He insisted on protecting me, but I escaped into the streets. Right into a mob fight. I was pummeled by both sides before they left me for dead. Ha ha. I crawled away, and made it back here. I made it. I..."

His head slumped to one side. A low hum, constantly rising, filling the air. Everyone stood erect, facing the body of Wolfgang, eyes closed, mouths open, uttering the ungodliest M-M-M-M-M I have ever heard. My brain tingled. I could not decipher their intentions; no telling how long it would last. I jerked out of the ring, back to the tent, to make my own journey to the city that had killed Wolfgang.

>>>50. WITH CARSON>>>

He visited my cell, or closet, briefly, before we had a formal interview. I graciously offered the bed, preferring to see him for once from a higher vantage point.

"I'm not supposed to be here, you know," he said.

"Neither am I."

"Did you know I've been elected Arbiter? Even the Governor approved. So now it's all set." He paused, took in my puzzled face, and continued. "The reorganization, I mean."

"Revolution."

"Oh, that too. Nothing will stop that. I don't like them much... too much blood and killing. I'm a man of the future, Castle. Got to keep in tune, in touch with the times. You'd be amazed at the tenacity of that silly idea about the social sciences not advancing. The rot they write in textbooks. I don't need books to tell me what's happening."

"I could use a window or two, as a start. Then I might know what's happening, too."

"Oh, no need of that. Sorry. For the time being, it's better that you don't have one. You understand, of course?"

"Look, I don't know what's going on out there, but I'm not just going to accept your word about two plus two equals four until I see for myself. This revolution business is all in your imagination, Carson; it hasn't happened and it won't. You're sick."

He smiled a secretive smile, the kind that I hate in normal

circumstances and now it drove me up the wall. He narrowly missed getting his teeth bashed in. The shadow of a gun across the threshold stopped me.

"But you're part of it, Castle. Without lifting a finger. Here, let me sing you our new national anthem." And in the most incredible theatrical manner, the Arbiter of Mars rose to bellow:

Mars! We have come from far
To-o build a better world
For all men
As stone by stone
We will join land and sky.
Mars! We are ready for...

"That's mine!" I shouted, cutting him short.

He grinned. "Yes, isn't it? And you'll get your name on it, too. You didn't copyright your wastebasket, did you?"

"Wastebasket, my foot, that's from my diary. Where did you get it?"

"You left a wide trail, Mr. Castle. Littered the landscape, you might say. It was hard to tell trash from gold... or grinch, wouldn't you agree?"

"Well, you picked a trashy one, all right. I'm ashamed of it. No, you wouldn't dare!"

"I've already declared it public property. It's worthy, Castle. I wish I could just sit down and whip out poetry. We men of action don't have time for words. That's the difference between you and me, you know. Words won't get you anywhere, not since politics. Who needs them?"

"Carson, I'll say this, because it's true, even though you might have trouble understanding. True words are written straight out of action. But there's no truth in that song. I wrote it before I had even touched down on the surface. It was a gag. It's a dream, Carson, a puff of smoke, just like your crazy ideas about Mars. You don't know what this place is like, you've spent your time in the town, indoors. You've never hunted the barbel, or slept in the open. You…"

"Who cares about that? I can assure you that my time was well-spent. Look where you are now, and look at me. Wake up, man. I'm not the man you knew; this isn't the planet you thought it was. Who's dreaming, hanh? You, you writers just sit by the sidelines, while we make things happen. All of us, everybody except the goddamned writers." His tone shifted abruptly from narrow prejudice to placating. "There's things to be done, Castle, if you're man enough. You're no idiot. Think of yourself for once. You'll come to see me tomorrow. Guard!"

Then the door swung shut, and I was alone, more alone at that moment than I had been in the desert.

>>51. JOURNAL: ADAPTING<<

Food was calculated for four weeks on this basis: if the means for sustenance were not found by then, that would be the conclusion of the experiment. By means of half-rations, quarter-rations, and fasting, this time period lengthened until I lost count of days.

The landing site, though of interest topologically, had been an unfortunate beginning for the search for food. Ultimately, simple chemical indicators demonstrated what would have been obvious to an alert observer. On rocks here and there, always on the sunward side, a light coat of bluish-gray material formed in the early morning, and at dusk. Tentatively, this scum proves the Oeltjen hypothesis: Mars, like the primitive Earth in that crucial 100-million-year interval between the original reducing atmosphere that had allowed organic molecules to form but not burn up ("The whole basic structure of cellular metabolism is anaerobic"—Wald), in which fermentation was the basic process of life... between that and the oxygen atmosphere created by the fourth and fifth stages of living processes, photosynthesis and respiration—in that delicate interim, Mars had an opportunity that might have been caught within perhaps half a million years. In other words, life-stuff abounded, but not the capacity for reproduction.

The last bit of Handimilk squeezed out of the tube at the very same time as I was struck by a new perspective. The body that stood on the plain was a form so advanced in terms of the bluish-gray matter, so huge in comparison as to be inconceivable. And yet, all life is one, and the cells of my body were composed of the same substances that had been flung around the sun in spiraling knots of matter, the same as were revived every morning and evening. The human pride that had brought me here was no longer a survival plus. I would be humble... like the whale, who spends all its time in the consumption of minute creatures, straining the soup of the ocean for nourishment.

At nightfall, the grayish material formed once again... its perseverance through centuries perhaps preceded the cooling of the Earth . Faint sparkles from the dying sun indicated the presence of water, or ice. On my hands and knees, I proceeded to scour the rock with my tongue. Progress was slow, and the low temperature of the surface forced me to be patient. Would my body accept these primitive organic molecules, and convert them into food? An hour past dusk, the faint taste had vanished completely. A good night's sleep was in order.

In the morning, the tongue was raw, but the stomach craved food. Slight indigestion, but no cramps and no vomiting. The air felt colder than ever before. There were glittering dots of ice, and breakfast, laid out on the same rock I had licked clean.

My tongue leaped to the task, but not my brain. Morning, of course, is not the same as evening... a full thirteen hours of night had sucked the heat out of everything. On one childhood winter's day on Earth, I had stuck the barrel of a toy pistol to my lips... tearing it away had take the skin off. Wishing to conserve the sensitive membranes of lips and tongue, Brer Rabbit (me) kissed Tarbaby (Mars rock) for twenty minutes, breathing as warmly as possible, using bare fingers. Finally, contact was broken, but not skin.

The coldness of the morning rocks brought up a second solution, a method which proved, finally, to be my main source of sustenance on Mars: sucking sand. The bluish matter appeared on the sand as well as on the rocks, in perhaps the same concentration, though invisible at first glance. By thrusting a handful of sand pebbles into the mouth, warming them until they released their nourishment, it is possible to consume a light lunch in about two hours. Half my time here might be spent in eating, but survival in terms of food was assured.

§

Something disturbed me about the life on Mars. There was little enough of it, and a number of similarities could be balanced off against a number of dissimilarities. What was the key?

The first clue came days after discovery of the deltons, predatory vertebrates with four unlikely longish limbs. They live in the hills, and are cunning hunters. The evidence is incontrovertible; I saw one of the deltons contrive a trap. The ingenious device seemed cruel at first: a wound spring made of barbed tough tendrils wrapped in a pulpy vegetable mass and then frozen. Déjà-vu: a scene in northern Canada among the Polar Eskimos, who used essentially the same technique for bear bait. This delton was duplicating an Eskimo trick. How was this possible?

At length, from examination of the exhausted body of a delton that refused to be ensnared... it preferred to run itself to death at the end of a rope... the original estimate had to be revised. Telltale signs—I couldn't be sure—yet the similarity was too close to be cast aside easily. The danger of anthropomorphic nostalgia had to be considered, but every checkpoint in exobiology that was possible to perform under field conditions gave the same answer. A hundred and fifty species had been spotted and classified by this time; no other Earth life-form appeared to have such a definite relationship to the native Martian flora or flora-fauna. The evidence seemed unmistakable. This delton, distorted into a spidery wraith, was possibly, impossibly, related to Earth humans. I placed my hand over the still paw... even the fingernails were there, even the flexible thumb.

§

The ease of my own adaptability to Mars, given the extreme conditions, led to more philosophical thoughts. I had to entertain the possibility that Man, or a type of man, had once lived here on Mars, probably prior to his existence on Earth.

Two possibilities: One, the life-form known as man is a universal phenomenon appearing wherever conditions for evolution are propitious... the anthropocentric view. Two, there existed at some time in the past a connection between Earth-men and Mars-men. Only the second theory offered a chance to be proved or disproven.

Several conclusions follow from this second theory, which I come to think of as the Riddle of Mars. First, it is unlikely that man made the trip alone... other forms of life not native to Earth should have appeared about the time man did. It was impossible to verify this corollary on the basis of memory, though, indeed, some animals shared a place in the Creationist pantheon by virtue of an appearance on Earth that would seem to contradict strict evolutionary lines.

But these were advanced forms; very few motile forms were in evidence here, though there were an abundance of the pre-life forms. If Mars had indeed been the cradle of man and other creatures, then it must have progressed through more stages faster; what could be seen was more likely to be the end, as it would be millions of years hence on the now-fertile Earth. Mars... very old, and very young. And Earth had returned, finally, to start again on this tired planet, re-enact the drama of life on these worn sands. Perhaps, in ten thousand years the means for penetrating and cooling the Venerian greenhouse would be more propitious. Would man end up on Mercury before the Sun snuffed us all out, like moths flitting around a candle? The teeter-totter balance of self-maintenance cost us more energy each eon... and would it be man that prevailed, or another version of the DNA?

Much later, I spotted another anthropocentrism in the argument. Suppose that man had indeed made the journey between planets millennia ago. What had happened then to make us forget the technology needed to make it happen? The extreme conditions of adapting? Perhaps. And perhaps it wasn't man who had the technology, but another creature, or several types of beings, who took us with them, along with other creatures... if that were the way it occurred. In this case, only man had the capability of understanding it.

At this point, I began to have dreams, which are worth reporting in general... dreams of fantastic ages ago, scenes that made me believe that I was delirious. Or that some substance in the gorsh... what I called my food... caused me to hallucinate. Otherwise, I was normal... a bit over-strained from bellows-breathing, that was all.

As the dreams took on a consistency, it appeared that, psychological or not, an unknown source was emptying into my subconscious. My body was slowly adapting to the new diet... perhaps these changes evoked a change in my psychic life. At night, in the middle of sleep, it seemed so clear, interior visions of a teeming planet, forms that registered emotions that I had never personally experienced, a youngness, leaping through fields of grass after small scuttling animals, rutting, shitting, being stroked.

The sensations were not objective; no chart or table could express them. Call it intuitive, I believe it not as a scientist, but as a man who wakes to see worn hills where mountains were in my dreams. I am a part of it here, sipping the sand, sitting under the sun, running naked across the land at midday.

My intention had been to prove that man could live on Mars. I now begin to believe that we descended from beings who did live here, and that the marvel is the first transition, from Mars to Earth, rather than vice versa.

>>>52. EMPEROR>>>

I was rudely shoved into Carson's office by two uniformed henchmen, one of them a former Radioman who, fortunately, didn't recognize me. The space was larger than anything I'd seen on the whole planet...the floor, the walls, the ceiling showed marks where more than a dozen partitions had been torn out to make room for the immense ego now seated behind a plain desk fifteen meters away. I made three first-downs and an end run before a snappy "Halt" slammed my ear. A sergeant-at-arms in attendance beside the desk, so rigid as to be part of the furniture, drew my attention. From his frozen military expression, his locked posture, I understood that we were alone, Carson and I. The bunkroom on the *Fledermaus* had been too small for the two of us... I was getting stuffy from the closeness already.

Carson had changed a bit. His honorary space cadet fourth class black and silver suit had acquired a few authoritarian embellishments. The caricature of authority stank in my radical nostrils. I had to give him credit, though...few men in history had risen so far so fast, and with so little help from right-minded citizens. So, the arguments we'd had before were no longer moot...he'd manufactured his own reality, and he was prepared to sell it to every man, woman and child on Mars. I, for one, wasn't buying.

"Long time, eh, Castle? Changed your mind?"

"About what? You? Not a bit."

His voice, always grating, had taken on an edge of cuteness. I gritted my teeth to keep from snarling.

"You know what I mean. I talked about it enough, even to get it through your thick head. The unification of Mars, man. We can go places, now. The stuff's on the ground out there, worth more than...hell, worth Italy and France put together. And we've got enough able bodies, we've got a ship, maybe more..."

"A ship?"

"Wentworth, good chap, he saw the light, after, ah, thinking it over. Valuable man."

"At the moment. For you. Don't count your schemes before they hatch."

"Yes, yes, at the moment. No telling what might happen. But we're prepared, you bet. Hardest thing at the moment is to recognize the enemy. That's what I wanted to see you about."

Uh-uh, here it comes. "Me?"

The eyes narrowed. A hand went beneath the desktop.

"Yes," he said. "You."

"Well?"

Several minutes elapsed while he riffled through a sheaf of papers, legal-sized. He withdrew one from the folder and offered it. The sergeant-at-arms sprinted over to snatch it, and marched around the desk to me. Yankee-doodle-dandy.

It began "People of Mars..."

Carson nodded amiably. "You had a hand in this, and more than that, if I know you."

" It's a fine document, but I didn't write it."

"You're joking. Oh, that's not your name at the bottom, and the sentences lack slickness. But I know better than to think this grew in the desert like grinch. Do you realize the impact this statement has had? You know, I wasn't quite ready when this came out...and yet, it didn't take long to fan the flames, did it? And now it's done. The pen is a two-edged sword, Castle... you might have learned that on Earth, but you ought to know by now. But that's several bridges by now. We've all had time to reconsider, I'm sure. The fact is, I could use a man of your abilities, to cool those flames, see, so we can get on with it. The real work lies ahead, and all we need to do is..."

"I know your plans. Carson. Trample over people's lives in order to rearrange the piles. You've got a pretty big one now, Carson. Why don't you stop?"

"Are you accusing me of personal ambition? No, man, you're wrong. That grinch...hate the name, we'll need to think up a better one when it reaches Earth markets...it's dynamite stuff. Have you seen what it can do?"

The Junkman would have been gratified to hear the effusive appreciation of his peculiar genius...but where was the Junkman now, in hiding? Shot in the back by Carson's personal army?

"I've seen."

"Well? think what it means, man. With that stuff, and just one ship to Earth, we can buy a fleet! That scrap of paper in your hand was just a foolish dream...until now. Let me tell you something, Mr. Big City. I grew up in tough conditions, and I can tell you one thing from experience: in the dead of winter, when there's no help coming and food is low, democracy is a fancy name for suicide. If we didn't have laws and enforce them, nobody would be happy, not the survivors, not the dead children..."

"Spare me the emotion, Carson. You said you had a deal."

"Deal? Well, you might call it that. I'm offering you a post in the new government. I'll pay you well, but you'll earn your keep. Everybody's got to pull their oar."

"In your boat? Where do you get this 'I offer' business, anyway? What happened to the Assembly of Electees?"

"What? Nothing happened to them. They're sitting on their asses somewhere. Maybe you didn't hear the news. As one of their first official acts, they honestly elected me Governor pro tem as well as Arbiter." He flicked an imaginary mote off his epauletted shoulder.

"Pro tem. Does that mean indefinitely, in your vocabulary?"

"For the duration, shall we say. Who knows how long it might take to restore order here? They never had it to begin with."

"In that case, I definitely refuse."

"Wait, Castle. You only heard one of the choices. There are worse things than working for me, you know."

"I can't think of any."

"Look, Castle, if you continue in this obstinate pre-revolutionary attitude, I'll think of something myself. Suitable for a traitor."

"Traitor! Now just a minute, King Carson, you may need some tall answers yourself. The usurpation of power..."

"...Is irrelevant. Listen, Castle, I write the laws around here, I am the Arbiter, the sole legal authority, derived from your precious Declaration of Martian Independence, If you want redress, you come to me, same as everybody. Me! Get that? Get it clear. If you walk out of here, you may not get very far."

"Now that's the kind of challenge I like. Forthright, on the square. I misjudged you, Carson."

"And I You. Oh, one last thing. The celebration this afternoon, I'll need you for that, regardless. Sergeant?"

"Yes, sir."

I was led away again, under double guard. I didn't know what to make of Carson's last remark. Perhaps I was to be the first of the purge, publicly shot for a demonstration. Crude, very crude. But given the chaos in town, it might work. For the forces of evil.

>>53. JOURNAL: CALENDAR<<

A rational calendar for Mars is of prime necessity, but while the sequencing is straightforward, the choosing of a starting date may be strictly arbitrary. I date this calendar therefore from an event both personal and purely Martian. While still an undergraduate, observing Earth's sky one crisp autumn night with telescope trained on the fourth Planet, almanac perched on my knee, I perceived that the published information relative to the position of Mars had all been collected and arranged just as I myself was doing...from the eyepiece end of the scope. After half an hour wrestling with figures from this particular point of view to interpolate the true situation of Mars itself, I uncovered a coincidence of sorts that has remained, for me, a symbolic linking of fates...mine and the red planet's. For that very night, April 24, 1999, a period of "opposition" or closest passage to the Earth, and the best viewing time, was, as closely as I could then determine, approaching the very beginning of the Martian New Year, its perihelion, the summer of summer...for unlike Earth's nearly circular orbit, Mars varied its distance to the sun by 42 million kilometers.

In my undergraduate way, then, I affected a shift in my point of view... henceforward I would be the first Martian, and all things that passed through my brain would be seen as by a Martian. I started work on a cosmology scrawled over poster paper that very night by candlelight, poring over the cosmic plan which included the Earth as the brightest star on a par with my other giant neighbor, Jupiter.

The notion that fired my youthful enthusiasm now comes

to the test. The Earth months I accept in the name of Mars, for they express seasons. A distinction should be made by inhabitants between North July and South July on the basis of usage...one hemisphere will not be as warm through the year as the other.

For lack of contradiction, then, this is the calendar I propose to follow: The Martian year consists of 668.6 days, which shall be counted in twelve months of 56 days each, with these exceptions:

March, June, September, and December, which shall have 55 days each.

At the end of each pentade, or 5-year interval, three days shall be added after December, these days to be known as Festival. January 1st shall be established as the perihelion, or closest approach to the sun, years shall be dated from zero on Earth-date January 29,1999. Weeks shall be marked off by seven days: Marsday, Tuesday, Wednesday, Thursday, Friday, Saturday, and Sunday: each month shall commence on Marsday. This calendar shall serve as a universal calendar for Mars until such time as discrepancies in the marking of the seasons shall require change. The Winter Solstice in the North is established as 1 February, likewise, Spring Equinox on April 47, Summer Solstice on August 17, and the Autumnal Equinox on November 57. These, it will be noted, mark seasons of varying length, since the passage near the sun goes swifter. These lengths are: Spring 193 days; Summer 177, Autumn 142, Winter (alas) 157.

Marsday	Tuesday	Wednesday	Thursday	Friday	Saturday	Sunday
1	2	3	4	5	6	7
8	9	10	11	12	13	14
15	16	17	18	19	20	21
22	23	24	25	26	27	28
29	30	31	32	33	34	35
36	37	38	39	40	41	42
43	44	45	46	47	48	49
50	51	52	53	54	55	(56)

and three Festival days on Pentade on the basis of the above scheme, constructed years ago, I date my own landing on Mars as January 13, 15, the first time men have landed on this planet and survived. May that continue to be the case.

I made two star charts: a complete Zodiac as seen along Mars' celestial equator, the second showing the constellations grouped around Deneb, the Martian Polar Star.

The seasons operate here in two cycles, each of which runs the period of a year. The first set I denote by terms relating our distance to the sun: Apocal for aphelion: Transal for the approach to the sun: Perical for perihelion; and Versal for the reverse motion away from the sun. The long Apocal period stretches over May, June, July and August: the Perical months are December and January.

The second set of seasonal variants run opposite in each hemisphere, and depends on latitude, for this set roughly measures the angle at which the sun hits ground. In the northern hemisphere, where the Polar Star is Deneb, alpha-Cygni, the height of comes on August 17. For convenience, the Summer months are July, August and September in the north; January, February and into March in the south.

The actual course of temperature range change combines these two concurrent cycles. In the more variable Southern hemisphere, the Perical months nearly coincide with the spring, and the warmth is enough to stand, but not to sit, naked during most of the daytime. The polar cap melts completely, and the growth of organic material from the Pole to the Equator covers nearly every available square meter of soil, at places up to 5 centimeters thick.

The season of Southern life quickens, and then dies as the cycle shifts again, away from the sun. Other growths, more truly reproducible, but also more patently parasitic, replace the early lush crops, but by late April everything is frozen again until October. And not just frozen, but caked with frozen air, for the Winter follows hard on the Apocal season, making the southern hemisphere inhospitable to liquid life of any sort. The most hardy plants form cysts, or shells, of their own, and from these will spring new life 300 days later.

To the north, the two seasonal cycles run opposed, and year-round growth can be found as far as 20° or 30° from the equator. The polar cap melts, but never completely, and this valuable resource forms the basis for some of the most interesting specimens of Martian life. Stems raise up little tufts of green and blue, the molecules forming them apparently pushing in this new direction with all their might, and succeeding.

I also found a few "flowers," which are really multi-hued plants with roughly-defined leaves that are utterly unlike the common sphagnum-type matting of much of the landscape. These queer plants, and others, apparently benefit from the constant water table provided by the ever-present cap.

Seeds. I brought a variety of seeds with me, in the hopes

that some Earth life might foster other growth on Mars. Contamination? Destruction? I believe that all life is one, and once I had unlocked a few of the secrets of this planet's biosphere, I had no hesitation to apply what I knew. After all, my own presence was a contaminant of far more consequence that pumpkins or apples might be. In any event, little progress is to be reported at this time.

>>54. JOURNAL: EVOLUTION<<

The sun so dominates the system of which it seems to be the parent that 99% of the angular momentum of all bodies lies within its circumference. The forming of the planets, therefore, while related to the Sun historically, may be more interestingly approached as peripheral phenomena. From the point of view of the center, a few flakes and mists that rose from the primal swirl refused to fall fast enough to enter the making of the solar body itself, and among those few insignificant particles, a tiny group also refused to fly away completely. That tenuous zone, then, between falling and flying, allowed those anomalies known variously as comets, meteors, planets, cosmic dust, what have you, to remain in existence as best they could.

What Keller said, both in class and in his roundly-but-wrongly-criticized book *Origins*, is that the makeshift solutions that matter a-making had found for temporary stasis (shorter-lived than stars, longer-lived than zero) might be thought of as a spectrum of responses to the stimuli of time and space. All of these possibilities were tried, and some are still workable. The dust, of course, did nothing, would never do anything in the way of coalescing... that would probably be the most durable answer, though, like most simple conclusions, it lacked finesse. "From dust to dust..." —so what? Keller went on to list the accommodations he believed the various light and/or luminous bodies had made... ranging from an etheric glue, a byproduct of the actual descent of mater-matter into individual elements, to the meteoric masses that were by then "classified" (which in his terse terminology meant "not understood"). The glue, he thought, allowed an alternate model to the standard Table of the Elements for a picture of the universe near us—that is, near us, for he disputed even the Pythagorean conception of a uni-verse, and as it turns out, with justification. Old Py had some queer notions; most of them derived from playing music too much. The idea of harmonies, though, had been so attractive to those who followed that they retained the method while rejecting the theological premises. Every framework of fictitious harmony that fitted most of the facts was clapped down like a cage over scientific thought whenever and wherever possible. Satisfying answers never satisfied Keller, though he ended up with a self-contained system of his own. His erratic career reflected his own preference for the interesting rather than the dull-but-solid.

Apart from the glue, though, and most pertinent to describing the strange mineral, "A"—which I have discovered—we should set forth Keller's planetary theory.

"Picture," says Keller, "a random assortment of particles... at this point it is bootless to consider universe origins, and random distribution will do as well as any other. Through dusty eons, particles collect in corners, as it were, while the housekeeper is away. Dust balls form increasingly larger masses after a certain originate mass has coagulated. Early in the career of a budding mass-node, energy from the impacting new arrivals are utilized directly in mater-matter transforms, of which a series can be deduced from the surviving elementals. Later, an ossification prevents further transforms, though the theoretical limit is physical infinity."

The Law of Matter-Energy Conservation gives few choices here for what to do with all the incoming energy. One is gravity, and its attendant mysteries. One is spin. Keller elaborates spin into a plausible way out of the mists.

"Assume," he says, "a still point in the center of a swirling mass. For the moment, this may be atom or sun or iron-nickel core; the point is that the still point is a mathematical abstraction, a way of making sense out of matter. Now, set the still point spinning, let's say at the speed of mass that would be contiguous. Standing on this still point, in imagination, we see energy flow in rather a different light. The direction of rotary motion now appears to go from zero, at the center, to higher and higher negative velocities... that is, in the opposite direction to what we had first observed. An unknown force, it appears, is whirling the outer layers around our still point with a definite progression.

"But we don't stop there. Imagine the still point expanded now into a hollow sphere somewhere in the middle of the swirl... it doesn't matter where... and its reference speed again matched to the actual motion of matter at that distance from the center. The observations now show both inward positive and outward negative velocities, each increasing with distance from the imagined shell. A true maelstrom, here. The contiguity is most important, the very fabric of space itself allowing only gradual changes, not discrete intervals, from one point to another.

"Now, flatten out this sphere mentally, along with the mass in which it is embedded, and a Euclidean model emerges in which velocities race one way on one side, the other way on the other side, in flat planes or fields."

Keller says that if you move the still plane back and forth... he gives a formula for it that incidentally allows the gravity constant on one side, but not on the other... the endpoints, too, must not be true endpoints, for in terms of the flat model, no distinction can be made of one from the other, and since one may be extended to infinity, so may the other.

Thus, not only does he provide a soluble expression for

gravity itself, but he reveals at one bold stroke the secret of energy-mass, which he labels the mater-matrix. Not only spin is involved, but a funneling through the center of any formed piece of matter... as if the sphere collapsed again to the still point, and kept on going into negative space. Energy and mass are not only two expressions of the same phenomenon, but are continually shading back and forth in the insubstantial statisticality of atoms. In larger bodies, this is evident in the very properties that men have struggled over since the Greeks got the intellectual itch.

Relative to the formation of planets, Keller concludes that the sun and the larger planets probably shared the same process I have just described, up to a point... their densities bespeak a softness, an incompletion which , in Sol, still rages, and in the majors may still be ongoing glows of lighter elements... failed stars, as it were, with pitifully small masses.

The minors apparently occupied a crucial zone of fire that burned hotter than the sun's exterior, hot enough to bake loose energies into denser and heavier elements. Earth, occupying the central ring of this band, is the densest of all; Venus next, then Mars, with Mercury close behind... Astra must have been just at the edge in those days when the gaseous giant sun encompassed the orbits of several planets, before it had fallen into its own funnel of negative space energy. Like a pot in an underfired kiln, Astra appeared as strong as the others for a time, but as the clay will crumble under stress, so did Astra. Thus, being neither close enough for true transformation into heavy stone-iron-nickel, nor far enough to remain unchanged light elements, Astra developed unique solutions through its double-history. Keller, one of those far-sighted men who stumble over everyday realities, may not receive the unjustly-deprived fame for his discoveries.

The proof of the pudding came yesterday. A substance,

which I have no more doubts is extra-arean, abounds here at this camp. The crater is so ancient I will not hazard a guess as to its age, yet Martian winds and weather have not disintegrated these "stones." I puzzled for days over its constituent elements. Though crystalline, it had a definite feel of fuzz. The structure of the lattice could only be represented as a double tetrahedron, six equilateral faces:

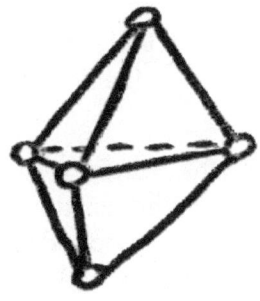

and each 4-bonded point is joined to three other atoms, so that each has a seven-fold bond with the others. Though this was clearly impossible, so were the properties of A. I pursued the logic of it. By extension, a cubit framework emerges. A few rough weight calculations showed that the atom in question was undoubtedly OXYGEN. Oxygen-five, or oxygen-x, with a valence of -2, shouldn't be observable.

But the diagram showed what had probably happened. Rather than -2, oxygen can also be +6, with its six electrons in an incomplete outer shell. Now, if each atom joined with seven others, that requires a total of 48 electrons to find places...musical chairs in the orbits. Each double pyramid held only five atoms, though, so that five complete shells of eight electrons yielded a total of 40 electrons present and accounted for (every other unit would have "none," though, since each atom was shared by two units, it hardly mattered where you started the count).

But what about the extra eight? "A" scintillated in my hand, an actual tingle through my palm told me that it had a more interesting possibility, imaginable only in Keller's terms.

The tight cages of these closely-packed oxygen atoms held electron-figura that were both there and not-there, neither matter nor energy, but a stable transition fluid-aura. Even my body temperature excited the "A"—I put it down on the cold dry ground.

So, in terms of theory, Bucky Fuller had been on the right track, after all, with his interminable constructions of the triangle.

Strongest form known. The fruitful search, however, had lacked a basis in Earth materials; the theory remained theory... until the key could be found on another world in the remains of still a third world. A freak of physics that might not have occurred in a hundred other systems had happened here. Magneto-hydrodynamics had barely reached the point of comprehensibility, but now you could hold it up and look at it. "A" had no counterpart in the whole system, except for the interior furnace of the Sun.

Such an incredible compound could only be explained as a result of Astra's own remarkable career. But it was one of the biggest ironies of Mars... oxygen-poor, the planet's surface must be peppered with "A," an oxygen molecule that could possibly supply not only the needed oxygen, but a source of energy unthinkable from common sources. The Keller funnel effect apparently creates and maintains stasis in a dynamic system.

Whew.

N.B. From this and other references that Weston made to "A," I'm convinced that it is identical with grinch. Carson knows only its worth for him, and either he is ignorant of, or disregards the real dangers. A marginal note alongside this passage, which I believe must have been inserted by the Junkman, affirms that grinch, like some fine wines doesn't travel well. I confronted the Junkman about that. He said, "Vat for travel? You go Erde maybe? (he winked) Hah! Grinch no go mit. No grinch, no you (a tearing gesture, hands clasping stomach, eyes rolling) Hah!"

>>>55. POWER>>>

So, it came down to this: Carson didn't just happen to come along on this trip...Mars wasn't his destination, I was. Or rather, the mission for which I was sent. He'd known all along... or had he?

The power monopolies were running out of monopoly. Earth had exhausted all but about 10% of the easily accessible and legal oil reserves. Geothermal plants had ruined the West Coast... increased earthquake activity had enlarged San Francisco Bay by drowning a few towns. The scandal had been brewing for years, and my book had begun an avalanche of criticism, Congressional inquiries, even sabotage.

Carson knew just enough of the inside story to know where to put his money; and the gamble was working. Mars had really very little to offer Earth in the way of minerals, considering the transportation costs. No one seriously considered Mars as a productive source...no one, except for Campbell. Old C had always stuck out an ear to every rumor of fuel sources. And he was wrong, of course, about fuel. Grinch wasn't a fuel.

Grinch had an entirely different meaning. Solid oxygen, not only solid but crystal-compacted electron-vibrant oxygen metal. You could burn anything with it, if burning was as creative as you could imagine for a totally new substance.

Carson had found another use for O_5. When eaten raw in tiny quantities, the grinch did what it always did so well; in the slow burning process of digestion, so a bit of the oxygen compound would eventually break down into molecular oxygen, a rare enough quantity on Mars. In the thin air, grinch could supply energy, build up reserves of oxygen in the muscles, and in general facilitate normal functioning. Apparently in an oxygen-rich warm atmosphere such as Earth, the grinch would facilitate to the point of rapid aging, deterioration of the body starting at the cell nuclei, boiling the blood with excess oxygen.

The nefarious Carson had been using the grinch on human subjects, like the zombie that had been Harry Lawrence. Had he forced it down his throat personally in the beginning, increasing the dosage until a physiological dependence set in, the ventilation inadequate to cope any longer without the added help of grinch? Had he pushed to the limit this man who once had rather die than submit? Sadie told me he was dead, seemed not to hear when I said I had seen him in the hall. She was probably right; in what sense could I claim he was still Harry?

Grinch had done it; though not an evil in itself, this powder was a new factor in power. Power for Carson, power for Earth.

Nothing at all for the Martians in that scheme, nothing but a bleak future dominated by the same old political swindle, the country bumpkins crossed by the city-livers. Not if I could help it!

The grinch... that tensive substance created by the Keller Jump, whatever that is; had apparently metamorphosed in a way unique in the solar system as we knew it. Carson could only imagine it as free energy, or a treasure to be squandered; a fortuitous blessing of Nature on his personal being for the greater purpose of political advancement.

Even before they hauled me out again, I could hear the crowd. Carson was doing it up big. And why not? Nothing but the best for the Emperor of Mars.

I was shoved into a corner, undressed, shaved, bathed by sponge, perfumed, and then dressed in a complex set of braces, covered by an outlandish costume, similar to the ones that Carson's men wore, but with additional epaulettes, braids, buttons and stripes. On my head was placed a square-billed cap in the French style. Fortunately, no mirror mocked back at the peacock in borrowed clothes.

Outside, a mob of people had gathered, some with the sunburned look of outlanders, even a small bloc of austerely dressed Chinese. From glimpses through the window, I could make out faces I'd seen before. Perhaps, but I couldn't be sure, some of the outlaws, now were milling innocently amid the townspeople.

Then it was time. Marched in a cordon of guards to an area behind the rostrum, I had a chance to see and be seen by most everybody. A few times I'd turn my head slightly, but the high collar hid a stainless steel ring that constricted me all around my neck. And the braces they'd put on my limbs seemed to drag me down. Still, I could hear my name called. I'd shout back, or nod, but my hands were in stiff lock under my coat, and I was too crowded in by soldiers to turn around. The two men in front of me were cunningly dressed in nondescript civilian clothes, so that my gaudy outfit stood out. Thus it was made to appear that I was leading the troop, instead of its prisoner. I accepted the role; it might have advantages.

The big moment came almost as soon as I reached the speaker's area. A stooge from a newly-created ministry was interrupted by Carson's dapper master of ceremonies for a special announcement. He introduced Carson himself, resplendent in a new idiosyncratic uniform on a scale with his own grandiose dreams. By appearance alone—and in that crowd of multilingual knots, it was by appearances that most of them would judge by—Carson looked like the king of the universe. In a science-fiction way, he epitomized the Lord Urglak of Zubenelgenubi. And I would be his second in command, by virtue of well-tailored costuming!

I looked summarily about, to see if I could spot a friendly group to run to for sanctuary. No, it was hopeless. There they were, huddled near the town wall, the whole lot of them. I cried out, but with every cry, someone switched the yoke tighter around my shoulders by remote control, and I went white with pain. These infernal robot handcuffs weren't cheapie models from Segal's. Old Rupert must have spent a good portion of his travel allowance on these babies. It was really very simple, though no one but Carson would ever think of using prosthetic devices... a complete set: arms, legs, neck, everything but the face... for such diabolical ends. Science could do no right, as far as I was concerned, at that moment. And with the heavy uniform, who was to know that some of the decorations were electrical?

And almost before I was aware of it, my body was clambering up the steps. I had to pay attention, use my mind to catch the right step at the right time, If I resisted now, I'd fall several feet without the possibility of moving my arms. No, that would be too easy a way to let him win.

But at the top of the platform, I stood next to Carson himself, apparently to be symbolic of the great cause stirring people into action, and he'd just say a little eulogy for the hero who had saved the town, written the constitution, the national anthem... in other words, me... of which the crowd was being prompted into singing... and a whole series of activities that made me sound like Napoleon cannonading the street mob in Paris. Law and order, that was his pitch, but there wasn't much cheering from my friends by the wall. I wasn't cheering either. What an atrocious bastard I was, from that introduction!

Then the microphone was thrust in front of me...really, it was my body being pressed up to it by automatic steps. But why? This was my chance.

I shouted out to those right below the speakers' platform! "It isn't true!" But at the same instant, I felt the high collar on my coat raise even higher. A hidden metal plate pressed on my jaw from below. I choked. Only my nose could breathe, and the best I could muster was a gurgle through clenched teeth. I had to find the man with those controls. He had to lie close by: the responses were quick, precise, practiced.

Meanwhile, I discovered that the mike was dead, but my voice was coming out of the P.A. system anyway, or a good approximation of it. "...declare the Assembly void. I am proclaiming myself dictator until further notice..." and my hand went up like a Hitler salute, only my fingers were free. But no amount of wiggling of fingers or obscene signs helped; past about thirty feet, no one could tell the difference. That really raised their hackles, and my cross-eyes and grimaces didn't seem to matter. They were boiling mad at me now, and I understood the point of it all. I was to be the classic mock-king, the pig that's killed instead of the king. Carson had done the same thing with poor Petten.

And he had done in Petten without any electronic tricks. Carson! It must be Carson himself doing the controls. I couldn't turn my head, but at least I could turn my eyes. Yes, amazing. He stood not two meters from me, he'd hooked up the controls so that his body movements controlled mine, though he was barely raising his arm while mine shot up above my head. I could have burst out laughing... these statements were his, these emotions. He really did want to be dictator, and proclaim it to everyone. Only he knew how to make it happen. Kill the old one. I was to have the briefest reign in Martian history, an inglorious footnote, an Aaron Burr.

So that meant he'd have to do the job himself. When? How?

The moment came sooner than I'd expected; The gun at my side was now pressing against my hand; Think quick, Sandy, Death is behind every door, but keep alive the hope that there's one door more. The gun might unlock that door.

Somewhere, Scheherazade tells the story in the *Arabian Nights* of two neighbors who had been enemies for years. One day, the first man found a magic ring, while stooping to petty thievery in the other's garden. Alas, he was caught. Caught by the collar, and the other man wouldn't let him go without "rental" on the ring, which he claimed to have lost. Unable to escape otherwise, the first man agreed. The "rent" would be, whatever the first man wished, the second man would get double.

As the days went by, the first man grew fat, had several wives, a big house and plenty of camels and servants. But he'd look over at his neighbor, who lived in a house twice as big, with twice as many servants and wives and camels. But what was worse, that neighbor gloated, bragged, and in general made a fool of the finder of the ring.

It was no use. He tried virtue, but his neighbor became twice as virtuous. He tried craftiness, but his neighbor had twice the guile.

Envy ate at his ambitions until he could stand it no longer. Finally, by accident, he wished for a well. His neighbor had two wells in that same instant. Thinking a minute, he wished half his yard to be covered with wells. His neighbor now had a yardful of wells. The neighbor came racing over. "Give me that ring!" he demanded. "You fool. Look what you've done!"

"And look what I'm doing," replied the frustrated man.

"Ring, take away one of my eyes." One eye was instantly gone, then two more.

"Hey!" screamed the rich man, groping around for support. The end was inevitable now. He fell straight into one of his own wells, broke his neck and died.

So, I figured, if Carson is hooked to me, maybe I'm hooked to him, just with the leverage rearranged. I tried it with a knee he wasn't applying any pressure on. Just a bit of movement. The gun waved in the air for rhetorical effect, now lowered to point at Carson, who faced me with a crouch straight out of the old Westerns. Sure, he was still strapped into me... But I had the power. My gun had to be filled with blanks... he wouldn't set up this scene otherwise. His pellets, of course, would rip right through me.

Quick, now, the magician's trick, the left hand knows not what the right is doing.... I inched up my left hand as far as I dared, and tossed the gun into it. For a split second, he'd be too surprised to think. And I snapped the gun up to the side of my head and fired.

Blanks?! An explosion tore at my scalp and I fell against the railing, knocking over the microphone stand on my way to the planks.

>>>56. AFTER PARADE>>>

When I awoke, Sadie was standing over me in the dimness. "Sash," she whispered. "Don't talk, you've got to rest."

"Where am I?"

"In the Arbiter's Building. It used to be Customs."

"What are you doing here?"

Her hair tumbled down to my face and a pained expression went through her eyes. "I left Harry. And then... Sandy, it's a long story. Anyway, I ended up here. But I'm not very happy about the way things are turning out."

"What'd you expect with that bastard Carson?"

"Sssh, not so loud. I know now. I saw what they did to you. I'm sorry, Sandy. Why does it have to be like this?"

"Hey, calm down. As long as I'm alive, I'm fighting. Sadie?"

"Yes?"

"I don't love you."

"But that doesn't matter..."

"It does. Now listen to me. You've got to get me out of here. I don't know what he's got planned now... maybe a public trial... or an execution... I'm having none of it. You hear?"

"Oh, Sandy, I love you."

"That's irrelevant. Just get me out. Where are the guards?"

With her help, my getting away was easy. They wouldn't

discover that I was missing for hours. Time enough, I thought, to clear out of town.

On the way, though, I spotted a familiar face. Pyotr was shuffling in the dust dejectedly, and he hardly paused when I dashed in front of him with a grin. No bear hug, no smile, no greeting at all.

"Pyotr, what's wrong? It's me! I'm free!"

He stopped to scrutinize my face. "You look like tchelovick I knew. Ptah!" he spat at my feet. "For you I give the seat of Assembly to Moncho. Now my debt is over. I have no more with you. No more."

"But wait! It was a setup. I didn't say those things. Didn't you see my mouth? I couldn't open it."

"I saw you, heard you."

"But it wasn't me doing that!"

"It wasn't you? Sasha, swear for truth," he grasped my hand so that our palms met, the old camp method of detecting lies... the slightest pressure could be felt by the whole arm, the slightest wavering. "...Was you on the platform?"

"Yes," I gulped.

"Was you to shoot gun?"

"Yes, but..."

He snatched his hand away. "Enough. Go before I kill you."

"But it was mechanical. I was a prisoner!"

"Mechanic, biology, electric, what difference?"

"I was in Carson's power, I tell you."

"He have strong spirit. You have weak one."

"Pyotr!"

But he had already clutched his head in his hands, shouldered me out of the way, and melted into the crowd. Stunned, I let him go. Now only Sadie was left. I'd arranged to meet her in half an hour.

With hardly anything on my mind except despair, I wandered along the streets, unmindful of my own safety. Somehow or other, I found myself in the midst of aimless knots of citizens and outlanders, some shouting, some fighting, all in confusion as deep as my own. And then, amid the mêlée, I spotted two militiamen and a ghost from the past...Governor Daniels! He must've kept alive by the expedient of ignoring everything and staying at home. But this was the wrong place at the wrong time for him. He'd dressed like a fool, his honorary military ribbons dripping off his chest, paunch held in by a tight girdle, a ceremonial military cap, and he was marching straight for the Administration Building!

I ran out to stop him, warn him that Carson already had had the building for days. Ten steps, eight, five, I almost reached him, he turned to me in surprise, and the explosion of a high-powered gun ripped into his chest.

I caught him in my arms, but his personal guards tore me away, drawing their guns. One fired, but he had been hit, his aim wild, and the other, realizing that I didn't have any weapons, looked smartly around to locate the sniper. Too late. He whirled and fell.

I was too numb to move, but there were no more shots. And no point in sticking around. Daniels was dead. I fled for shelter.

>>57. JOURNAL: CRATERS<<

The craters can be accounted for by the thin atmosphere, and vice versa. Volcanic craters and fissures, of course, are only part of the active geology of the planet. But the meteoric craters also fall into two types: bowl-shaped and flat or even convex-bottomed craters. No meteor splashes down like a pancake. The flat-bottoms seem to be caused by erosion, both of wind and of water.

This process has gone on longer and faster in the southern hemisphere, presumably because of the greater temperature differences.

When a meteoroid strikes, it penetrates the surface and generates heat, which is a rare commodity on Mars. Most of the land is underlaid by permafrost, so that when an object collides with the planet, an almost immediate thaw changes the below-surface conditions and, depending on the depth of the crater, may induce permanent change in local ground conditions. Often, such an impact will open up possibilities for thermal forces to come to the surface. And the process continues on its own.

>>>58. JOURNAL: ASTRA<<<

October 29

The problem of Astra: Freed from Earth-perspective, the evidence is piling up. On emerging from my tent in the morning, the ancient devastation lies all around at my feet. Craters, blasted features, still-blackened rock-faces. Even with all this, there is no way of telling for sure how ancient... 50 million years, a billion?

But the most significant proof has been my work with the tiny life and pre-life forms that exist here. From all experiments I've been able to devise, only one theory appears to account for the observations: there are two full-scale systems of life here, with very little overlap.

At first, Heisenberg's principle seemed to explain it. My own presence was affecting the surroundings; after staying in one spot for more than a few days, slight variations in the aboriginal flora were detectable. And on examination, it has always seemed to be new growth, rather than a change in the old. It is now over 500 days since my arrival... the arrival of an Earth vessel...and the changes now occur much less than before. I myself am being changed, as the planet is changed by me.

But the two forms have nothing to do with me. As I arrive in a new patch area, I can note with reliable prediction the demarcation between Form A and Form B... separated by a band of gray. Form A is light green-dark green-black, a thin scum that protrudes out of the ground with tiny flower-leaf-tendrils which follow the sun in its daily course.

In 72 variants, all Form A plants are based on a triangle-cum-rhombus structure. At night, the tendrils appear to withdraw, though my observations are spotty after dark. The generative light still functions, but one bulb has burned, and I am conserving the others for as long as I may be here. If worse come to worst, it might be possible to break the glass and re-tie the tungsten, with care to keep this away from the oxygenator. Suffice it to say that I have observed Form A rarely later than one-half hour after sunset.

Form B appears to have no effect on the other form. Form B is bluish brown and is not soil-bound, but shifts about... not by any discernible independent means of locomotion, but by wind or gravity. Yet whenever the two forms come together, neither seems to have any relation to the other. Not only that, but a distinctive gray band forms between them... in which they both wither and die. Yet the organic substances left by them both are indistinguishable...until I tried to eat them. By ingestion, and considerable indiges-tion, I learned that the greenish varieties, which may be related to chlorophyll, are edible. The brown and the gray are not.

From rough polarization experiments performed on the dusts of the two types, Form A is optically active in the opposite direction from Form B. And if this corresponds to the amino acids present, this levorotatory form is compat-ible with my own Earth system. Form B is not.

Now, two possibilities arise. Either Mars in its original fecundity gave birth to two rival life-forms, both of which continue to exist in advanced stages, despite the trying conditions, lack of continuous liquid water, etc. Or, one or both of these forms originated elsewhere. Given the almost ideal primitive atmosphere and temperature of Mars in primordial times, it is unlikely that life would not have begun here as it did on Earth, and perhaps earlier than Earth. My guess, and at this point it is only a guess, is that Astra had a role to play in this drama. That as the Sun and planets cooled, Astra would be the first terrestrial-type planet to offer the possibility of life, even while Mars was sweating out an atmosphere from the many volcanoes and fissures that now lay scattered and eroded everywhere I travel, even while Earth itself spun liquid-like without a Moon, without even a crust to stand on.

If this were so, then we have the next clue to the reconstruction of the cataclysmic events that obliterated the very origin... the first origin... of life in the entire solar system (leaving the giant planets out of the question for now, until they are within ken). The Form B plants may be living fossils, but we must expect, and account for, changes that must have occurred if there were a transition from Astra to here.

For the record. I note the efforts of Earth scientists to establish the biological origins of the carbonaceous chondrites...the meteoric remains, if I am correct, of the crust of the enigma called Astra in honor of the asteroids that now mark its oblivion. The scientists' puzzlement over trying to match the substances found with the components of Earth-life now becomes understandable, but not for that reason excusable. Earth is no longer the measure of all things, indeed there may have been... I believe I have held in my hand... living things that have no reference at all to anything Earthly. And yet they have as much right to exist, they express just as well the glory of the universe, with a different voice.

I feel a kinship, a universality, here that I have never felt before, not in the Redwoods, not in the forests of New England, the swamps in Asia, the Australian Outback, the polar stations. Here we may be touching for the first time a link to the past...and the future...a connection with the rest of the universe, a first halting step. We will fall back to Earth again and again, but we will rise once more, and soon…a thousand dreams later…we will walk amidst the stars in equality with every level, every variation of the theme of which we are a part.

That is why I came to Mars; that is why I stayed. I'll celebrate today… with my last pad of peanut butter and my last meal, turkey noodle soup. Hooray! Our side and their side are the same side!

October 32.

The past three days went quickly. There is enough here to feed me a week. Questions kept me here. Are there only two possibilities for life-systems? How do they compare? Reviewing my notes, I began to realize that Form B likes the colder places; it may survive longer, in that case. There is a possibility that Form A is the indigenous form; certainly it fits the planet better. The two seem to operate on entirely different levels.

Form B, in a brief duststorm here, almost entirely vanished. Only a few particles floated down as if on little parachutes. The spores, if that is what they are, gave sign, then, of being true wanderers.

Yet the puzzle is not complete. What brought them here? Or, in wilder fantasy, who brought them here? Let us set forth what is surmised of the lost planet, Astra. It circled the sun dangerously near the Keller Transformation…that point beyond which matter would follow a different path to planethood, the path of the giant planets.

Astra, then, was already at the focal point of stresses barely noticeable on either side of the imaginary boundary. And in this hybrid world, we can imagine remarkable juxtapositions, transitory states, and undoubtedly a struggle of elemental forces in the teeth of which the energy from the Sun speeded processes of chemical evolution…first the elements, then simple compounds, breaking down and being built up again, each atomic brick needed for its functions, the ultraviolet radiation pushing each atom toward the next, until amino acids formed... and all the rest followed from that: pre-biotics, nucleotides, and finally the soup was ready.

How long it all took is a matter of conjecture, but we can pinpoint the end of Astra, within a few million years, given equipment and the data here. But between the beginning and the end, the picture is almost blank. Only the comets, the meteors, the asteroids, and the craters here told us about Astra. Until now.

The specks, I call them, interest me more than anything else I've found. The little 30x magnifier scarcely permits me to make out their features. This drawing is the closest I can come.

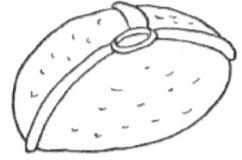

Both sides are identical...like a fat three-sided football. The three raised protrusions end in a cap, which usually projects outward. This cap appears to be a break mark, leading me to suspect the existence of a mother plant that seasonally releases the spores. One or two of them, out of thousands, have been cracked, or split slightly.

The bumps have no obvious function, though I will often find dust particles stuck between several of them. The weight of a speck must be between 0.1 and 1 milligram, much like the common dust of the Edom plain. Through the magnifier, their color appears yellow-brown, a vivid hue scarcely noticeable among the orange-buff sand particles.

‹‹‹59. FAREWELL‹‹‹

So, it was over. A few shots could be heard from beyond the wall, nothing serious. Lawrence's house was out that way, but Sadie was never going back. Her lip trembled and I patted her on the cheek. From her downcast look, I knew that she expected at least a kiss.

"Sadie, it's over. You know that, don't you?"

"Yes. I'm sorry."

"So am I, believe me…"

"No, don't ask me to do that. I once thought, believed, dreamed… but never mind now." With a brave shake of the head, she edged nearer the shattered window. "Get down!"

"What's up?"

"It's Garrigan. I thought he was dead."

"Thinking doesn't do much good in Garrigan's case."

"Come on, this is serious. He's got a dozen men with him."

"We've seen worse."

"Not this time. He's got Lechay with him."

"God, that means he knows about me, or he will, soon enough. Lechay can't lie, he doesn't have the brains. He's on Garrigan's level."

"Get down," she whispered.

A ringing in my head prevented me from answering, and

by that time, a fist had plunged straight through the thin wooden door. The side window was our only chance. I heaved it open, and started to pull Sadie toward it.

"No, I'm not in danger. You are. Get."

I didn't stop to argue. An arm was already reaching around to unlock the door from the inside. Headfirst into a somersault and a sprint directly across the yard took me no more than three seconds. By then, they would be slapping Sadie around... she had just had time to slam the window down as the door crunched open.

Only Lechay knew where I had been, or that I had anything to do with the night raid, and those were innocent escapades compared to the complicity of Carson and his minions. Something else was behind this, and I meant to find out. The whole town might fall for his story, but to build on his veracity was more foolish than jumping into quicksand. Lechay... we were mad to trust him. Of course he was trustworthy, like a child. But a child is not responsible. Neither was Lechay.

I ducked into a shed next door to watch what was going on. My name was in the babble as the men moved out, fortunately in the opposite direction. Then Sadie emerged, weak in the knees. They had beaten her.

‹‹‹60. GRINCH‹‹‹

"Grinch! You mean the ship's cargo is grinch?"

"That's right," Billy said. "Got a bit of my own. Want some?"

I slapped the offered package out of his hand angrily. "You fool! Where did you get it?"

"Cool down, man," he retorted, retrieving the matted fibrous ball.

"But that's poison, Billy. Don't you know that?"

"I don't know no such thing. It's no worse than grass, you just…"

"Float into oblivion. Grinch, eh? Billy, you know the drug scene. Tried them all, right?"

"Sure. Just once for most of them."

"Or watch someone tear his guts out over it."

"Well, yes. But not with this stuff, it's sweet, baby, sweet all the way down."

"Look at it this way. You can get your body in really fine shape, do some yoga, tone up the muscles. Feel good, right. But it's not enough. So you shove in food, or coffee, to throw the balance off, give you a thrill, a speed trip, or downers, or flipped out. Doesn't matter really. It's life feeding off life, off the magic mushrooms of Mexico, or Siberia."

"Yeah, but this grinch is something else, Sandy."

"That's what I'm coming to. Plenty of grinchheads on Mars. People get time to adjust, get the inner ecology so they can take it. You've tried it, haven't you?"

"Sure, boss. Great stuff. It's a high in a million."

"Listen, Billy. I talked to a man who knows the chemistry of it. If he's right, grinch may be fine for Mars, but off the planet, it's a killer."

"Oh, boss, you're puttin' me on. Here, try some. We're not on Mars, are we?"

"But we're not on Earth either. Look, remember the transition sequence? That won't happen to us until Skyhook, or Landing. But what he said was, the direction that life took on Mars is like a separate branch of organic matter, and when you mix the two branches together, in this particular case, nobody wins."

"So, why is the Captain set on carrying this load to Earth?"

"It's in the special properties of grinch. One, it's habit-forming. Worse than that, it affects human body chemistry, changes it so that the grinch becomes an essential part of the homolog. Take my word for it, Billy. Don't touch the stuff."

"Too late for that."

"Look, you've got to clean your system out of that crap before we touch down, every last bit of it. Two is the hooker. You know how easy it is to breathe after grinch? It's the myoglobin."

"My-oh-myo!"

"This is serious, Billy. Myoglobin is what whales and seals use to store oxygen, it's about one-quarter the size of hemoglobin and it's in the muscles, but it does the same thing, really. On Mars, you need it. On Earth, it builds with the unused grinch into a monster molecule right in the blood."

"Right in the blood?"

"So that causes a whole series of imbalances that don't get flushed out. Especially to the brain."

Billy looked at me expectantly. Finally he said, "You done?"

"Done what?"

"Done with the lecture. Done so we can set back and have some grinch."

"Billy! Have you listened to a word I said? Put that down!"

"Hey! Give me that back. Hey! Come back here!"

I didn't know what got into me. It was a foolish thing, on the face of it, running down the corridors, bouncing off walls to escape Billy's unthinking grabs for the poisonous grinch. I evaded him just long enough to duck into the engine room. Either I'd be able to destroy the prize, or I'd have a good chance of tricking him and sneaking back out, and then getting rid of the grinch.

Amid the multitude of pipes, he carried on a threatening monologue, trying to rouse me, give myself away, but I bided my time until he was far enough away from the door to make a soundless break for it.

And he was rampaging and yelling, swearing at me because I was keeping the grinch all to myself! Fat chance. I'd seen the results of Carson's grinch experiments on a human guinea pig, a man who had once been highly educated. And then in the hallway, he'd looked at me blankly, as if he'd never known me. Harry Lawrence. I can't wipe those eyes out of my mind.

But it was obvious from all the shouting that Billy was all

right, so far. He carried on against me and my kind at high volume, too high.

I stumbled over a valvehead, caught myself, but he'd heard me, and he was on me before I could get up. Then we were wrestling on the floor like children, over the little bag.

"Aha yourself, Spaceman," a voice said from the door. "What is this ungentlemanly conduct? Break it up, break it up, I say."

Sheffield! We snapped to our feet without time to glance at each other.

"Now then, what seems to be the trouble? What were you fighting about?"

"Nothin', sir," Billy said, his eyes wide. "We was just fooling."

"A rather uncivilized scuffle, it looked to me like. Oho, what's this?

Give my that bag. Yes, you. What's your name, Spaceman?"

"J...J...J...Jones, sir." I stammered. Could there be a Jones? Did he look like me?

"This, hummmm...," he sniffed at the grinch. "Yes. I see. All right, you Jones, and Brown, I want you both to report to the Captain at a reasonable hour. Is that understood? You will relate what went on tonight, including the, ahem, object of contention."

"Yes sir," we chorused.

"And as for this material," he paused. "You understand that it is illegal to be in possession, of course. I could have both of you locked away for the rest of the trip. But that really doesn't make much sense out here. We need every able-bodied lad at transfer points. In this case, I'm going to make matters expedient. Since this parcel was the object of dispute, I believe that its absence may promote the absence of a reason for common scuffling. Is that correct?"

"Yes sir," two voices came together.

"Then I will remove the cause of conflict. There." He tucked the parcel into his pocket, glancing sideways at us. "I think we understand each other. Oh, and as long as we all understand, I think there's little point in bothering the Captain with this little... breach of discipline, eh?"

And he walked out. The pair of us stood like dumbbells for a second until the door slid closed again. Then we were talking at each other.

"Hey, what are we..."

"He just walk in like that and..."

"...going to do? He'll..."

"...take the grinch as if..."

"...check on Jones and then..."

"...he owned it. Damn!"

"Billy!"

>>>61. JOURNAL: FOOD<<<

June 19.

A lethargy has seized me, dangerous this time of year. Nothing to do but write. I can barely scrape the soil; permafrost here takes longer to melt in my mouth. No free water at any depth. As soon as I am able, I'd better move north.

June 24.

Sick. Only the solar batteries keep me alive through the night...the worst is before dawn, when the current weakens and cold seeps through the sleeping bag. Pulse 55... very low. I sweat, the sweat vaporizes. A bath...where on this godforsaken world can I get a bath?

Food. A plate heaped high with steak and rice and potatoes and string beans, cauliflower, spaghetti, ice cream, peanut butter, French fries, chicken liver, crackers, sawdust, peaches, mushrooms...it fills my consciousness, and it is there, hovering in space right before my eyes...too weak to reach out for a mouthful...chocolate cake, pineapple, raisins, pastrami, catsup, chow mein, cinnamon...the fruits of Earth, how I long for hamburgers and milkshakes, just a swallow of Coca-Cola, or hot dogs roasted over an open fire, marshmallows...

I'm letting this get control of me. Better sleep now. useless energy.

Feeling better now. The banquet table is gone. I am a bit shaky.

>>62. JOURNAL: ALASSOM<<

The air that had been moving down the little valley halted, hesitated, started up again, but with a slight shift in direction. I had been kneeling over a bare area, brushing aside the remaining grains of coarse sand to examine a large swirl-pattern flagstone. But now I stood up abruptly. Yes, it was true, the wind now tossed my hair from the side. How had I known? It hadn't entered my conscious thought, but even without the delicate signals of the hair, I knew. I just knew, with clarity and precision, each tiny variation of the wind. A low-throated throb, with overtones ranging two octaves, reached my ears. It was a wind-whistle, that Swiss cheese rock that shouldn't have been on top of that hill according to any quirk of probability or geology.

The music of the rock paused, transformed into another interval...measured, but not by a twelve-tone scale. The textures of the several sounds wove whole scales together like an immense complex harmonica. The vibrations reached right down into my soul... and somewhere behind my brain, ancient juices flowed forth. For half an hour I stood fixed by the melody, and associations of specific memories in my life as I knew it sprang forth in delicate visions, a dance of beings right there in the square, almost in my sight, clearer when I half-closed my eyes and let the music roll over me. What a peaceful place to be!

It was the silence that followed that woke me out of the trance, a few brief moments of utter stillness. I wasn't ready for that. But the spell was broken. Unformed questions flocked to my vacant thought-arena, and I sat down to write this out before the freshness of it cools.

A presence lives here. I will not accept that this was not man-made, or made by a being so fantastically elevated in spirit that I would turn every stone on Mars to meet him. One look...but I'm carried away. It has been four long Martian months now since I have tasted human food, nearly six months... 302 days... since I have talked to a human being. I have lost much weight, my head is light with a touch of dizziness. But my eyes and ears function perfectly. Let this record stand, as written.

June 36. Camped outside the valley, last night. No human trace should mar this site. Its utter rightness astounds me...but so subtle are the changes that it is impossible to tell where nature left off and man... whatever creature it was, though the images of human beings keep coming into it... began. No solid relics yet...a great number of incidental impressions... data is a poor substitute for describing El Hacienda, as I have come to call this site. As yet, no trace of the peoples of the culture.

A cave, or concave opening in the rock wall... one of several. Seating arrangement around a semicircle, the acoustics seem to be finely tuned to a point in the center, as if a speaker, teacher perhaps, held meetings here. The valley itself resembles a three-sided stadium... thousands could have sat at games or other spectacles. But that's just fantasy. Something is happening to me. A fluid has been forming on my skin, creamy yellow, and brittle in the cold: physiological, probably.

More important, I've begun to have full-scale daydreams, of a romantic sort. If I don't shake this, the whole point of my staying will be lost. This is a tough place; it'll take some doing on my part just to survive... and this is summer. What if the whole planet hibernates, come winter? Already I lick my boots for water; my very steps squeeze moisture out of the sand.

June 39.

My perception is changing. Amid the strangeness, a fondness, a tickling expectancy. I am learning much. By familiarity, the puzzle pieces fall into place. I sense, too, that I am part of the puzzle.

June 42.

To pick up the pen to write... useless. In meditation with... whoever. I respect, almost revere them. I live in a chamber now, that is warm, not hot. Day or night, the same temperature. The wind whistle talks to me in my sleep, all day, all night. I can't leave yet. The cycle is not complete. Something in the air here... I hardly need to eat. Yet food is all around... I discovered one morning, not yet quite awake, that if I let my body rise up, there was a place to go, a thing to do. So hard at first to trust... who?... but that had to happen. I am with the planet now, learning so much of its beauty by being here. El Hacienda... today I know the name...the wind whistle repeats it over and over like a mantra. Alassom is the wind name. Alassom Molango Famothan Somoro... I hear sentences like this, and listen to the everchanging melody or resonance. By listening, I learn; by being here, I am part of... by living, I add to Alassom. A beautiful sadness that quickens into animation as soon as I direct my attention inward and outward. I am enchanted by magic... a good magic. More later, too dark to see.

June 43, morning.

I need less sleep than before. Last night I discovered a remarkable section of a cave. The floor in daylight gave a dim record... tiny grooves in smooth rock, all in the same east-west direction, as if a giant many-toed claw had swept across the floor. I had swept sand to the side for more peaceful sleeping. And during the day, on top of this very hill, I had found a beautiful large spherical crystal on the surface... black, but strangely lit, as if it had its own source of illumination. Now, at night, I discovered its meaning. For, tiny spots of light appeared in the darkness...they were all over the floor, mostly in the grooves, or near them. I rubbed my hand at them at first, but felt nothing more than stone floor polished smooth by an artificial process. I tried to brush them away...but the brightest of them leaped onto the back of my hand, then back to the groove. Of course! These tiny bits of light were just that. Their pattern, which was vaguely familiar before, now became entirely comprehensible. They formed the constellations, backwards and upside down! I looked up. Yes, very faintly I could make out that same "stone" I had noticed on the outside... it was a lens, and I was in a little planetarium!

For a long time, I stared at the floor, and more and more stars became visible to my adjusted sight. I felt as if I were gazing into the black emptiness of space once more. With the data, I'm sure that the age of this construction could be calculated, by checking the variance of stars from their grooves... but I had no way of comparing. It must be very old, though. No moving parts...the same principle as the wind whistle, and the same eternal subtlety. They must have been extremely sensitive creatures, as well as very intelligent.

June 48.

A thought on the planetarium. No large grooves for Deimos or Phobos. Could it be that this was built before their arrival? Another explanation is that their courses are so rapid that they change too often, as well as their faintness against a background of stars.

And what about the planets? Earth and Jupiter should be very bright here. I will check tonight.

June 49, morning.

Jupiter was approximately in its groove, a complex curve that I hadn't paid attention to before, because it appeared to be a slight mistake in alignment... but there it was, an elongated sawtooth. Earth was not visible, but it, too, had a path in the floor. Another matter... a series of faint scratches in the same orientation... I could not be sure that I was seeing this, but it appeared to approximate the band of the Asteroid Belt, which circles the Sun just outside Mars' orbit. Outside, it was faintly visible, like the Milky Way, but much fainter.

At some time in the distant past, a planet had exploded, leaving a trail of about 10% of its former substance. The Martian astronomers must have puzzled that one out. Could it be that William Keller was right? He'd predicted, on the basis of sophisticated math, that the division between giant planets, (starting with the biggest anomaly of all, Jupiter), and the minor planets (the last and nearly the smallest, Mars), was produced by the interplay of fluid atomic structures before the elements were created... and that a planet formed at the nodal transition from dense and compact to diffuse and huge... such a planet would be precarious indeed. Thus, the Asteroid Belt would be entirely explainable: the question would then become—what happened to the pieces? Perhaps the anomalous moons of Mars came from such an extraneous source. Another consequence of the Keller formulation might have ramifications for Mars itself...was it truly out of the transitional zone? Some of the features already observed indicate a magnitude of stress that no volcano could have produced. Angular momentum around the Sun should match and stabilize. Everything should be settled in. But is it?

June 53.

Alassom is a thousand miles behind. Without her, I would be forever lost; now, I'm flying, borne on the wind with cloth patched together from my pack, my clothes, every shred of material I could think of... and it is enough for flying leaps up to twenty seconds.

>>63. JOURNAL: ANNIVERSARY<<

12 January, 28.

Three years have passed, and no sign of another expedition. The middle of May this year marks the third opposition. I worry about what may have happened to Earth in the meantime. But about that I have no way of knowing.

The time I've spent here has not been wasted, though. By now I have a clearer comprehension of the status of areobiology. The more stringent requirements here have produced an entire spectrum of solutions to the basic problem of survival. From these forms I myself have learned how better to sustain myself.

A curious example of the extreme adaptability occurred more than a year ago...a long year for me. I would sleep in the open, if the stars were clear, and no signs of dust storm were apparent, with my electric sleeping bag set on low. A cover under me was essential, to trap water vapor squeezed out of the ground by the very low temperatures. As time went on, I adjusted my own system to maintain heat balance. A consequence of my being here on the ground was to create a warm spot in the middle of coldness. The warmth, even if it were just my body, kept a tiny area clear of frost under the ground where I slept, and in the morning I would find fresh green tendrils in an attentive circle around my bag.

One morning I woke to discover that my hand showed green when I passed it over my face. The mirror showed green splotches running in a line from my left cheek to my forehead and into my beard and hair. At first I was panic-stricken. With scarcely sufficient water, I determined to scrape it off, all of it, and I shaved away as much of the hair as seemed to be necessary, which was a nuisance for the cold, but I thought at the time that it was a necessity. Afterward, I looked down at the little pile of scraped skin, hairs, and green scum. The first principle I had practiced was extreme economy: now that came into play. I had even started to save my own excrement...though distasteful, at least it wasn't poison.

My procedure with any new organic material has been to consume a little bit...the rare chance of a specific poison is too slight to consider. The worst that could happen would be that I'd suffer for a day or two, or lose my lunch.

By following these rules, I determined that the green growth, combined with the sweat of my skin, had a tang scarcely to be believed. I nurtured its growth that day, and the next, but there was a flaw in my reasoning that my body discovered before I did. While the scum was delicious, and while it was rich food, my first reaction had been the correct one. All that was happening was a recycling of my own substances back through my mouth: the drain on my skin proved more than any counterbalancing food value the growth might have.

On analysis, the scum bore a striking resemblance to another curiosity I had encountered long before. This substance I first met as a dull ochre-red rock. On closer inspection, it became obvious that this specimen was no ordinary rock. A fine powder came off on my hands. I proceeded to clean it, brushing off the crust. Ten minutes later, it was as dusty as before. In fact, it was noticeably smaller than when I started. My training, my western, or should I say human, education stood in the way of seeing what was right before my eyes.

"Rock," I had concluded, judging by the look and feel of it.

There should have been a pile of dust on my table, too. But no dust remained. My hands had earlier taken on a reddish hue. I looked at the caked mixture of palm sweat and dust in the weak sunlight, holding my hands open. I must have engaged in a reverie for a few minutes, for when the mud should have been dry, I saw only my own two hands, dry and clean, staring back at me.

Determined now to capture and analyze this phenomenon, I encased the remaining piece of rock... I dared not call it clay, or hang yet another Earth label on it, for fear of losing the game by stumbling over my own limited conceptions. It would sit while I took a stroll.

With my magnifier, the "rock" revealed its secret... its particles were densely packed fragile filaments or crusts that appeared to have been living at one time, perhaps were living now, in the extended definition of that word that I had been forced to employ on Mars. The structures bore a kinship resemblance to the green scum, which grew out of nothing, and perhaps the disappearing act was simply the other end of that.

‹‹‹64. EXIT‹‹‹

It was a simple matter, after all, once Sadie lured one of the space-suited figures out of the Farewell Parade and into the now-deserted shed that Wilkes had used for his nefarious operations (before he'd been caught in the final crunch of the last few days), to substitute myself into the spacer's costume. With the unlucky, unconscious mariner tied to a post, Sadie and I made our last goodbyes. So hard to leave her, after all. But at least she knew the real story. A kiss, a hug, and she had to jam the helmet on and push me out the door into the milling crowd.

I rejoined the departing spacers just outside the wall, jostling aside well-wishers, looking as official as I could manage. We were then lined up, in the open, like an infantry detail. I ducked unnoticed into an open slot just a second behind the others, and we marched the next mile or so to the ship. Patchwork on the upright landing girders now enabled the ship to point proudly upward, to the stars. Ah, the dream of space still held strong in that ultimate symbol of aggression, the phallic man-force of our genital power, sleek and abstracted into glory.

Inside, I slid into the nearest empty seat; one man came over to protest, but thought better of it and sank into another seat on the second perimeter. They hadn't much time left for takeoff; Carson's "celebration" had taken most of the day.

The familiar thunder, the downward pressure, fighting back nausea... I hardly noticed these things. More important to me was finding a place to hide just as soon as I could climb out of the seat and get out of the suit. If all went according to rule, I'd have less than a minute. Time and again, I'd raise myself on my elbows when it seemed that the thrust surely must be lessening, only to find that I didn't have the strength.

When the time did come, I was too late. The man next to me made such a production getting up that there wasn't enough room to get through without arousing suspicion. So I settled back to wait for another opportunity. As long as I could safely remain in the suit, I stood a chance of escaping detection.

Finally, all the others had gone up a gangway into a little hall that apparently led nowhere, and each emerged sans suit. I glanced down at my left sleeve again. "Gpmn. Shelton, X09837241."

Sheffield looked down at me from the first tier.

"Desuit, spacer! We've got work to do."

"Yessir." I clambered out and up, or what used to be "up," filed past a couple of crewmen unzipping. One of them noticed my insignia.

"Hello, Jack. Here, let me help you get out of that fishbowl."

I waved him off with a brush-off motion, but he had already undone the back clasps.

"Later," I said.

"OK." He stood puzzled for an instant, then dodged back out of the little entryway. I was alone now, briefly, but there was no way to close off the area from view. I fumbled around, found Shelton's locker. The door opened the right way; I could hide most of my body behind it while unsuiting. Quickly, I shed the suit and stuffed it in half of the locker. Everything else cluttering the bottom I shoved into the little shelf on top, checked the handle... yes, it could be worked with difficulty from the inside... and climbed in, closing the door as softly as possible behind me.

"Hey, Jack. Jack?" He was just outside the locker. I held my breath.

Then he shuffled off.

It had been the inspiration of a desperate moment, but I was to be in that locker, except for a nightly trip to the john and the kitchen, for the next month. There I began writing this account, and there I almost went mad. Until Billy found me.

‹‹‹65. FINIS‹‹‹

So there it is, the story to date. Rogers promised to get this to you—he's a good lad. I trust him—but there really isn't any choice. Billy and I are going to see it through on Wentworth's ship. Wherever we end up, you'll be hearing from us again—I hope.

So keep the world spinning: if there's a moral to this tale, it's what a mess we monkeys get into, left to our own devices—or not.

About Weston—he's crazy, but what else he might be depends on who you are, I guess. I'm not a Westonite myself. but it wouldn't take much more to make me a believer. One thing I'll say though: I admire his guts. Makes a man feel like there's a life to be lived that's full and rich.

§

Hi! This is Billy Brown, the spacer's racer. Sandy says say high. O...High! This here story Sandy's been scratching out's true, so you go ahead and get the presses rolling. You hear? Any questions, you ask me, care of Florence Brown, 743 Wildwood, Indianapolis. That's my mama; she know how to get to me. And here, Sandy help me write these notes down; maybe you can print it in the book:

You know you're a long way from home
You've gone such a long way from home.
That bottle you're in
Will pickle your skin,
It's a long, long way you roamed.

Space got a hold on your soul,
Yeah, space got a stranglehold on your soul,
That space is so big,
Hold onto your rig,
Space chill your soul stone cold.